Right Package, Wrong Baggage

Right Package, Wrong Baggage

Wanda B. Campbell

www.urbanchristianonline.net

Urban Books, LLC
78 East Industry Court
Deer Park, NY 11729

ISBN 13: 978-1-60162-861-9
ISBN 10: 1-60162-861-7

First Printing October 2010
Printed in the United States of America

10 9 8 7 6 5 4 3 2 1

Distributed by Kensington Corp.
Submit Wholesale Orders to:
Kensington Publishing Corp.
C/O Penguin Group (USA) Inc.
Attention: Order Processing
405 Murray Hill Parkway
East Rutherford, NJ 07073-2316
Phone: 1-800-526-0275
Fax: 1-800-227-9604

Dedication

For my brothers and sisters in the Kingdom whose background doesn't consist of perfect parents, white houses with picket fences, two and a half children, a dog, and church every Sunday. To those who trudge every day through hell-like circumstances, but never give up.

There is therefore now no condemnation to those who are in Christ Jesus, who do not walk according to the flesh, but according to the Spirit. For the law of the Spirit of life in Christ Jesus has made me free from the law of sin and death.

Romans 8:1-2 NJV

Acknowledgments

First and always foremost, I thank my **Heavenly Father** and **His** son, **Jesus Christ,** for using me to minister to His children through the written Word. Without Him, the words would just be incoherent thoughts on a page.

Once again, I extend my sincerest gratitude to my family members who have supported me without reservation.

Craig, my husband of twenty years: Thank you for allowing me to give birth to the vision with which God impregnated me.

My children, **Chantel, Jonathan,** and **Craig, Jr.:** Thanks for the fuel I needed to keep writing.

Cassandra and Sabria: Thanks for reading every one of my crazy stories and setting me on the right path.

My friend **John Edwards:** Thank you for blowing me up around the post office. Your support means more than words can express.

God has placed angels in my life, also known as my literary friends. Without these individuals, I would be completely lost.

Tyora Moody: Thank you for your unselfish acts of kindness in opening doors for me. Without you, I'd still be trying to figure out what a URL is.

Tinisha Johnson: Thank you for making a sista look good!

Lacricia Angelle, Linda R. Herman, Bernard Boulton, and the **Urban Christian** family: Thank you for the encouragement and for teaching me about the craft of writing.

Acknowledgments

Book Clubs and **Readers** everywhere: Thank you for investing your money and time in support of this novel.

I thoroughly enjoyed writing this story. *Right Package, Wrong Baggage* is the sequel to my first published short story, *Mommy's Present*, in the anthology *The Midnight Clear*. The continuation of Micah, Pamela, and Matthew's story will make you laugh, cry, and think. Enjoy and be blessed.

Who are you to judge another's servant? To his own master he stands or falls. Indeed, he will be made to stand, for God is able to make him stand.

Romans 14:4 NKJV

Prologue

Little Matthew ran to the reception in the fellowship hall in search of his mother and grandparents. He found them standing near the Christmas tree. *Perfect,* he thought. Brother Stevenson couldn't fit under the tree, but at least Matthew could give his mother her present near the tree. After receiving hugs and accolades from his family, Matthew instructed his mother to close her eyes.

"Wait right here, Mommy. I'll be right back with your present." Matthew smiled at his grandmother before he went off to find his mother's present. He returned shortly thereafter and said, "Okay, Mommy, you can open your eyes now."

Pamela assumed her son would have the present in his hand. Upon opening her eyes, she automatically looked down at her son who was wearing the biggest grin. Then she looked over at Micah standing next to him with the same grin on his face.

"Merry Christmas, Mommy!" Matthew shouted and started giggling.

"Merry Christmas, Matthew, Merry Christmas, Micah." Pamela said, wondering what happened to her Christmas present.

"Do you like your present, Mommy?" Matthew asked with expectancy.

"I don't know." Pamela shrugged. "You haven't given it to me yet."

"Mommy, it's right here." Little Matthew held out Micah's hand to his mother.

Pamela searched Micah's eyes for an answer; he didn't give her one, just continued grinning. Pamela then turned to her parents for an explanation. They had the same goofy grins on their faces Matthew and Micah had. It was obvious to her they knew more than she did.

Finally, Pamela knelt down to Matthew. "Sweetheart, I don't understand."

Matthew blew into the air in frustration. "Mommy, Brother Stevenson is your present!"

Pamela looked up at Micah who was still grinning. It wasn't until then that she noticed the flowers in his hand and that he was wearing a blue and gray suit. Since neither her parents nor Micah were going to point out Matthew's error to him, she took a shot.

"Sweetheart, Brother Stevenson is a person, and you can't give a person away as a gift," Pamela explained to her six-year-old son.

"Yes, you can, Mommy," Matthew said, nodding his little head. "God gave us His son, and Jesus was a person."

Pamela laughed at her son's analogy. "Baby, that's different. God gave us His son so that we could have a chance at eternal life."

"That's not different. I'm giving you Brother Stevenson so that you can have a chance at life and not be by yourself anymore." Matthew's revelation left Pamela speechless. "Mommy, you asked me what I think you need. You need a husband like Mary had."

Pamela looked back at her parents again. Now she understood why they were still smiling. They agreed with her son. Inwardly, so did she, which is why tears now rolled down her cheeks. Matthew, in his innocence, had reached a part of her she thought was hidden.

"Don't cry, Mommy," Matthew said, after he handed her the handkerchief Micah had given him. "I made sure he is right for you. His name starts with an 'M' like mine. He's tall so he can reach the top shelf, and he likes vegetables and keeps his room clean. And, Mommy, he never falls asleep when Pastor Jackson preaches. I know because I've been watching him."

Pamela couldn't help but laugh along with the group at Matthew's scale. When she finished laughing and crying, she looked over at her son and wondered when he had become so wise and insightful.

"Thank you, baby, for looking out for me," she said while hugging him tightly.

"Does this mean you like your present?" Matthew just had to know.

On her feet again, Pamela looked over at Micah. "Are those for me?" she asked, referring to the flowers.

"That depends on if you're going to keep me or return me," Micah joked.

"My son didn't pressure you into this, did he?"

"Matthew just told me his plan two days ago, but I've been watching you for months." Micah was still smiling, but the sincere look in his eyes told Pamela this wasn't a game to him. Micah was seriously interested in her. Pamela was definitely interested in him too.

"Mommy, do you like it?" Matthew pestered.

"Baby, don't be stupid," Pamela's mother whispered in her ear when she hesitated.

"Yes, sweetheart, I like it," Pamela said, finally answering her son's question, but holding a steady gaze with Micah. "Can I have my flowers now?"

Watching his mother accept the flowers from Brother Stevenson, Matthew jumped up and down and then giggled uncontrollably when his mother said, "Micah, that suit looks good on you."

"Thank you, Pamela. Does this mean you're going to keep me?" Micah winked.

"Well, I'm certainly not going to send you back," Pamela blushed.

"Once you get to know me, you won't want to send me back." The strength and confidence in his voice gave Pamela goose bumps.

"Confident, aren't you?" Pamela asked.

"I have to be. I come with a lifetime warranty. One hundred percent satisfaction guaranteed!"

Pamela giggled along with her son. She couldn't wait to get acquainted with her real-life present.

Chapter 1

Pamela pressed her notary seal firmly into the document, then glanced at the clock on the wall. *Almost done,* she thought, looking in the direction of her clients. She loved assisting first-time home buyers the most at the title company where she worked as senior escrow officer. Pamela took pleasure in helping new homeowners purchase their piece of the American dream, particularly, single mothers like her.

At age twenty-nine and widowed, Pamela understood firsthand the pressure of making ends meet. If it weren't for her parents' help with a down payment after the untimely death of her husband five years ago, Pamela would still be renting a one-bedroom apartment instead of owning a three-bedroom town house in Berkeley.

Today, her clients were newlyweds, married seven months and already purchasing their first home. Every so often, Pamela would look up from the pile of documents and catch a glimpse of the couples' interaction. The husband and wife constantly touched one another and addressed each other by cute nicknames. The wife blushed constantly. Every so often, the husband kissed her cheek.

Pamela wondered what that kind of love felt like. What did it feel like to love a man and for him love her back? That question made her check the clock again. If she didn't hurry, she may never find out.

Thirty minutes later, Pamela stood at her desk buttoning her coat, or at least trying to button her coat. Her hands trembled and her palms dripped with perspiration.

"Girl, let me help you with that." The offer came from her best friend and fellow escrow officer, Jessica.

"Are you nervous?" Jessica asked, and then rescinded when Pamela twisted her face and at the same time rolled her eyes. "You're right, that's a stupid question. A blind man with two seeing-eye dogs can see that you're nervous. You almost look petrified." Jessica then laughed.

Pamela waited until Jessica finished buttoning her coat for her before she smacked her lips and said, "Forget you."

"Watch it now. I'll let you go on this date looking like John Witherspoon in *Boomerang*."

Pamela couldn't help but laugh at that scenario. "Jessica, I'm just so nervous about tonight," she said, now serious. "I haven't been on a real date in years. Up until yesterday, I wasn't aware that such a thing as 'dating etiquette' existed. I don't know how to dress for the occasion without sending the wrong message." Pamela took a deep breath in an attempt to calm her nerves. "Thanks so much for helping me select a dress and shoes for tonight. I probably would have worn one of my Sunday-go-to-meeting suits if you hadn't intervened."

"I know," Jessica said as she reached for her own coat. "Why are you so nervous? You and Micah have been hanging out for over a month now."

"But this is the first time we're going somewhere without Matthew," Pamela explained.

Jessica shrugged her shoulders. "I still don't get it."

"It's easy to talk with Matthew around. We focus our attention and conversation on him. With him gone, I don't know if we'll have anything to talk about." Pamela wrapped her scarf around her neck.

Jessica shook her head. "Girl, you are really letting your nerves get the best of you. I think the two of you will have a whole lot to talk about with Matthew away with your parents for the weekend. I bet Micah is ecstatic to finally have some one-on-one time with you."

"I hope so. I'm just so out of touch with this dating thing. I don't know what an appropriate or safe subject is anymore. I usually limit the scope of our phone conversations to church or the Bible."

"That won't be the case tonight." Jessica paused to tie the belt on her coat. "But just in case you can't find anything to talk about, ask that fine, saved man if he has a single brother for me."

Pamela laughed.

"Why are you laughing?"

"Jessica, you are too funny."

"Girl, I am not playin'. I need God to send my soul mate while I can still produce eggs."

Pamela finished laughing and placed her arm around Jessica's shoulder. The two headed for the door. "I know he doesn't have a brother. He told me he's an only child."

"What about a cousin, or an uncle?" Jessica persisted.

"I'll ask, but I believe Micah Stevenson is one of a kind." Pamela prayed and hoped he was authentic.

The cold January wind beat against Pamela's face the moment she stepped from the building. She pulled her scarf up over her face and braved the blustery weather. By the time she'd made it across the parking lot and into the confines of her Altima, she was so cold her bones ached. That's the only thing she disliked about the Bay Area—the traditional January winds and rainstorms.

On the drive home, she was more cautious than normal. At yellow lights she applied the brakes instead of speeding through the intersections. Pamela prayed all the way home against mechanical failures and unexpected traffic delays. Arriving late might cause her to miss her destiny.

* * *

Micah pulled his SUV into his parking stall so fast that when he applied his brakes, they screeched. He was running behind schedule thanks to his last customer, an elderly gentleman who decided he wanted cable in his bedroom. However, the nice man didn't bother to tell Micah the task would require him to crawl underneath the house until after Micah had agreed to do the installation. That was the one thing he hated most about his job with the local cable company—crawling underneath houses.

Micah grabbed his lunchbox, and after slamming the door, raced to his apartment on the third floor in the St. Moritz complex building. It was a good thing he climbed telephone poles on a regular basis; otherwise, he would have been winded by the time he reached the third flight of stairs. Once inside his unit, Micah tossed his lunchbox on the kitchen counter, and then headed straight for the shower.

Under the therapy of hot water pellets, Micah's mind relaxed as he reflected on his short life in California. Two years had flown by fast, and his life had changed dramatically. It was hard to believe he was the same person. When Micah Stevenson arrived at the Oakland airport on that rainy December night, he was just a shell of a man. Back then, he compared his life to the chocolate Easter bunny, solid on the outside but hollow and empty on the inside. Self-esteem and security had vacated the premises of his spirit, along with his will to live. He loved God, but wasn't sure God loved him anymore because he'd repeatedly done the very thing that was an abomination.

Today, with the help of his uncle, Pastor Jackson, and his new best friend, Minister Anthony Combs, Micah Stevenson was a mighty man of valor, and he knew it. He valued his relationship with God above anything material or tangible.

He'd spent the past two years totally devoted to God. Micah learned to hear His voice and learned God's plan for his life.

The only leisure activity Micah afforded himself was coaching the church's baseball team. That was only after God had shown him how to use his past experiences to help keep the younger generation from falling into the same trap he had fallen into.

Up until six months ago, he was satisfied with his life. Church, work, and baseball brought him complete contentment. Then he met his little buddy, Matthew, and everything changed.

He'd met six-year-old Matthew Roberts one Sunday while the child played with the water fountain in the church's vestibule. Matthew was conducting an experiment, trying to see if the water would touch the ceiling. After gently scolding the little boy, they became buddies. When Micah met Matthew's mother on the following Sunday, Micah wanted to become her buddy also.

Pamela's natural beauty captivated him months prior, but he was too shy to approach her, so he admired her from afar. The mocha skin and soft brown eyes drew him in, and her warm smile hooked him. Micah thought she resembled Sanaa Lathan, especially when she wore her shoulder-length hair down in loose curls. Micah never voiced his interest in Pamela Roberts, but he did learn about her from a distance and from the subtle inquiries made to his uncle. He also observed her every Sunday and Wednesday night. Although impressed, he decided not to pursue her until later. Then the unimaginable happened. Little Matthew handpicked him as a Christmas present for his mother! When he pried the plot out of his little buddy, Micah fought hard to keep a straight face. He felt like break-dancing, he was so happy. His happiness swelled when Pamela accepted him as her present and agreed to start a relationship with him. That was twenty-seven days and nineteen hours ago.

With a steady hand, Micah trimmed his goatee. The second he realized tonight was their first date without Matthew, he nicked himself. "Why am I so nervous?" he asked audibly. Normally, they went to places like Chuck E. Cheese or caught the latest animated feature so Matthew would be entertained and not feel left out. It was important to them both for Matthew not to feel neglected now that they were dating. Matthew didn't mind at all. He was happiest walking between them with one of his hands resting safely inside theirs. What Matthew really loved was for Micah to ride him on his shoulders. Micah loved that too. He laughed just as much as his little buddy, if not more.

There will be no laughing tonight, he thought, *unless she's laughing at me.* Micah quickly shook that thought away.

"You are a twenty-eight-year-old mighty man of valor," he said, looking at his reflection in the mirror. "You can have a conversation with a woman without the aid of a six-year-old." Micah made the statement in his deepest, most masculine voice, but deep down, he hadn't succeeded in convincing himself. Micah continued talking audibly at his cloudy image in the steamed mirror.

"What kind of questions should I ask her? How much information should I disclose? Should I ask about Matthew's father? Should I ask about her dreams and aspirations?" Micah looked around the bathroom as if waiting for a voice to answer back. Then he remembered what Pastor Jackson said: it was all right for him to talk to himself, just as long as he didn't answer himself back.

Micah chuckled at the thought of him being scared to talk to a woman. But then again, this was new to him, and right now he needed reassurance he wasn't going to make a complete fool of himself. No sooner had the thought left his mind, the phone sounded, alerting him that he had a visitor.

"Yes," he answered, annoyed that someone would disturb him in his time of crisis.

"Man, buzz me in."

Micah breathed a sigh of relief. It was Anthony Combs. He pressed the button for the security gate, and then quickly stepped into his pants and slipped on a turtleneck sweater. In the middle of tying his casual dress shoes, Anthony finally knocked on the door.

"Man, are you hyperventilating yet?" were the first words from Anthony's mouth once Micah let him in.

"AC, what are you doing here?"

"Making sure you don't stand Sister Pamela up."

"I'm not going to stand her up. I may sweat like a pig before I get there, but I am going to show up," Micah said, right before splashing on cologne.

Anthony's eyes lit up. "Man, when did you start wearing Sean John?"

"The day Pamela told me she likes it."

"You really like her, don't you?" Anthony asked, although the smile on Micah's face told the story.

"Yes, I *really* like her," Micah answered. "Which is why tonight is so important. I need to make sure Matthew isn't the only thing we have in common, and that outside of church we're still compatible."

"I understand your concern," Anthony said as he helped himself to bottle of water from the refrigerator. "But, Micah, my man, I honestly don't think you have anything to worry about." Anthony closed his eyes and pretended to receive a revelation. "The Spirit is telling me she's sprung."

Once Micah stopped laughing, his expression turned serious. "I hope she's also open-minded."

Anthony nodded his understanding of Micah's dilemma. "If she's the one God has for you, she will be."

Chapter 2

Pamela nervously applied the finishing touches to her make-up, then checked her hair one final time. Micah was due to arrive any second, and she didn't want to keep him waiting too long. That might give the impression she wasn't interested. Lord knows that was far from the truth.

"Jessica, you were right again," she whispered at her reflection in the mirror. The long-sleeve crepe dress flattered her size twelve shape nicely and complemented her mocha skin. *Perfect*, she thought. Not too dressy, not too casual. She didn't have any idea where they were going, but this dress could adapt to any environment. The doorbell sounded. She quickly stepped into her new pumps, and then dashed for the door. She hesitated before opening it. "How long are you supposed to make the guy wait?" she mumbled. "Oh, forget it. I've been single for five years, that's long enough." Pamela put on her friendliest smile and welcomed her guest.

"Good evening, Micah." She thought he was handsome in his black slacks and leather parka. Around his neck, she could see the collar of his cream turtleneck.

Micah stood there motionless and stared at her. He held flowers in his hand, and his mouth hung wide open. His face was perplexed, like he'd forgotten what he wanted to say. Seconds later he still hadn't returned her greeting, so she spoke again.

"Good evening, Micah."

"Hello, Pamela." As if suddenly remembering something, his facial muscles relaxed. "These are for you." He extended the flowers to her.

"Thank you." Micah watched her put the flowers in water and place the arrangement on the living-room table inside a crystal vase. Her back was turned, and her shoulders remained still. He couldn't tell that she considered his momentary memory loss hilarious. She turned to face him. "I'm ready; I just need to grab my coat." Her smile made him smile. He exhibited more confidence.

"Pamela, you're beautiful. I like that dress on you, and your hairstyle is very flattering."

The richness of his voice gave Pamela goose bumps, and she blushed uncontrollably. Yesterday's visit to Portia over at the *Top it Off* hair salon for a fresh relaxer had paid off.

"You look nice too," she replied, then reached inside the hall closet for her coat. In two long strides, he was at her side assisting with her coat. "Micah, where are we going?"

"It's a surprise, but trust me, you'll like it."

"And just why should I trust you?"

He had a quick comeback. "Because your son chose me; remember?"

"I'll be sure to thank my son later." She offered him a smile, and he exhaled.

Riding alone with Micah in his SUV proved more awkward than Pamela had imagined. She didn't know what to say now that she didn't have to turn her head to the backseat to warn Matthew to be still or to answer a question from her inquisitive son. Pamela directed her attention to the red taillights in front of them as they traveled eastward down Interstate 80. She started to comment on the heavy traffic, but figured that would reveal how desperate she was for conversation.

She looked at Micah. His palms were so sweaty they kept

sliding down the steering wheel. He popped in a CD, she assumed, to calm his anxiety and also to break the silence.

"I didn't know you listen to him. He's my favorite praise and worship artist," Pamela said, relieved they had more in common than Matthew and church.

"Mine too." Briefly, he grinned in her direction. "What's your favorite song?"

"All of them. I have all of his CDs and DVDs," Pamela answered proudly.

"I haven't seen his DVDs, but I have all of his CDs also."

Pamela sung and moved to the beat of the song. "I'll let you borrow my DVDs if you want," she offered then resumed singing.

"I'd like that." He pumped the volume and the two continued singing and chatting about the popular gospel artist the remainder of the way.

"Micah, I didn't know you were bringing me here. I have wanted to try this place for months," Pamela said when they pulled into the parking lot of the Dead Fish.

"I know." Micah smiled mischievously before he continued. "I heard you mention it to Jessica one Sunday after church."

As she watched him walk around to the passenger door, Pamela was impressed. He'd remembered a conversation from at least a month ago. After he assisted her from the vehicle, she interlocked her arm with his, and together, they walked toward the restaurant's double wooden doors.

"I like your cologne," Pamela complimented before stepping inside the waterfront seafood restaurant.

"A pretty girl once told me she liked it, so I picked some up."

Pamela didn't have a response, she was too busy blushing.

"Micah, this is lovely," Pamela said once they were seated at a corner table along the glass wall overlooking the Zampa and

Carquinez bridges. The romantic atmosphere was complete with candlelit tables and fresh-cut roses. Soft jazz played in the background.

"You sure are. Your beauty enhances the atmosphere."

"I was referring to the view of the lighted bridge," she responded just as the waiter introduced himself, and then asked for their drink orders.

Micah touched her arm. "Allow me." He looked up at the waiter. "We'll have a bottle of nonalcoholic White Zinfandel, please."

"How did you know I like White Zinfandel?" Pamela asked after the waiter left.

"I saw a bottle in your kitchen."

"Micah, I'm impressed. You notice everything."

"Thanks, but I must admit, I've been a nervous wreck about tonight."

"Is that how you cut yourself?" She had noticed the fresh cut just below his lip.

"I was hoping you wouldn't notice," Micah admitted.

"That's nothing; I almost put my eye out trying to put on eyeliner."

"Why were you nervous?" he asked once he stopped laughing.

"Probably the same reason you were."

"It's different without him, isn't it?" Micah referenced Matthew's absence.

"Very. I was scared we wouldn't have anything to talk about."

The waiter returned to chill the wine and to take their dinner orders. Pamela chose the stuffed salmon and Micah, the blackened catfish. They agreed to share crab cakes for an appetizer.

Pamela tried not to stare, but it was hard. Micah Stevenson

was by her account a handsome man: over six feet tall and milk chocolate with a goatee and a full set of lips. Every time she looked into his warm smile, she was nearly mesmerized. And his body, that was enough to make any woman thank God for creating man. But what she loved most were his eyelashes. They were so long, they almost curled.

"Micah, you said on Christmas Eve you'd been watching me for months. What exactly were you looking for?"

He took a sip of wine before answering. "At first, I don't think I was looking for anything. When I saw Matthew sitting next to you that first day, I thought you were pretty. That's how it started; I enjoyed looking at you. Especially when you danced in the Spirit."

Pamela blushed again.

Micah rested his arms on the table. "I know you're not shy, the way you dance all over the place."

"Don't sit there and act like you don't get your praise on nearly every Sunday," Pamela replied, placing her hands on her hips.

"So you were watching me also?"

She took a sip of wine. As the cold liquid lubricated her throat, she wondered why she favored the watereddown drink so much. "After I realized how fond Matthew was of you, I had to check you out." He nodded his understanding. "Did you like anything else?" She had to know if he were sincerely attracted to her or if Micah's purpose for being in her life was only as a role model for her son only.

"I love the way you take care of Matthew," Micah answered sincerely. "Coming from a home without a father and an alcoholic mother who sometimes forgot I was alive, I can appreciate a woman who cares for her child as well as you do."

Micah's unsolicited history surprised her, but she didn't let it show. "Thanks for the compliment. I do my best, trying to make sure he has everything without a father. I'm sorry you don't have a close relationship with your mother. Is that why you moved here from Chicago?"

Micah pondered his answer before responding. "No. I moved here because my uncle was here, and he was willing to help me turn my life around."

Pamela was curious just how much turning he needed to do, but decided to wait for him to disclose more of his past on his own.

"Exactly how are you related to Pastor Jackson?"

"He's my mother's oldest brother."

The waiter placed the crab cakes and two small plates on the table. They savored the aroma, then dug in after Micah said grace.

"Um, this is so good," she said, relishing the taste. Micah agreed, but Pamela discerned he was more interested in her than the crab cakes. He'd barely touched his cake.

"Pamela, tell me about your late husband, if you don't mind."

Pamela finished her crab cake and sipped more wine before answering him.

"While attending junior college, I worked part time as a cashier at Walgreens. Just before closing one Friday night, Marlon Roberts came running through my line. He flirted. I blushed. Three years later we were married. Then he died. That's it in a nutshell." Pamela shrugged her shoulders as if her marriage was no big deal. A coping mechanism to remain emotionally detached from her late husband's memory.

"Were he and Matthew close?"

"No. Marlon was killed in a motorcycle accident when Matthew was a year old. The only thing Matthew knows about his father is what I tell him. Beyond that, he doesn't remember him."

Micah took a sip of wine before asking his next question. "Do you think you'll ever marry again?"

Pamela looked him dead in the eyes. "If God sends me someone who'll love me and love Matthew as his own, and love God, I would marry him before the ink dries on the marriage license application."

The waiter approached the table to clear their dishes before Micah could respond to Pamela's declaration. "How would you want this man to look?" he asked once they were alone again.

A lot like you, is what she thought. What she voiced was, "As long as he's good to me and my son, I don't care what he looks like." Then with a smile, she added, "Just as long as he's not ugly and weighs five hundred pounds."

Micah laughed.

"What about you, Micah? Do you think you'll ever marry?"

"Of course, I told you on Christmas Eve, I come with a lifetime warranty."

Pamela blushed again. She was tired of blushing, but as long as Micah kept saying the right words, she had no control.

"What type of woman are you looking for?"

"The true and honest type," Micah answered frankly and without hesitation. "The type of woman I can share my goals and dreams with and she in turn does the same. A woman I can share my heart with and trust her not to intentionally break it. A woman who will open her heart to me and trust me with her fears. Quite simply, the type of woman who will love me for me and allow me to love her back. It goes without saying, she has to love God."

Pamela needed a sip of water after that. Micah appeared to have heard her secret prayers. The ones she whispered in the dark snuggled against her pillow. "And what does your type of woman look like?"

"If you have a mirror, I'll show you."

Pamela really needed some water after that statement. She finished off the entire glass. Afterward, Micah was amused as he watched her try to figure out what to do or say next. She looked from the window to the couple at the table next to theirs. Then to the front door; she even looked down at the floor. Pamela looked everywhere except in Micah's eyes. When the waiter delivered the main course, Pamela wanted to jump up and scream, "Hallelujah!"

Micah gently touched her hand. "Don't worry; I'm not going to propose tonight."

"No, this man didn't sit here and break every dating rule in the book, implying he's going to propose," she mumbled underneath her breath as she sprinkled salt on her vegetables.

The dinner conversation took a funny turn when they discovered they both enjoyed watching commercials. They ranted and raved about their favorites through dinner and over the hot fudge sundae they shared for dessert.

"Did you see the one where the dog barks, 'I love you'?" Pamela asked, just before popping the maraschino cherry into her mouth.

"What about the one where granny goes flying into the air and lands doing the splits?" Micah countered.

"What about the one where the bridesmaids tumble down the hillside?"

Pamela was ecstatic; she thought she was the only person in the world who preferred commercials over sitcoms. During the ride back to her place, Micah held her hand. It seemed appropriate as they laughed and sang commercial jingles.

"Micah, I had a wonderful evening," Pamela said when they reached the door of her town house. "I was really afraid we wouldn't hit it off after the novelty of you being my Christmas present wore off."

"Well, do you think we *hit* it off?" he asked, but he knew the answer. Pamela Roberts was everything he was looking for in a woman—saved, sweet, funny, loving, and pretty.

"I think we at least have a base hit," she answered, but failed to prevent a satisfied grin from escaping.

"Is that all?" Micah pouted, pretending to be offended. Then he embarrassed her. "Pamela, the way you downed that glass of water back at the restaurant says I hit a home run. Maybe even a grand slam."

"Every major-league player starts in the minors," she said unlocking her door.

"Pamela Roberts, you are too much. It's a good thing you have a pretty face, or I'd send *you* to the minors."

She flicked the light switch and stepped into the doorway so she could face Micah. "All jokes aside, I like you, Micah Stevenson."

"I know you do." His smile was wider than normal. "I like you too, Pamela Roberts."

Pamela nearly jumped when he kissed her hand. Her first thought was it had been a long time since a man was romantic and genuine toward her, then she realized this *was* the first time.

"I hope you don't mind me kissing your hand," he remarked. "Don't worry; I won't kiss you anywhere else without asking first."

"I don't mind," she answered faintly. "Not at all."

"Good night and sweet dreams, Pamela. I'll call you tomorrow."

Watching Micah disappear down the walkway, Pamela knew it was time to pray. Micah was the kind of man she could love, really love. He was God-fearing, caring, attentive, and romantic. "Maybe my son really does know what I need," she said before closing the door.

Chapter 3

"Talk to me!" Jessica didn't bother waiting for Pamela to say hello.

"Are you crazy calling me this early on a Saturday morning?" Pamela asked, although she'd been up for over an hour.

First she prayed, then read her Bible. Pamela needed direction from God about her new relationship. Thoughts of Micah Stevenson had invaded her mind since his departure ten hours ago. With every thought, she longed to see him again.

"Girl, stop playin'. I want details now. You know you should have called me the second you got in."

Pamela strung her along. "There's nothing to tell. We just had a little dinner, that's all."

"Pamela Roberts, don't make me come over there and beat it out of you," Jessica warned.

"I told you, we went to dinner, that's all."

"I'm putting on my coat and searching for my boxing gloves." Pamela remained quiet. "That's it, I'm on my way."

"Girl, we went to the Dead Fish!" Pamela screamed into the phone.

"No, you didn't."

"He overheard us talking about it. Would you believe that man chose the best table in the house?" Pamela took a breath. "Let me back up. He brought me flowers, and he was wearing Sean John. The food was good; the conversation great. We even shared a sundae for dessert."

"This is just ridiculous. The man looks good, and he's attentive, plus he has manners. Over here, Lord!" Jessica yelled. Pamela envisioned her waving her hands in the air to get the Lord's attention.

"But the best part is he loves commercials just as much as I do." Pamela was bubbling.

"Humph," Jessica smirked. "I knew something had to be wrong. He sounded too good to be true. He's crazy just like you are."

"Keep making fun of me, and I won't tell you how we ended the evening," Pamela warned.

"Spill it!"

"He kissed my hand!" Pamela giggled. Jessica remained silent. Pamela figured her friend was too busy shaking her head to respond.

"You really like him, don't you?"

"Yes, but I'm not rushing into anything. We're taking the time to get to know one another."

"One thing's for sure. I've never heard you this giddy over a man before."

"Seriously, Jess, I'm going to take my time and make sure I hear from God on this one."

"God had better speak quickly before you find out he likes latching as much as you do. It's a wrap if he does."

"That depends on what the Lord has to say about it."

"When the Lord finishes telling you what you already know, ask Him where He would like for me to stand so I can be found." Jessica's request had Pamela bent over with laughter.

"Good morning, Pastor Jackson." Micah respected his uncle to the point he addressed him as pastor even when they were in private. Micah joined him at the breakfast table and helped himself to a glass of orange juice.

"Good morning to you," Pastor Jackson said, adding emphasis to the word *you*. Micah suspected his uncle wanted the details from his evening with Pamela.

"Is that Micah's voice I hear?"

"Yes, sweetheart, it's him," Pastor Jackson answered his wife.

"Good morning, First Lady." Micah kissed the woman who'd taken on the role of mother in his life for the past two years.

"You tell me how good of a morning it is," his aunt responded as she sat in the chair opposite him. "You know I was waiting for you to call me last night."

"I'm sorry, Auntie, I was too excited to talk." That was the truth. After leaving Pamela's town house, Micah went home and tried to relax. It was useless, because every time Micah thought of Pamela's smile or the touch of her hand, he'd get excited all over again. Like a CD set on auto repeat, the evening replayed continuously from start to finish in his mind until he finally fell asleep with a smile on his face.

"What about now? Can you talk now?"

Micah appreciated his aunt's directness almost as much as he did the love and care she lavished upon him. He finished his juice to find his aunt and uncle staring at him with oversized grins.

"All right, I'll tell you," he surrendered. "Pamela and I had a wonderful time last night. I took her to dinner at a place she wanted to try and found out we have a lot in common; from our taste in music to our shared love for commercials."

"I didn't know she's a little touched like you are," his uncle chuckled.

"Robert, leave that child alone. It's all right for him to like commercials, just like it's all right for you to like pickled pig's feet and hot sauce." First Lady turned her attention back to Micah. "Do you think she's the one?"

Micah's smile was a dead giveaway to the positive answer they were seeking. "I'm praying about it real hard. So far, she seems like the one, but it's still early."

"I think she is the one. The mere fact that her male child picked you is enough for me." His aunt sat back and folded her arms.

"I think she's the one also, but there's still a lot she doesn't know about me."

"I assume you are referring to your past?" his uncle questioned.

Micah nodded.

"Son," Pastor Jackson began, "you are in Christ now, and that makes you a new creature. Your past is just that; the past. If she's the one God has ordained for you, she won't hold it against you."

Micah agreed with his uncle in theory, but in many cases reality and theory didn't match up, especially in the church.

"Son, have you talked to your mother lately?" his uncle asked.

Micah knew the unpleasant subject of his mother would eventually come up, but he still didn't want to discuss her. What would be the point? His mother hadn't changed. For as long as he could remember, Helen Stevenson did two things every day— drink and curse until she passed out. Some days she added eating to the list.

As a child, there were many days in which Micah was left to fend for himself. Some nights he had to find his own place to sleep because Helen was passed out and had forgotten to leave the front door unlocked, or she'd bring home a *friend* and needed her privacy.

"I called her last weekend, but she passed out in the middle of the conversation," Micah said. "I did send some money to the electric company to make sure she's not living in the dark again."

Pastor Jackson shook his head. "I don't know what happened to my sister. She hasn't been the same since your father was murdered in that robbery. All I can do is keep praying for her."

"That's all anyone can do until she decides to stop hurting herself," Micah surmised.

"I'm not going to stop praying for my baby sister until the day she dies," Pastor Jackson said. "But in the meantime, I'm also praying for your new relationship. I can see great things happening for you."

Micah refilled his glass, hoping his uncle was right.

Pamela unplugged the vacuum and placed it back inside the utility closet.

"Finished," she said out loud to the empty apartment. It had taken her nearly the entire day, but she'd managed to clean every room in her town house. The only thing left to do now was to take a hot bubble bath. Before she reached the stairs, the telephone sounded. "This better be important," she mumbled before answering the phone.

"Pamela, I need to talk to you. It's very important." The seriousness in Micah's tone caught her off guard. What serious matter did they have to discuss?

"I'm listening," she responded.

"What I have to say to you, I need to say it in person."

Micah was making her nervous. Their relationship was too new for this type of urgency. "When do you want to talk?" she asked, hoping the good feeling she had about their relationship wasn't about to end.

"Right now, I'm outside your door."

"Okay," she answered and wished she had more time to prepare for whatever news Micah was about to broadcast. She replaced the cordless phone on the charger and slowly walked to her front door. She took a deep breath, and then opened the door.

"Pamela, I have to tell you something." Micah stepped inside.

"Oh God," she mumbled. What did Micah have to say to her that would cause such a grim expression of distortion on his normally handsome face?

"What is it, Micah?" She still held the door open, thinking she might need it for support in the near future.

With a straight face, he looked her dead in the eyes and said it. "Pamela, I just saved a ton of money on my car insurance."

It took a moment for her to realize Micah had just reenacted one of her favorite commercials. "Micah Stevenson, are you crazy?" she yelled and at the same time slammed the door. "Coming over here scaring me half to death. I thought something was really wrong with you."

"Something was wrong," he said once he stopped laughing. "I was missing you."

"You missed me, so you decided to come over here and scare me?" she asked with her hands planted on her hips.

"No." He stepped toward her and reached for her left hand. "I missed you, so I came here to hear you laugh." He then kissed her hand and got what he wanted. Pamela giggled and blushed.

"I owe you one, Denzel," she said, after reclaiming her hand.

"Denzel?"

"You deserve an Oscar for that performance."

"You have to admit, that was funny."

She thought about it and agreed. It was funny. She shared a laugh with him until she remembered she was wearing old sweats and a hair scarf. Instantly she was embarrassed. She smelled like pine and disinfectant, which only added to her sudden discomfort. Micah didn't seem to mind at all.

"Looks like you're in the middle of housecleaning. Would you like for me to help you?"

Pamela was taken by surprise with his offer. "Thank you, but I've just finished. I was about to take a bath when you pulled your little prank."

"I won't keep you then. Like I said before, I missed you and wanted to hear you laugh, that's all. I've gotten what I came for. I'll let you enjoy your quality time alone. I know you don't get much of that." Before Micah turned the doorknob, he made her an offer. "If you ever need help with Matthew, call me. I'd be more than happy to take him off your hands for a few hours so you can rest, run an errand, or whatever."

"I appreciate that, Micah. Thank you." She really meant that. No one but Jessica had ever made that offer. It was challenging being a single mom with a limited support system. Her parents lived forty-five minutes away, so she couldn't rely on them to pick up Matthew from afterschool care on the days she ran late at the title company. Or take him to the park or the movies. Pamela promised Matthew she would sign him up to play T-ball in the spring, but she didn't have any idea how she was going to keep up with the practice schedule and games. Baseball was her son's love, and she would find a way.

"If you need something fixed around the house or your car worked on, call me," Micah added. "I'm not a handyman or mechanic, but I'll make sure it gets fixed."

"What if I don't need anything? Can I still call you?"

"Pamela Roberts, you can call me anytime." His wink caused her to blush again.

Pamela didn't wait to lock her door before she started praying. She called on the Lord with her hand still holding the doorknob. All the way up the stairs and into her private bathroom, she sought direction.

So far, Micah was everything she desired. He was like no other man she'd met. Micah was a leader, and she liked that. He didn't wait for her to ask for assistance, he freely made himself available to her and to her son. He respected her as an individual and even respected her space. She didn't receive that kind of veneration from her late husband.

"God, give me some direction before I fall in love with this man," Pamela mouthed, and then closed her eyes and succumbed to the soothing bubbles of the bath she had prepared.

Chapter 4

Sunday morning, Praise Temple Church lived up to its name. The praises were extra loud and plenteous. It all started with Deacon Blake's opening prayer. Every time Deacon Blake prayed, the presence of God would fill the house. This was amazing, because when Deacon Blake wasn't praying, he was sleeping. He would sleep right on through the choir's "A" and "B" selections and Pastor Jackson's sermon. But when he prayed, Deacon Blake was wide awake. Often people would be slain in the Spirit by the time he yelled his final hallelujah. Deacon Blake was so dedicated to praying, one Sunday he double-parked his Cadillac on one of the busiest streets in Oakland, just so he wouldn't miss his spot on the program.

Pamela closed her eyes and listened carefully to words the choir echoed. "*God's got a blessing . . . with my name on it . . . God's got a blessing.*" She wondered what blessing God had for her. Was it a husband for her and a father for her son? Pamela opened her eyes and looked across the sanctuary in his direction.

Watching Micah praise God, a smile instantly creased her face. Pamela imagined Micah praised God the way King David had done after returning with the Ark of the Covenant. She looked slightly to the left only to find the first lady whispering something into Pastor Jackson's ear, and then pointing in her direction. No doubt they knew how well Micah's and her date had been. By their smiles, they were certainly pleased.

"Look at that," Jessica nudged Pamela. "They're already welcoming you into the family."

"That's a little premature, don't you think?"

"Try telling that to Micah. I saw the way he was watching you earlier."

Pamela found Jessica's adequate observations irritating. "This is why I don't like sitting by you; you talk too much."

"Would you like for me to trade seats with Brother Stevenson?" Jessica rolled her eyes, but didn't miss a beat with clapping her hands and receiving her blessing.

"Would you like for me to trade seats with Minister Combs?" Pamela shot back. Those words made Jessica lose her rhythm and her smile. Jessica rolled her eyes again, but she didn't say another word.

Pastor Jackson took his sermon from Matthew 7:1.

Judge not, that ye be not judged.

"There are some people in the church who have become professional judges although they haven't spent five minutes inside of a law school. They haven't been appointed or sworn in, but they've taken it upon themselves to judge the lives of others. The worst part is they hold people in bondage long after God has set them free."

"Talk about it, Pastor!" Pastor Jackson always had an amen corner.

"God forgives anyone who comes to Him with a sincere heart, and He is able and willing to deliver all of us from sin. The Bible clearly tells us if we confess our sins, He is faithful and just to forgive us and to cleanse us from all unrighteousness."

"That's right!" the amens were in high gear now.

"But now we have these self-appointed judges, who have the audacity to hold the past over our heads and question our deliverance. They have the nerve to want you to prove to them that you're free when God has already declared you free. They want to condemn you for mistakes in the past and totally discredit your present victories. The worst part is these judges have just as much *active* sin in their lives right now, but they're hiding theirs by focusing on ours."

"Preach, Pastor!"

"Tell the truth up in here!"

"Saints," Pastor Jackson wiped his forehead with the engraved hand towel, despite the fact he wasn't sweating, "some of you who have just finished dancing all over the floor and shouting hallelujah the loudest sit on your high bench and judge others."

The amens quieted down.

"If someone looks, acts, or dresses differently, their salvation is called into question. Today, I want to pose a thought for you to ponder. Maybe God uses people in diverse ways because He's a diverse God. He is not limited to our small minds and these four walls. We can't box God into our tiny mind set."

Pamela listened, thankful she wasn't one of the people Pastor Jackson was talking about. She was careful to treat everyone with respect and was always open-minded to new people and ideas.

Micah listened too, praying Pamela wasn't a self-appointed judge.

No sooner had Minister Combs recited the benediction, Jessica lit into Pamela. "What do you mean by implying I like Anthony Combs? I have never said that."

"I've seen you stealing glances at him on more than one occasion. During his last sermon, you jumped and yelled hallelujah more than his mama," Pamela answered calmly, completely ignoring Jessica's attitude.

"You know he is not my type. He's bald and too short.

Besides, I can't stand those bright shiny suits he wears all the time. Plus he has an eight pack across his midsection and I like six packs."

"So, you have been checking him out." Pamela looked in Minister Combs's direction. He was receiving another home-made cake from the first lady. Pamela waved, and he waved back.

"Ugh!" Jessica stomped out of the sanctuary.

Micah met Pamela in the vestibule and offered to drive her to her parents' home in Vallejo to pick up Matthew. She gladly accepted.

After changing into casual clothing, Micah met Pamela at her town house. To his surprise, she wasn't quite ready to leave.

"Come in," she said. "I have something for you." She pointed to her granite countertop where two empty glasses were placed.

Micah didn't have any idea what the glasses were for, but her smile was so welcoming he obeyed. He followed her over to the counter and watched quietly as she filled the two glasses with milk. She then reached inside the cookie jar for her favorite chocolate cookies with crème filling.

"Bet you I win," she said, offering him a cookie.

Micah's laughter echoed in her medium-sized kitchen. He couldn't believe it; she was challenging him to a crème-licking and cookie-dunking contest.

"Come on, you've seen the commercial, you know the rules," she baited.

"You can't be serious." Micah, still laughing, leaned against the counter.

"I told you, I owe you one."

Micah enjoyed the commercial in question, but he didn't want to look like an idiot, racing to lick all the crème from a cookie in front of the woman he was trying to impress. Then Pamela touched his hand.

"Please." Her voice was as soft as her touch, and Micah knew he would try his hardest to walk on water if she made the request.

He threw his hand in the air. "All right, all right."

Pamela counted down. "On your mark, get set, go!"

It was a sight to behold, two adults licking the crème from cookies like crazed maniacs. Goo-goo eyes were replaced by intense stares and aggressive grunts.

"Ah-ha!" Micah roared when he finished first and slam-dumped his clean cookie into the milk. Pamela talked him into a rematch, and the madness started all over again.

"I can't believe I let you sucker me into this foolishness," Micah said after winning for the third time.

"Foolishness? That was fun, and you know it." Pamela finished her milk. "I didn't sucker you into anything."

Micah stepped closer to her and used his thumb to wipe the milk that settled in the corner of her mouth. "Yes, you did sucker me. You know I can't refuse that smile of yours."

Micah was too close to her. He smelled too good; his touch too soothing. "We'd better get going." Pamela was still smiling, but distracted her thoughts by cleaning up the mess they'd made.

"Do you want to grab a bite before heading out?" Micah asked, also feeling the need to leave the confines of her town house and get into a public place.

"I'm sure my mother has prepared dinner."

"Good, I could use a home-cooked meal. That is, if your parents don't mind me joining you." He assisted with her coat.

"My parents don't mind. In fact, they expect it."

"Micah!" Matthew must have been sitting by the front window of his grandparents' home, because Micah barely had a chance to shut off the engine before Matthew came running from the house to the SUV.

"Hey, little buddy." Micah stooped, and Matthew jumped onto his shoulders. Pamela remained in the vehicle, and her parents watched from the porch as Micah ran around the front yard with Matthew on his shoulders. He then dropped Matthew on the ground and tickled him.

"I missed you, Micah," Matthew said between giggles.

"I missed you too, but I bet you had fun with your grandparents."

"I did, but I still missed playing with you." Matthew giggled when he saw Micah prepare his hand to tickle him again.

"Did anyone miss me?" Pamela's voice startled both of them. Matthew and Micah were so caught up in their play, they'd forgotten all about her.

"Hi, Mommy." Matthew gave her a quick hug, then turned his attention right back to Micah.

"I'm sorry, sweetheart; I forgot to open the door for you." Micah couldn't believe he'd left her sitting inside the vehicle while he played like a child on the front lawn with Matthew.

"Hello, Mr. and Mrs. Jacobs." Micah waved and her parents excitedly waved back from the porch.

"Come on inside, dinner is almost ready," Pamela's mother called.

Matthew looked up at his mother's eyes, then placed his little hand into hers. Pamela could tell by the smile on her son's face he was about to say something to embarrass her.

"Mommy, he called you sweetheart. Did you get married yet? Can he live with us now?" Matthew questioned.

She was right, Matthew embarrassed her, then Micah did the same.

"Matthew, don't worry, when I marry your mother, you will be right there and so will your grandparents," Micah replied.

"Okay," Matthew giggled and ran inside.

Thoughts thronged Pamela's mind as she walked into her parents' home. *Micah just said he's going to marry her. He couldn't have been serious. Did she want to marry him? Was he the one?* She didn't have any answers.

"Pam, come in here and help me set the table," her mother called from the kitchen.

Pamela wondered since when did her mother set the table? Aside from holidays, she hadn't set the table in all the eighteen years Pamela lived at home.

"Son, have a seat." Pamela's father invited Micah to the sage-colored couch.

Son? Pamela looked at her father strangely. He'd never addressed her late husband as son.

"Thanks, Mr. Jacobs." Micah was barely seated on the couch before Matthew jumped in his lap.

"Son, please call me Henry."

"And feel free to call me Dorothy," Pamela's mother added from the kitchen archway.

"How about Mr. Henry?" Micah considered it disrespectful to refer to his elders by first name.

Henry nodded and smiled, appreciating the respect Micah afforded him. "Tell me about yourself. Every time I ask Pam about you, she starts giggling and can't get any words out that I can understand." Henry shook his head, and Micah grinned.

"Sir, I'm originally from Chicago. I'm an only child. I've worked for the local cable company for almost two years. I have my own car, and I'm saving for a house. I am saved and love Jesus. I don't have a criminal record, and I have good credit."

"Son, you've just about covered everything. No wonder my baby girl likes you so much." Micah joined in with Henry's laughter.

"I like him too, Grandpa." Matthew added his two cents.

"I know you like him," Henry said to his grandson. He looked over at Micah. "You're all he's talked about since he got here on Friday. 'Micah's going to show me how to ride a bike' 'Micah said he's going to play baseball with me.' 'Micah pulled my teeth.'" Henry shook his head again. "That boy is crazy about you."

Micah squeezed Matthew and rubbed his head. "I'm crazy about you too, little buddy."

Henry watched the play between the two. "If I didn't know any better, I'd swear you were Matthew's biological father. The two of you blend well. And anyone who makes my daughter and grandson this happy is all right with me."

While setting the dining room table, Pamela tried to suppress the excitement she felt bubbling deep down inside of her. Micah was such a good fit for her and her family. Matthew loved him, and today it was apparent her parents approved of him. They wouldn't oppose their union at all. But did she approve of him? It was still early in the relationship, but in a short period of time, Micah made her feel special and made her enjoy life again. She felt free to be herself around him, like today. From the second she saw the cookie commercial, she'd wanted to try it, but was too embarrassed to tell anyone about her desire to act like a kid. With Micah she wasn't embarrassed at all. She actually looked forward to their next antic.

"You really like him, don't you?" her mother asked, noticing Pamela's smile.

"A little bit." Pamela tried to be modest.

"By that smile, I'd say it's more than a little bit."

Pamela didn't even know she was smiling. "Mama, Micah is a wonderful man, and I enjoy the time we spend together and our talks. Matthew loves him. But I'm not sure if he's the one."

Her mother finished buttering the hot rolls before responding. "What is it you're not sure about? Are you saying you don't have feelings for him?"

"Yes, I do have feelings for him, strong feelings. I just want to be careful. I've been down this road before and still have the scars to prove it." Pamela continued filling serving bowls with greens, cornbread dressing, and candied yams.

Dorothy placed the platter containing baked turkey wings in the center of the table. "Pam, this road may look the same to you, but trust me, it's not. Micah is a saved man, and he loves God more than he loves himself. God sent Micah into your life; Marlon just dropped in. Micah is here by divine appointment. Don't forget, your son prayed and asked God to send someone for you, and He sent Micah. A good man is a gift. Baby, don't give your gift back."

"I hear you, Mama, I just want to be sure. I have Matthew to think about."

Dorothy removed her apron and placed her arm around her daughter. "Matthew is going to be fine. He's already talking about how great it's going to be having a dad around the house. You need to start thinking about how good it's going to be having a good-looking man around."

Pamela smiled, knowing her mother was right. Micah Stevenson was her gift. He was what she'd prayed for and hoped for. During dinner she sat next to him and found she gave him more attention than she gave her food. She noticed things about him that she hadn't before. Like the way he held his glass tilted just slightly when he drank and how many times he chewed his food before swallowing.

"Mommy, did you sign me up for baseball?" Matthew's question broke her concentration.

"Matthew, it's not time yet. We still have a few weeks," Pamela replied.

"Oh." Matthew then turned to Micah. "Are you going to coach my team like you coach the team at church?"

"If I can work it into my schedule, I will," Micah answered before helping himself to another serving of collard greens. Matthew saw how much Micah enjoyed his vegetables, so he asked for a second serving like Micah. "Ms. Dorothy, you sure can cook."

"Thank you, Micah." Dorothy then smiled at her daughter. "Pam can cook as well as I can, if not better."

"I wouldn't know," Micah answered before filling his mouth with yams.

"Pam, you haven't made this man any of your meatloaf or peach cobbler?" her father asked.

"No, Daddy, I haven't." Her father was full of surprises today. He hadn't cared if Marlon ate or not.

"Micah, you've got to try her meatloaf and peach cobbler. The fried chicken is good too, but the meatloaf and cobbler are her specialties," Henry said.

Micah smiled at Pamela. "I love meatloaf and peach cobbler among other things. You know what they say: the way to a man's heart is through his stomach."

"I'd better start cooking then," Pam responded, and then quickly turned her attention back to her food, trying hard not to answer the urge to run into the kitchen and start kneading flour and Crisco.

Once they were back at the town house, Micah carried a sleeping Matthew inside and tucked him into bed. Pamela had given her son a bath and put on his pajamas before leaving her parents' home.

"I've enjoyed our time together this weekend," Pamela said while walking Micah to the door.

"Me too. I didn't laugh this much as a kid. Pamela Roberts, you're good for me. I hope you feel the same." The softness of his eyes showed his vulnerability, almost as if he were pleading with her.

Pamela swallowed hard. "Yes, Micah, I do feel the same," she answered softly.

"You don't have to cook your way into my heart; you're already in there." Micah stepped closer to her and stroked her cheek with the back of his hand. "Can I kiss you?"

Pamela nodded, then closed her eyes. Micah's lips brushed her cheek ever so slightly. The kiss was sweet, but she was a little disappointed. She wanted to know what his lips felt like against hers. She'd have to wait for the proper time to find out. Pamela didn't wipe her face until the next morning.

Chapter 5

Micah couldn't remember Monday mornings ever feeling this good. He felt surprisingly well rested, considering he'd gotten only five hours of sleep. His jubilation was the result of hearing Pamela's voice first thing this morning after his devotional time. They only exchanged a few words, but that was enough to bring an abundance of sunshine into his life and brighten the still-dark morning sky. By early afternoon, Micah was climbing telephone poles to a rhythm no one but him could hear, because the music was in his heart. Life was good, his spirit was free, and his heart was occupied by the woman whom he believed to be his future wife.

Micah grinned constantly while he reminisced about the tons of fun they shared over the weekend and their good night kiss. Micah acknowledged only to himself that he wanted to kiss her lips, but his uncle and AC had warned him against that. "Tongue action will lead to hip action," is what Pastor Jackson told him after Micah shared his interest in Pamela. Micah was content to wait. When he gave himself to a woman, he wanted it to be on his wedding night anyway.

Micah doubted if Pamela really understood how deep in his heart she had settled. Micah himself didn't understand how she'd gotten there so fast. He didn't have an explanation. It was like she belonged there; like she was the missing part of his life. Pamela had a way of releasing his playful side, something he'd never been able to do. With her, Micah could reveal his silly side and not feel ashamed or immature. What could he say about Matthew? He was an added bonus. As he had tucked Matthew into bed the night before, he felt like a father. Micah liked that. The thought of fatherhood brought his savings account to mind.

In six months, he'd have enough saved for a good down payment on a house. Another first. Having grown up in apartments on the south side of Chicago, he hadn't experienced living in a single-family home. Six months was also enough time to build a solid relationship with Pamela, or at least he hoped. Pulling into a customer's driveway, Micah made a mental note to ask Pamela what size house she wanted, just in case.

"Jessica, I can't believe you're still mad about yesterday," Pamela said when she entered Jessica's office. Jessica hadn't spoken two words to her all morning. Pamela even caught her rolling her eyes in her direction during the weekly office meeting. The silent treatment was expected, but Pamela considered the eye action a bit much.

"You know you were wrong for implying I'm attracted to Anthony Combs." Jessica rolled her eyes yet again and smacked her lips.

"By your juvenile behavior, I'd say I was right on the money." Pamela leaned against Jessica's desk and helped herself to some peppermint candy. "I don't know why you won't admit it. Anthony Combs is a good catch. He has a job, owns a home, a decent car, and he takes very good care of his mother. That's always a good indication of how well a man will treat his wife. In my opinion, the only thing wrong with him are those bright shiny suits he insists on wearing." Pamela plopped into one of the chairs reserved for clients.

"Girl, yesterday looking at him reminded me of that disco ball in *Saturday Night Fever*." Pamela laughed, then stood and imitated John Travolta's dance steps.

Jessica laughed too, but she still didn't agree with Pamela. "Since you want to have confession, when are you going to confess you're in love with Micah?" It was Jessica's turn to watch Pamela squirm.

"Wh-what are you talking about? I like Micah a lot, but—"

"But nothing. I've been watching you. You've been humming and smiling all morning."

Jessica was right. Pamela felt extra good today, especially after starting her day with Micah's voice on the other end of the phone. He'd called just to say he was thinking about her and to wish her a blessed day.

And a blessed day it was. Everything was going well for Pamela today. Matthew didn't protest when she dragged him out of bed. Traffic was light and all of the documents had come in for the escrows scheduled to close in the next few days. Everything was going well, and Micah Stevenson was a big part of the peace she felt. Yes, she did care about him; she might even love him, but it was too early to expose her heart to the possibility.

"Jess, I do care about him, but I think it's a little too soon to call it love. We've only been dating a little over a month." Pamela treated herself to a piece of chocolate this time around.

"If my memory is correct, two days after you met Marlon Roberts, you swore you were in love," Jessica reminded her.

"My point exactly," Pamela said, balling up the foil candy wrapper and tossing it into the trash. "I made the mistake of moving too fast before. I'm not falling into that trap again."

"This is different. Marlon was the devil in disguise; Micah is a man of God," Jessica explained.

"You sound like my mother," Pamela said rising to leave.

"You should listen to your mother *this* time."

"I know Micah has been sent to me by God," Pamela admitted with a smile. "But I'm not going to rush getting emotionally attached. I have a son to consider."

"If my godson had his way, you would have married Micah on Christmas Eve."

"True, that's why I'm the parent. Now you should listen to me. Admit that you like Anthony *Saturday Night Fever* Combs and give the man a call." Pamela had to run out of the office to keep from being hit by the box of paper clips Jessica tossed.

Two days later, Pamela was the middle of clearing a paper jam in the printer when her office telephone rang. She answered on the third ring. The voice on the other end caused her cheeks to warm. "Hello, Micah, how was your day?"

"Perfect now that I've heard your voice again." Pamela giggled at his reply, and he continued. "How about dinner at the Chinese buffet in San Leandro?"

"Micah, you know we can't go out tonight." It was Wednesday, Bible Study night. "By the time I make it across town and pick up Matthew and feed him dinner, I'll barely make it to church on time."

"I know. That's why I'm going to pick Matthew up for you, and we'll meet you at the restaurant. I'll even help him with his homework. This way you can enjoy your dinner without feeling rushed. What do you say?"

Following Micah's offer of assistance, Pamela was glad she'd added his name to the list of adults allowed to pick Matthew up from the after school care program. Today her work ran behind schedule. Not having to rush in commute traffic would truly be a blessing. She wondered how Micah knew his help was needed, but didn't ask.

"Micah, you're a godsend. Thank you so much. I owe you one."

"Don't worry about it. Watching you relax and enjoy yourself is payment enough."

Pamela blushed again. Micah always knew what to say to make her feel special.

Two hours later, Pamela walked into the Chinese restaurant, starved. She'd worked through her lunch to ensure she'd get off on time. Pamela headed straight for the buffet figuring she'd make her plate first then look for her men later. "My men? What am I thinking?" she mumbled. Pamela was about to reach under the heat lamp for a warm plate when she heard the sound that made her heartbeat accelerate.

"Over here, sweetheart."

Pamela turned to see Micah and Matthew waving and smiling at her. Anticipation and excitement took control. Her stomach would have to wait. At that moment, she wanted nothing more than to give her men a big hug and kiss— both of them. That's what she did. Upon arriving at the table, naturally, Pamela hugged and kissed her son. And almost just as natural, she hugged Micah and kissed his cheek.

Micah stood holding a chair out for her. He didn't say anything, just grinned and returned the embrace.

Matthew slapped his little hands to his face and giggled.

"Have a seat," Micah offered.

"Can I get something to eat first?"

"We'll take care of that." Micah pointed to Matthew. "You've had a busy day, now relax and let us take care of you."

Pamela obediently sat down. As soon as they were out of sight, she checked Matthew's backpack. All of his homework was completed and neatly organized in his homework folder. "Thank you, Lord," she mumbled. "I can get to bed early tonight."

She then scanned the buffet. There were people coming and going in all directions selecting everything from chow mein to steamed oysters. Through the throng of people only one person held her attention: Micah. Even in his company uniform, he was attractive. At that moment, it wasn't his physical attributes that mesmerized her. It was him. His personality; the concern he showed for her; the way he interacted with Matthew; the way he smiled at her like she was the only woman in the world. All that made Micah Stevenson the finest man she'd ever seen. Once again, Pamela prayed for her emotions to remain in control, before she made another shipwreck.

Pamela was impressed. The plate Micah placed in front of her contained all her favorite items.

"How did you know what I like?" she questioned.

"I told him, Mommy," Matthew answered after setting down a glass filled with her favorite diet beverage.

Pamela's eyes roamed from her son to the new man in her life, both of whom were smiling. They were so good together and even better to her. "Thank you," she said softly.

Micah caressed both her and Matthew's hand and said grace. At the end of the prayer, Pamela had to force herself to release the comfort of his hand to eat her dinner. His touch was so soothing that she was tempted to eat with her left hand and risk staining her white blouse. She'd decide to take the challenge until Micah released her right hand and began eating.

"Thank you for helping Matthew with his homework," Pamela said after savoring a snow crab leg. "Micah, you are so good to us. What would we do without you?"

"I hope you never find out." Micah winked and continued eating.

He was doing it again, planning *their* future, and this time the vision of Micah as a permanent fixture in her life completely agreed with her.

"Micah, how was your day?" Pamela figured she'd change the subject before she gave in to the urge to kiss him again.

"Except for falling off a roof, it was uneventful."

Pamela dipped the crab leg into butter "What happened? Did you hurt yourself?"

"I was thinking about you and missed a step. Just the thought of you is a safety hazard for me nowadays." Micah winked again, and Pamela suddenly became parched.

"Mommy, you're really thirsty," Matthew commented, watching Pamela down the diet soda without stopping. She then sent Matthew for a refill.

"Micah, hold up!" AC, carrying a pie from the first lady in his hand, caught up with him in the vestibule after Bible Study. "Man, has love made you forget about your friends?"

"What are you talking about?"

AC shook his head. "Man, you've got it bad. I saw you and Sister Pamela and Matthew enter the sanctuary together looking like the perfect family."

"We met for dinner." Micah beamed. "But what does that have to do with anything?"

"You were supposed to help me move my mother this evening, remember?"

"Oh, man!" Micah shook his head. He'd totally forgotten he'd agreed to help AC move a refrigerator, stove, and a couch into AC's mother's new senior citizen complex. "I'm sorry. I'll meet you at your mother's house in ten minutes."

"It's too late now," AC responded. "Mama said to tell you, if her food spoils, you're cleaning up the mess and buying her a freezer full of groceries."

"Man, I'm really sorry, but Pamela had a busy day and needed my help."

"And you were just the one to help a sista out," AC teased. "It's cool. For a three-piece meal from Popeyes, my nephew helped me at the last minute, but next time . . ."

"I know, man." Micah's voice trailed off. Pamela approached, and he lost his train of thought.

AC shook his head. "Man, you are one sick puppy."

"What's wrong, Micah? The food from the buffet didn't make you sick, did it? Do you need to see a doctor?" Pamela asked after overhearing AC's comment.

The concern in her eyes and the soft feel of her hand on his shoulder only added to Micah's absentmindedness. He couldn't think of an answer. AC had to help the brother out.

"Sister Pamela, the kind of sickness he has can't be cured with modern medicine," AC laughed. "But I'm sure *you* can cure him."

Pamela blushed.

Micah dismissed his friend's musings with the wave of his hand. "Come on, sweetheart, I'll walk you to your car."

AC watched his friend disappear. The three of them, Micah, Pamela, and Matthew, truly did display the perfect family image. In all the time he'd known Micah, he'd never seen him happy until now. AC bowed his head and prayed. "God, please let everything work out for my friend."

Chapter 6

Pamela thought the knocking and ringing was all in her head until discerning Micah's voice. It was then she realized he was outside her front door trying desperately to awaken her. Micah Stevenson was the sweetest man she knew, but he was also crazy. He had to be. Why else would he think it was normal to bang on someone's door at 6:00 A.M. on a weekday?

"Wake up, sleeping beauty," she heard him call.

"Micah Stevenson, are you crazy?" She swung her front door open only to find him grinning like his name was called as the next contestant on *The Price is Right*.

"Yes, I am, for you."

Pamela placed her hands on her hips. "Can you at least act like you have a little common sense before 7:00 A.M.?"

Micah laughed. Pamela didn't. She was furious. How dare he rob her of her last thirty minutes of sleep? She was so mad, she didn't care that she had a red and white scarf tied around her head and dried drool on the side of her face. She folded her arms and glared at him.

"Lighten up, sweetheart; it's a special day. I'm on my way to work, but I didn't want to wait all day before expressing how special you are to me."

Pamela didn't have a clue about what he was talking about. All she knew was the sun hadn't come up yet and this cute madman was getting on her nerves.

"Micah, if I'm so special, you'd let me get some sleep, and you wouldn't come here uninvited at 6:00 A.M.!" she yelled.

Micah frowned. "You sure are grouchy in the morning. Here, before you mess up my day."

"Mess up *your* day," she started to scream, but stopped when he revealed the single red rose and the huge card in shape of a heart that he had been hiding behind his back.

"Happy Valentine's Day," he said solemnly. "I know it's early, but I wanted to see you before I went to work. True, I could've called, but I wanted to surprise you. And yes, I could've waited until this evening, but I didn't want you to be the only one at your office without something special on this day." He then bent over and picked up the gift box and handed it to her. "Have a good day." With that he left.

Pamela was stunned. She'd totally forgotten about Valentine's Day. She hadn't celebrated the day set aside for love since before Matthew was born. She didn't even purchase cards for Matthew to exchange at school. Pamela closed the door and slowly walked over to the counter and laid her unexpected gifts down.

Slowly, she sniffed the red rose and savored its fragrance. Next, she examined the big red heart made from construction paper. Her eyes watered as she read the handwritten sentiment.

Good morning, sweetheart.

Today would be dull and boring without you.

You make every day special to me.

My day would be incomplete without your warm smile and the sweet sound of your voice.

Every day, I thank God for blessing me to be a part of your life.

Happy Valentine's Day,

Micah

Pamela grabbed a paper towel from the kitchen counter and wiped her face before opening the neatly wrapped box. The red and gold paper was so pretty she hated to tear it, but she bubbled with anticipation. "Oh, Micah," she whispered after lifting the fuchsia silk pantsuit from the box. It was the same pantsuit she admired on the mannequin in the window at Macy's two weeks ago when Micah accompanied her and Matthew on a shopping trip for shoes at the mall. At the time, Micah acted like he wasn't paying her any attention when she expressed interest in the ensemble. Turns out, he had paid close attention. Micah had also purchased jewelry and heels to match. Everything was the right size. Pamela was impressed. She also felt like an idiot for the way she'd treated him. "I've got to catch him," she announced, then quickly ran to the door. She opened the door and gasped; Micah was standing there, arms folded, wearing the biggest smile on his face.

Pamela didn't bother hiding how she felt. She hugged him with such force she almost knocked him off balance.

"Thank you," were the only words that she would allow to flow from her. She wanted to say more, much more, but was afraid to. She wasn't ready to vocalize what she felt inside for this sweet man in the cable company uniform. Not just yet.

"I guess this means you like your gifts," Micah said after forcing himself to release her.

"I love them, especially the card," she whispered, trying to interpret the look in his eyes. Then he did something she didn't expect. He stepped away from her and placed his hand over his nose.

"Pamela, sweetie, I'm really enjoying this moment, but it is early and you have drool stuck to the side of your face and that morning breath is killing me!"

Micah was laughing, but Pamela was embarrassed. She turned her head and covered her mouth with her hand.

"That's what you get for coming here so early uninvited."

"You're still beautiful, but I have to go." He turned to leave then stopped. "Don't work too hard. I'm picking Matthew up from after school care. We have plans for you." He blew her a kiss, then trotted to the cable van.

Pamela stood in her doorway enjoying the morning air and the orange rays peeking through the gray morning sky. Her irritation a distant memory. The forecast called for rain, but Pamela didn't care. It could snow and her day would still be wonderful, thanks to Micah.

"Good morning, Ms. Pamela."

Pamela's neighbor startled her. What was Mr. Larson doing up this time of morning, watering his lawn without a shirt, she wondered, but didn't dare ask him. She quickly greeted the middle-aged gentleman and hurried inside.

Pamela stared at the stack of documents in front of her; she really needed to review them. Her clients were due in half an hour, but she couldn't focus. Micah's early-morning visit filled every corner of her mind. Even when she was married, Valentine's Day didn't mean anything to her. Micah changed that this morning. All morning, she'd been thinking about their relationship. She finally admitted to herself she liked where they were headed and loved the attention and appreciation he showered on her. She loved how he looked after her, not wanting her to worry about anything. Like the other night after Bible Study when he followed her to the gas station where he filled up her gas tank and put air in her tires. He was so thoughtful, he even prayed with her once a day. She couldn't imagine what Micah had planned for that evening, but whatever it was, she would enjoy it, of that she was sure.

"What are you smiling about?" Jessica asked, taking a seat in Pamela's office.

Pamela hadn't heard her enter or realized she was smiling; she should have. Thoughts of Micah always brought a smile to her face.

"It's Valentine's Day," Pamela answered.

"That has never made you smile before, and neither did it give you a reason to dress up," Jessica said, checking out Pamela's outfit.

"That was before Micah," Pamela whispered, although no one was in her office but the two of them. "This is one of his Valentine's Day gifts to me."

"What are you talking about, girl?"

Pamela giggled like a schoolgirl. "Jess, that crazy man showed up at six o'clock this morning with this entire outfit. I even got a rose and a card."

"Pam, you're kidding."

"No, I'm not. But the funny part is I didn't even know it was Valentine's Day!"

Jessica laughed so hard she cried listening to Pamela tell her about the drool and morning breath.

"You two are a mess." Jessica was smiling, but Pamela knew her friend wished she could trade places with her. It wasn't a secret that Jessica desired to be a wife and mother.

"Have you talked to Anthony lately?"

Jessica rolled her eyes. "Why did you have to go and mention him?"

"Because I know he's on your mind. Jess, why don't just admit it, you like the man." Jessica pouted. "Come on, Jess," Pamela coaxed.

"All right, all right. I like him. Happy?"

"I knew it!" Pamela shrieked. "I think he likes you too."

"How do you know?"

Pamela recognized the desperation in her voice. "Well," Pamela leaned back in her chair. "I've seen him watching you in church, and Micah told me he asks about you from time to time."

"Why didn't you tell me?" Jessica snapped.

"Because you kept denying your attraction to him."

Jessica glanced at her watch. "My clients will be here any moment, but the next time Anthony Combs asks about me, tell him to talk to me!"

Pamela laughed watching her friend stomp away like a two-year-old, until she realized she had ten minutes to prepare the documents for her next appointment. She blocked everything out of her mind and focused on her work. That is, everything but Micah. She couldn't think about him enough.

Three hours later, Pamela practically skipped along the concrete walkway of her complex leading to her town house. The cable van was parked outside. That meant Micah was there, but where? She retrieved her mail and unlocked her door and stepped inside.

At first she thought the sight of Micah and Matthew dressed as waiters in black suits and white shirts waiting to serve her was a hallucination.

"Happy Valentine's Day, Mommy." As if on cue, Matthew stepped forward and handed his mother a red rose.

"Thank you, sweetheart." After hugging her son, Pamela added the rose to the vase that contained the one Micah had given her earlier that morning.

"I hope you don't mind Matthew showing me where you keep the spare key," Micah stated. "We wanted to surprise you, and by the way, you look beautiful in that outfit." Micah winked at her, and Pamela's breath caught in her throat. He was simply gorgeous. Micah's well-defined physique made the black suit look good, instead of the other way around.

"I am surprised, and thank you," she said, hesitantly look-ing away at the dinner table. It was set with china and crystal topped off with candlelight.

"Do you like it, Mommy? Micah said you would like it because you are our Valentine, and this is what you do on Valentine's Day." Matthew anxiously awaited her approval.

"I love it." Pamela knelt to hug her son, but held eye contact with Micah. "And I like you," she cooed.

The smile Micah afforded her sent a warm feeling that started in her chest and then flowed throughout her entire body.

"Come on, Mommy, sit down." Matthew pulled out her chair. After Pamela sat, he placed a cloth napkin across his mother's lap with ease.

"How did you learn to do that?"

"Micah taught me," Matthew beamed.

"What else did Micah teach you?"

Micah cleared his throat. "You ask too many questions. I hope you're hungry," Micah interrupted, pouring sparkling apple cider into her flute. "We have all of your favorites, so sit back and enjoy."

"Where did all of this come from?" Pamela knew the china and crystal didn't come from her cabinets.

"If you must know, Ms. Nosy, I borrowed a few items from my aunt."

She noticed the table was set for one and not three. "Aren't the two of you going to eat?"

Micah shook his head. "The help never eats with the mistress of the house. Besides, we ate earlier. Now please, no more questions. Matthew and I have worked very hard to make this evening special. So settle down, relax, and enjoy your meal."

Pamela wanted to tell him she didn't care what the food was or what it tasted like. Micah made her evening special by simply showing up. But instead, she just whispered, "Okay."

"Here, Mommy." Pamela was impressed with the skill her son used to place a basket of warm rolls on the table followed by a Caesar salad.

Pamela enjoyed her food as her men served her like she was the Queen of England. Micah made sure her the drink in her glass never dropped below the halfway mark. As soon as she set her fork down upon taking the last bite of her salad, Matthew removed the dishes, and Micah promptly set a neatly garnished plate with grilled salmon, asparagus, and wild rice in front of her.

"Micah, did you cook this yourself?"

Micah shook his finger at her. "You ask too many questions."

Pamela didn't say another word until she was done.

"They say the way to a man's heart is through his stomach, but I think that may be true for women also," Pamela said after Matthew removed her dirty dishes. "Micah, that was delicious. Thank you."

"I hope you saved room for dessert. I have your favorite—chocolate cake with rum custard filling."

Pamela was full, but since Micah had taken the time and effort to cater to her, she wasn't going to deny him the pleasure. Besides, she enjoyed the attention. "Okay, but just a little piece."

Pamela tried to help in the kitchen after finishing her cake, but Micah made her sit down on the couch while he and Matthew cleaned the kitchen and packed away the borrowed dishes. That's when she noticed the bag from the Dead Fish. She softly laughed to herself; thinking the food tasted familiar. She didn't mind that Micah hadn't cooked it himself; it didn't matter. Micah had done more for her in one day than any man ever had.

"Good night, Mommy. I'm going to bed now. I already took my bath. I hope you had a happy Valentine's Day."

Pamela hugged and kissed her little man. "I had the best Valentine's Day ever." She smiled and watched her son trot up the stairs and into his room. Matthew was turning into a replica of Micah. She turned back toward the kitchen to find Micah staring at her.

"Did you mean what you said about this being your best Valentine's Day?" he asked.

"Yes."

"What about when you were married?"

"Like I said, this is the best." Pamela wanted to redirect the conversation away from the time she spent with Marlon Roberts. "I bet you've heard that a lot."

Her statement confused him. "I don't understand."

They had never discussed his past relationships, but she figured this was as good a time as any.

"Come on, Micah. You're a caring and romantic man. I bet you've brought joy to more than a few women on this day and many other days as well."

"Is that what you think?" Micah asked, joining her on the couch. "You think I'm a player or used to be one?"

Pamela raised her eyebrows. "Let's just say, you know how to make a woman feel special, so special that she'd want to pay you with her gratitude." Pamela held up two fingers on each hand to emphasize the quotation marks on the word gratitude.

"And you think I've had my share of gratitude?"

"I think you're a man who definitely knows how to get next to a woman."

Micah laughed out loud, and Pamela thought she had him figured out. He took her hand in his, and after slowly bringing it to his lips, gently kissed it. "I'm flattered, but I have a newsflash for you, Ms. Pamela Roberts. You're the first woman I have had a relationship with. Today is the first time I have celebrated Valentine's Day."

Her head jerked forward. "Micah, are you trying to tell me you're a virgin?"

Micah exhaled a long slow breath. "That's not what I'm saying. What I mean is I have never dated before. You're the first."

Micah's words were unimaginable to Pamela. "You are a twenty-eight-year-old attractive man. How can that be?"

Micah rested against the back of the couch. "Sweetheart, you forget. I come from the home of an alcoholic parent. Like I said before, my mother would sometimes forget I was there. That meant there where days I went without food, and most of the time, clean clothing. Naturally, I got teased at school and didn't have many friends. I couldn't blame the other kids though. I mean, who would want to be around the smelly, dirty kid with the nappy afro?" Micah half smiled, but Pamela didn't. Her heart ached for him. "Anyway, I didn't have any social skills. If you ask me, I still don't. The girls didn't like me, and I wasn't cool enough for the boys to hang out with, so I stayed to myself."

"What about after you became an adult?"

Micah hesitated before answering. "That's when my life took a downward turn. I got involved with reckless behavior and didn't have time. Beside, my destructive behavior didn't allow dating."

Pamela was curious. "How destructive are we talking?"

"For now, let's just say, I've done things that could have killed me. Thousands have done what I did and died, but God saw fit to spare me. For that I am so grateful. That's why I praise God as hard as I do. I know I shouldn't be here, and I wouldn't be if it weren't for His mercy."

"Me too." Pamela nodded her head in agreement.

Micah steered the conversation back. "Now, back to my original statement, you're the only woman I've shared this day or any other special day with. So if I make you feel special, it's because you are special, and I am designed to make you feel that way."

Pamela looked away with that statement. He was doing it again. First, he tells her son he's going to marry her, and now he's saying he was created for her. She had to redirect the conversation again. "What about your birthday? You do celebrate your birthday, don't you?"

"When my mother was sober enough to remember my birthday, she would bake me a cake, but I've never had a birthday party or anything like that. My aunt made dinner for me last year, but that's as far as it goes for celebrations."

Pamela now felt bad she didn't get him anything for Valentine's Day. "Micah, I'm sorry, but I didn't get you anything. To be honest, I didn't know it was Valentine's Day until you showed up this morning."

"I know, I could tell by your reaction. And that's okay; the only thing I was looking forward to was your beautiful smile."

"Are you sure?"

"Positive. All I want is for you to be happy and not have to worry about anything."

Pamela's breathing accelerated as the warm feeling in her chest returned. Their eyes locked, and she wondered if he were thinking the same thing she was. That he was right; he was the one created for her and her for him. That without him, there was no happiness. She felt her face moving toward his. "You're doing a wonderful job. I am happy. Very happy," she whispered before kissing him softly on the cheek.

He smiled and welcomed her head against his chest, right above his heart. Listening to the rhythm, Pamela couldn't decipher his heartbeat from her own, so she stopped trying. She awakened an hour later alone on the couch and covered with a blanket.

Chapter 7

"He's here, Mommy, hurry!" Matthew called up the stairs for the third time.

Pamela couldn't recall a time she'd seen her son more excited about anything. It was Saturday, but Matthew had risen before dawn just to make sure he didn't miss the big event: T-ball sign-ups. He'd marked off the days on his Sponge Bob calendar to make sure the day didn't slip by him, and every day, he reminded Pamela of the number of days that remained.

"I'm coming!" Pamela called back, and then continued styling her hair. Her morning would be spent in long lines and filling out a small mountain of paperwork. Still, she wanted to look good. Micah was coming with them.

Pamela and Micah were nearing the end of the third month of their relationship, and in her opinion, things couldn't be better. Pamela was in love, and she knew it. She hadn't told him yet, but she loved Micah Stevenson, and she believed nothing would ever change that. Micah was permanently etched in her heart. He hadn't shared his feelings with her either, but Pamela knew he felt the same. His actions showed it, like on the previous Saturday.

Having worked ten-hour days at the title company all week, Pamela was exhausted. It seemed as though every family in the Bay Area was buying a house and using her title company to do so. That Saturday morning she slept in and prayed

Matthew would let her rest until noon. That didn't happen. Shortly after 10:00 A.M, the aroma of bacon and fried onions floated up the stairs and into her bedroom. Then the smoke detector blared. Pamela panicked and jumped out of bed and ran down the stairs, praying all the while that Matthew wasn't burning down the house.

"Matthew!" She stopped at the bottom of the staircase when she saw Micah standing at the stove cooking. Matthew was setting the table. "What's going on?" she yelled over the piercing noise.

After a brief glance, Micah turned his back to her. "Sorry if we scared you. We were trying to surprise you with breakfast," he said after turning on the stove fan.

"How did you get in?" Pamela was grateful the noise ceased and she didn't have to yell over it.

Matthew's eyes bulged at the angry edge in his mother's voice. "Mommy, I'm sorry. I opened the door. I thought it was okay because Micah is not a stranger."

Pamela softened at the sight of Matthew's tears. "Matthew, go upstairs. I need to talk to Micah alone."

"Okay, Mommy."

Pamela waited until she heard her son's bedroom door close before she attacked the gorgeous man with the long eyelashes wearing her apron.

"Micah, what makes you think you can just barge into my house any time you want to?"

Micah kept his back to her. "I'm sorry. I didn't mean to upset you."

"Then why didn't you call?" When he didn't answer, she yelled again. "Micah, turn around and talk to me!"

"I will, just as soon as you put some clothes on or at least a robe."

Pamela looked down at her body and gasped. She wore a

button-down nightshirt that barely covered her thighs. The top two buttons were undone, leaving her breasts nearly exposed. She ran back upstairs so fast that she missed a step and fell. Thankfully, she didn't break or sprain anything. When she returned wearing fleece sweats, Micah was waiting at the bottom of the staircase. But before she could open her mouth to resume the argument, Micah opened his, making her regret her earlier tantrum.

"Pamela, you're right. I should have called, but that would have disturbed your sleep, and I knew you wanted to sleep in. You told me so last night. I wanted to make breakfast because I know you're tired, and I wanted you to rest without having to worry about Matthew. After breakfast, I'm taking Matthew with me so you can have the day to yourself to do whatever you want." He held out an envelope, and she cautiously accepted it.

"If you choose to lie around all day, that's fine. If you want to get your nails and feet done or even a massage, that's fine too. There's enough money in there for that." He brushed her face with his fingertips. "Today, I don't want you to worry about anyone or anything but yourself. Don't even cook; I'll bring dinner back this evening."

Micah's deed had left her speechless. She'd never felt so special and as cherished as she did at that moment. Like the fog suddenly lifting from the Bay, Pamela accepted the fact that she was in love with Micah and he loved her in return.

After apologizing, then allowing her men to serve her breakfast, Pamela spent the day alternating between sleeping and reading. Upon their return, they not only brought dinner back, but Micah had taken Matthew shopping and had gotten everything needed for T-ball, including a glove. Both of them sported new haircuts. After dinner, Micah and Matthew cleaned the kitchen while Pamela camped out on the couch. Her day was perfect thanks to Micah.

Pamela now smiled at her reflection in the mirror. She was positive Micah loved her, but she wasn't going to push him to share his feelings before he was ready. Pamela wanted him to make the decision that would drastically alter their lives without any nudging from her.

"Mommy!"

Now her son was getting on her nerves. "Coming!" she yelled back. She checked her makeup one last time, collected Matthew's birth certificate and school photo, then floated down the stairs.

"Hey, sweetheart." She greeted Micah with a light hug, and he returned her embrace with a smile.

"Hey, beautiful. If we don't want to stand in line all day, we'd better get going."

Pamela grabbed her jacket before Matthew bellowed lyrics to the mommy song again.

During the ride to the field, the three of them were the epitome of family. Micah and Pamela sat in the front holding hands, and Matthew sat in the back asking the million dollar question of "Are we there yet?" The field was only ten minutes away, but Matthew's constant pestering made the short journey feel like a cross-country road trip. At the stoplight, Micah slowly outlined Pamela's face with his eyes. She was a beautiful woman, and she was his woman. Of that he was sure. He knew in his heart Pamela was the one he wanted to share his life with. He believed she felt the same but was afraid to push her. He wanted her to open up to him in her own time. That way, he would know her feelings were genuine. Then he would share his complete history with her and pray for the best.

***

"Yes!" Pamela threw her fist in the air. Finally, the redundant paperwork and emergency information was completed. With Micah's help, they were able to get Matthew registered in half the time. As she neared the front of one line, he'd stand in the next line. That was truly a blessing because there were so many parents trying to do the same thing as Pamela, make their son's dreams come true. The only thing left to do now was pay the fees.

"Micah, tell me how did baseball become your passion?" she asked while they waited in line.

"Baseball was more of a lifesaver than a passion."

"I don't understand."

Micah placed his arm around her shoulder. "Remember my mother is an alcoholic. That meant I had a lot of free time to myself. On the weekends and sometimes on weeknights, I'd walk to old Comisky Park and watch the White Sox play through the fence. I'd come around so much the security guards knew me by name. Finally, they stopped shooing me away and allowed me to watch the game from the outfield and would even buy me food to eat." Micah chuckled. "I guess they could tell I was hungry most of the time by the way I eyed their hot dogs. That went on until I started high school, then I went to work in the concession stands. Baseball kept me from hanging in the streets and selling drugs. I did steal a few times so I wouldn't starve, but baseball gave me something to do, so I didn't get into too much trouble. My best childhood memories were at the ballpark. That's the main reason I coach baseball, to give kids who may not have anything else something positive to look forward to."

Pamela didn't understand how a woman could neglect her child the way Helen Stevenson had. Pamela determined someone like that shouldn't be blessed with the gift of motherhood. She would never put Matthew in harm's way. No

matter what, she would always keep her baby safe and pro-
tected, even at the cost of her own safety.

"How is your relationship with your mother now?" Pamela
asked him.

"My mother and I have an understanding; I'm her son,
and she's an alcoholic. She loves me, I know, but her lifestyle won't allow her to be a mother to me. There are some
days, far and in between, when she's sober and we have good
conversations. Those are the times when she tells me she's
happy because I've made my life better than hers and warns
me against the danger of drinking alcohol."

"What happened to your father?" Pamela noticed the blank
stare on his face. "You don't have to tell me if it's too painful."

Micah continued. "I was around five years old when my
father lost his job at the steel plant in Indiana. One night he
and my mother had a big fight because there wasn't any food
in the house. My father stormed out and attempted to rob a
liquor store. Unfortunately for my father, the elderly store
owner kept a loaded .22 underneath the register."

Pamela blinked back tears. Micah's story went from bad
to worse. She was amazed that Micah shared his traumatic
history without emotion. If he still had remaining scars, she
couldn't tell. Micah was a strong man; he had to be in order to overcome all those obstacles and still be sane. That's
the kind of man she wanted. He was what she and Matthew
needed. He wouldn't run when faced with difficulties. He
wouldn't leave her hiding behind the couch trying to dodge
the landlord.

"Is that the reason you're so drawn to Matthew, because
you know what it's like to lose a parent?"

"When my father died, I lost both of my parents. That's
when my mother started drinking. I'm drawn to Matthew

because he's a wonderful kid . . . and his mother is cute."
Micah winked, and she blushed. "Seriously, I love Matthew. I
couldn't love him more if he were my very own son."

Pamela believed that. Matthew loved Micah too. She felt
it every time they were together. Watching the two of them,
a stranger would have a hard time believing Matthew wasn't
his biological son. Micah spent so much time with Matthew
that the two were beginning to look alike. They even sported
the same haircut. Matthew imitated Micah to the point he'd
started opening doors and pulling out chairs for Pamela. The
first time he offered to pump her gas, Pamela was worried
Matthew would spill the gas and waste her last twenty dollars
until payday, but Matthew insisted. "Mommy, I got it. Micah
showed me how to do it. He says this is what men do."

When Matthew asked Micah to accompany him to Back
to School Night, Pamela couldn't tell who was more proud,
Matthew or Micah. The other day while collecting Matthew's
laundry, Pamela noticed he'd replaced the picture of his biological father he kept on his dresser with one she had taken
of him and Micah together. She found his father's picture
tucked away in his sock drawer. She began to wonder why she
still kept the urn that contained her late husband's ashes on
her own dresser.

Finally, they reached the front of the line. Pamela asked
the volunteer how much she owed for the league and was informed that the fees for Matthew Roberts were already paid.
All they needed from her was the paperwork.

Pamela smiled at Micah. "When did you sign him up?"

"When I came to the coaches' training last weekend."

Matthew returned from playing catch with some boys he'd
met in line before Pamela could thank Micah and find out
what else he had done. "Are we done yet?"

"Yes." Pamela breathed a huge sigh of relief.

"Micah, are you going to coach my team?" Matthew tugged Micah's arm.

Micah looked down at the little boy he considered to be his son. "Yes, but don't think you're going to get any special treatment." Happily Matthew ran off to tell his new friends.

"What about me?" Pamela asked. "Do I get any special treatment?"

"You, my dear, get everything," Micah said after kissing her hand.

Chapter 8

There is therefore now no condemnation to them which are in Christ Jesus, who walk not after the flesh, but after the Spirit.

Micah read the scripture for the third time. "I will not allow myself to feel condemned any longer," he declared. Micah had been telling himself that quite often lately. The closer he came to disclosing his past to Pamela, the more guilt and doubt tried to creep in. The more shame tried to overwhelm him. The more fearful he became.

"God has forgiven me. I am a new creature; old things are passed away and all things are new. My mind is new, and my spirit is new. The enemy no longer has control over me." Following his professions, Micah closed his Bible and knelt on his knees to pray once again.

Later, seated in his chair, Micah was enjoying the peace that had enveloped him when the phone rang. He didn't want to answer it, but the caller ID displayed a number from the 773 area code in Chicago. It was his mother calling. She'd remembered his birthday.

"Hello, Mother." Micah prayed she was sober, but that was not to be.

"H-happy bir-birth-day." Helen's voice sounded as if she were waking up from a comatose state.

"Thank you. I'm surprised you remembered." Micah tried to sound pleasant, but the thought of his mother being sloppy drunk before noon disturbed him. It shouldn't have, but it did.

"Of course I re-remem-ber the b-birth of my on-ly ch-child." By the time Helen finished the simple sentence, Micah had a headache.

"How are you doing? Do you have any food?" Micah rubbed his forehead.

"I'm f-fine. The lights are on. I d-don't need no f-food."

Micah wanted to get off the phone. Trying to hold a conversation with his mother was nearly impossible. It was hard to cope with the defeat and hopelessness that permeated through her voice. The despair was bringing him down. Micah decided a long time ago that if his mother insisted on destroying her life, she'd have to do it alone.

"Mother, thank you for calling, but I have to go." Micah didn't know why, but he added, "I love you." He hadn't told his mother that in years, but it felt appropriate at that moment. He hung up, and then knelt on his knees again, this time to pray for his mother.

Later, seated on the futon, Micah checked his watch. It was only two o'clock.

"The day sure drags on when you don't have anything to do," he mumbled. Normally, he spent Saturdays with Pamela, but she and Matthew had something else planned for the day. She wouldn't tell him what the plans were, but promised to be back in time to share his birthday dinner with him. Micah grabbed a bottle of water from the refrigerator, then pulled out his coach's handbook for the T-ball league. He was just about to doze off when the phone rang, alerting him of a visitor. Grateful to have company, Micah hurriedly let AC in.

"Happy birthday, man." AC greeted him with a brotherly hug.

"Thanks, man. What brings you around here?" AC sat on the futon. Micah leaned against the kitchen counter.

"Come on, man, you didn't think I'd let my boy's birthday slip by without stopping in, did you?"

Micah shrugged his shoulders, but didn't verbally respond. He wasn't accustomed to friends who genuinely cared.

"Man, you know me better than that." AC leaned back. "So how does it feel to be entering the last year of your twenties?"

"You tell me, you left the twenties years ago."

"Whatever, man, it's only been three years." AC stood and posed. "Tell the truth, I don't look a day past twenty-five."

Micah smirked. "Yeah, in dog years. If you keep eating all those cakes and pies my aunt keeps making you every Sunday, you and the Goodyear blimp will pass for twins."

"Forget you, man. I have a sweet tooth, and everybody knows it. There's nothing wrong with that as long as I exercise. Besides, First Lady can bake."

"Flexing your arm from the plate to your mouth is not exercise," Micah chuckled.

"I guess you're exercising your arm every Sunday when you're trying to relieve me of my goodies."

Micah shrugged his shoulders. "It's like you said, my aunt can bake."

Micah went on to share the details of his early-morning call from his mother with AC and his plans to have dinner with Pamela and Matthew.

"Sounds like you have some free time. Let's run over to your uncle's house. I just know the first lady made you a peach cobbler," AC suggested while casually looking down at his watch.

Micah really didn't want to go anywhere other than to see Pamela and Matthew, but the idea of warm peach cobbler with vanilla ice cream was too tempting. Micah would never admit it to AC, but his sweet tooth was just as bad as AC's if not worse.

"Give me a minute to change clothes."

***

"Jess, hurry up; they'll be here soon!" Pamela yelled. The only response Jessica offered Pamela was the sound of her lips smacking together.

Pamela turned to her father and Pastor Jackson. "Are the two of you almost finished with the balloons?" Her voice wasn't as loud as with Jessica's, but Pamela was just as firm.

"Baby, we have it all under control," her father answered.

Pamela whirled around. "Mama, are the hors d'oeuvres ready? First Lady, is the table set?" Pamela continued drilling everyone like she had stripes marked on her shoulder that identified her as a high ranking-military official, until she noticed they all were laughing at her. "What's so funny?" she asked, looking around the room.

"You've got it bad!" her mother started.

"No, she has got it REAL bad!" the first lady added.

"Baby, your nose is wide open." Her father patted her shoulder. "It's all right; Micah is a good man."

"What are you guys talking about?" Pamela knew exactly what they were talking about. She was in love, and by her anxious behavior, everyone knew it except the man she loved. That would change tonight. "I just want Micah's first birthday party to be a success. I want him to be happy, that's all."

"And *you* want to be the one to make him happy," Jessica teased.

"And not just today," Pastor Jackson added, causing Pamela's face to flush. She wasn't familiar with this playful side of her pastor.

Her mouth fell open when Matthew asked, "Mommy, is that why you're always smiling and singing about Micah at home?" Everyone continued laughing, but Pamela failed to see the humor.

"Matthew, go and change your clothes before Micah gets

here!" Pamela stomped into the kitchen to check on Micah's peach cobbler. She wasn't mad; she just didn't want everyone to know they'd figured her out.

"Shush!" filled the house when AC's car pulled into the driveway. Pamela quickly straightened her clothes and fingered her hair. She looked around the room with pride. The house was decorated from top to bottom with Micah's favorite superhero, Spiderman. A life-sized blowup of the Marvel character was positioned at the door to greet visitors. Balloons and streamers in the form of spiderwebs covered the ceiling. Pamela even had Spiderman plates and napkins.

The buffet table was loaded with all of Micah's favorite foods, most of which she'd made herself. Fried chicken, ham, catfish, macaroni & cheese, greens, hot water corn bread, candied yams, green beans, meatloaf, mashed potatoes & gravy, pineapple coconut cake, sweet potato pie, and, of course, peach cobbler. She kept Micah's own personal cobbler and homemade vanilla ice cream inside the kitchen.

Pamela surveyed the guests. Micah would be so happy. She beamed. Several coworkers from the cable company were present and a good number of members from Praise Temple. The entire church baseball team was there. She guessed at least seventy-five people were present to celebrate Micah's first birthday party.

After ringing the bell a couple of times without a response, Micah used his key.

"Surprise!" thundered through the house.

Micah was shocked to the extent he almost fell backward. He would have if AC's stomach hadn't blocked him. He was speechless, listening to the crowd sing Stevie Wonder's version of the "Happy Birthday" song. He looked back at AC who was grinning. His eyes then surveyed the group trying to figure out who was responsible for the pleasant sight before him. Who thought enough of him to go through all this trouble? The second he looked into Pamela's wet eyes and smiling face, he knew.

As he took quick long strides in her direction, Micah felt like he was floating. He didn't feel his feet touch the floor. When he finally reached her, Micah hugged her so tightly, that he thought he might suffocate her. He loosened his grip, but didn't release her. Pamela was right where he wanted her, and he didn't care who saw.

"Thank you, baby," he whispered repeatedly in her ear. "I lo—"

"I helped too," Matthew said, patting Micah's arm.

Micah released Pamela and picked up Matthew so that he held him with one arm; the other arm still around Pamela.

"Thank you, little buddy." Micah kissed Matthew's cheek, and Pamela's mother made him repeat the pose so she could snap a picture of the three of them.

"I helped too," the first lady said. "I want me some sugar too."

Micah laughed so loud, he nearly roared. The contentment that bubbled within him poured out and filled the room. Inwardly, Micah wished he could have been graced with his mother's presence. He went around the room greeting and thanking his guests. He had no idea this many people cared enough about him to celebrate his birthday with him.

Pamela watched him for a few moments, then went to find Jessica to solicit her assistance with serving the food. She spotted Jessica standing away from the crowd speaking with AC and decided give her friend some space.

***

"Minister Combs, is that you?" Jessica asked AC, taking note of the black dress slacks and sweater he wore.

"Sister Jessica, you know it's me," AC smirked.

"I almost didn't recognize you without your big, bright, shiny suit." She was teasing, but the look on AC's face told her he didn't appreciate her making fun of his taste in clothes. He softened his glare when she added, "Your outfit complements you well. You should dress like that more often." With that she turned and left.

"Wow!" Micah said, looking at the smorgasbord before him. "Baby, you've outdone yourself. Did you cook all of this?"

Before Pamela could answer, her mother and the first lady started in again.

"Did you hear that? He called her baby." Dorothy nudged the first lady's arm.

"Look at her smile; she likes that," First Lady baited back.

"Wonder what pet name she has for him?"

Pamela ignored the nosy women. She didn't like the endearing term, she loved it. Tonight was the first time he'd openly affectionately addressed her, and she hoped it wouldn't be the last.

"Baby, aren't you going to eat?" Micah asked when Pamela sat down next to him after handing him his plate.

"I'll eat later; I want to make sure you're satisfied first."

"If only you knew how satisfied I am, Pamela Roberts." She blushed and giggled uncontrollably. "I've never been more satisfied in my life."

Pamela sat there with him, and in between bites he shared his food with her until Jessica called her into the kitchen. Pamela rolled her eyes and pouted before leaving Micah's side.

"What is it, Jess?"

"I need help refilling the chicken." Jessica paused. "And I want you to admit to it."

Pamela placed her hand on her hip and cocked her head. "Admit what?"

"I saw you out there. Admit it; you're in love with Micah. Deeply in love I might add."

Pamela waved her friend off with the back of her hand. "Girl, please. Bring that tray over here so I can refill it before someone starts fighting over the last chicken wing."

"You know how black church people can act when there's only one piece of fried chicken left at a buffet table," Jessica laughed then added, "You still need to admit how you feel."

Pamela took the tray and turned her back to her friend. "Why don't we talk about you? I saw you over there talking with Anthony Combs."

Jessica smacked her lips. "All I did was tell the man to stop wearing those loud shiny suits."

"Are you sure I didn't hear you say, 'I like you. I need you'?" Pamela teased.

"You know, Pam, the first step to recovery is to admit that you have a problem. Go on, girl, admit that you're in love with Micah."

Pamela handed Jessica the tray and turned back to the stove and stirred the huge stock-pot of collard greens.

"All right, I'll admit it," Pamela said just as Micah appeared in the doorway of the kitchen. "I'm in love with Micah, but don't say anything because I haven't told him yet."

Pamela's back was turned so she didn't know Jessica had scurried out of the kitchen the second Micah appeared. "I love everything about him," she continued. "His smile, his eyes with those cute eyelashes. Girl, I can't get enough of those. I love the sound of his voice, his laugh, I even love the way he chews his food." Pamela giggled. "I love the way he smells and the sweet things he does. I love his devotion to God and his integrity. There, are you happy? I've said it. I'm in love with Micah Stevenson!" Pamela's giggles stopped abruptly at the sound of Micah's voice.

"I love you too, Pamela."

Pamela gasped and dropped the big spoon into the pot of greens. She was too afraid to turn around. Pamela stood there frozen with her eyes bulged and mouth gaped, trying to figure the easiest way to wring Jessica's neck.

Micah walked over to her and gently turned her body to face him. Pamela hung her head to avoid eye contact with him. With his thumb and forefinger, Micah lifted her chin and gazed into her eyes. "Pamela Roberts, I do love you. I love your smile. I love the way your cheeks flush every time you blush." The soft feel of his fingertip against her cheek made her knees weak; she placed her hand on the stove for support. "I even love the way you snort when you laugh. I love the way your nostrils flare when you're angry and how you chew your food exactly twenty-eight times before swallowing. I especially love how you give of yourself unselfishly, like tonight."

"Micah-I-um," Pamela couldn't form words. This was not the intimate moment she'd imagined. She wanted her first declaration of love to be made while they sat under the stars or ate by candlelight— anywhere but in the kitchen over a large pot of greens.

Micah moved in closer. "Do you really mean what you said? Are you really in love with me?"

"I was going to tell you later on tonight; it was part of my present to you. I guess it doesn't matter now," she whispered.

"How you feel about me will always matter."

Pamela allowed him to wipe the happy tear from her cheek before speaking. "Yes, Micah, I meant it. I love you."

"My love," Micah said just before kissing her softly on the

lips, and then wrapping her into a warm embrace. "You're the only woman I have ever loved, and the only one I want to love," he whispered in her ear.

"Pam, we need some more greens out here." Dorothy barged in. Instantly they separated.

"Coming, Mama," Pamela stuttered and at same time reached for the spoon.

"Maybe I need to eat in here since this is where the action is," Dorothy said, observing her daughter's red cheeks and Micah's sudden interest in the picture of a fruit bowl hanging on the kitchen wall.

Micah relieved the bowl from Dorothy's hand and Pamela quickly refilled it.

"I'll be back to check on y'all," Dorothy warned before leaving them alone again. She'd barely made it through the door when they burst into laughter and resumed their embrace.

For the remainder of the evening, Micah and Pamela were inseparable. Micah kept his arm around her or held her hand, making it plain that both he and she were spoken for. The new level of intimacy in their relationship didn't go unnoticed by their families either. Pastor Jackson and the first lady couldn't stop smiling and pointing in their direction. Henry grinned proudly and patted Micah on the shoulder when he sat beside him. Pamela guessed Jessica had told everyone about what happened in the kitchen because Jessica was careful to stay out of Pamela's arm's reach. Like always, wherever Micah went, Matthew was close by.

The best part of the evening for Pamela, outside of Micah's profession of love, came when Micah opened his presents. He was so overwhelmed with emotion that he found it difficult to talk. "Thank you," were the only words he could manage after opening each package. Micah didn't trust himself to speak. He could hardly control the quiver in his voice with just those two words. Pamela and the First Lady read the cards.

***

After the last gift, Micah went into the bathroom. He need-ed to be alone in order to release his emotions. He turned on the faucet, then leaned over the sink and cried tears of joy. This was the first time he'd experienced anything like this; people coming together to celebrate him without a hid-den agenda. If he combined all the Christmases of his child-hood, it wouldn't compare to the gifts he received today. They weren't grand gifts, but they were simple things *he* liked. Each gift was picked with him in mind, unlike the unlabeled gifts he used to get at the community center from the security guard disguised as Santa. From the Starbucks and Barnes & Noble gift cards to the Oakland A's and Chicago White Sox memorabilia, he liked and appreciated everything.

His life would never be the same after tonight thanks to Pamela. He knew now more than ever that she was the one God created just for him, his soul mate. Now that he knew she felt the same about him, the time had come to discuss their future. However, he couldn't do that without first dis-closing his past. With everything in him, Micah feared what would happen; how Pamela would react, but he had to tell her. He refused to have any dark secrets hanging over their life together; he loved Pamela too much for that.

"As long as I live, I'll never forget today," Micah said, stand-ing next to Pamela's car door after loading the last box of decorations into her trunk.

"Glad I could help you make good memories."

"Pamela, every day with you is a good memory." Pamela leaned against her car to keep from falling. Her knees were weak again.

"It's late; y'all can do that cup-caking tomorrow. I need to get some sleep," Dorothy barked from the front passenger seat. It was then Pamela second-guessed her suggestion that her parents stay at the town house tonight instead of driving all the way to Vallejo. Pamela, well aware of the time, didn't want to leave Micah's presence. She'd never felt this connected to another human being before, and the clock on the console reading ten minutes before midnight didn't deflate her happiness at all.

Micah leaned inside the car. "I'm sorry, Mother Dorothy. I know you worked hard today. Thank you so much for helping Pamela plan my party."

"That's all right, baby, take your time," Dorothy smiled back at him.

Pamela's head jerked in her mother's direction. Dorothy was still smiling. Micah had won her mother over with one simple word: *mother.*

"Your mother is right," he said moving closer to Pamela, "it is late and you need some rest. You worked hard today. Thank you again for everything. I love you." Micah was about to kiss her on the lips, but his eyes caught a glimpse of her father in the backseat, staring at him, and this time, Henry wasn't smiling. Micah settled for kissing her hand. "See you tomorrow, love."

"I'll save you a seat in church," Pamela whispered after returning the sentiment.

Pamela strapped on her seat belt and prayed her mother wouldn't nag her all the way home about the future of her relationship with Micah, because she didn't have any answers. All Pamela knew was she didn't want to spend one more day of her life without Micah Stevenson.

Chapter 9

Sunday service was exhilarating. Neither Pamela nor Micah could keep still. Pastor Jackson danced so hard, sweat actually dripped down his face. Halfway through service, he removed both his suit jacket and tie. In fact, the Spirit was so high he didn't get to preach. Praise and worship started off with "Lord, You Are Good," and the congregation praised God for just how good He is. In the end, Pastor Jackson exhorted a scripture, and after the deacons raised the general offering, service was dismissed.

"I know the two of you worked up an appetite with all that dancing you were doing," AC teased Pamela and Micah after service. "How about dinner at the Chinese buffet; my treat?"

"Um-man-I-um," Micah fumbled.

"Let me guess. The two of you have plans?"

"Actually we do," Pamela answered, then looked at her friend. "But Jessica's free."

Jessica's mouth fell open. AC smirked.

"Payback is something, isn't it?" Pamela whispered in Jessica's ear.

"That sounds like a great idea," Micah quickly cosigned.

"Come on, honey, let's leave before they lay hands on us." Pamela grabbed Micah's hand and took off in search of her parents and Matthew.

Later, during dinner, Micah tried to hold a conversation with Henry, but it was hard, almost impossible. His mind was cluttered with thoughts of Pamela. Dinner was a show of gratitude to the Jacobses for helping Pamela plan his birthday party. Right now, what he desired most was some quiet time with the beautiful woman seated on his right, but Henry wanted to talk. *I'll send a thank you card next time,* he thought as Henry went on and on about the upcoming baseball season.

"Grandpa, I start playing T-ball on Tuesday," Matthew announced. "And my dad is going to coach my team."

Pamela suddenly became parched and downed her glass of water.

Micah stopped chewing his food.

Dorothy didn't appear to be bothered at all by Matthew referring to Micah as his dad; instead, she teased her daughter. "Baby, I've seen you drink more water since dating Micah than I have in the past year."

"The dry weather makes my throat dry," Pamela explained.

"That's interesting, especially since the Bay Area just finished a record-breaking rainy season." Dorothy giggled and Micah chuckled.

"Is that right?" Henry baited his grandson. "Your dad is going to coach? What position are you going to play?"

"First base, but my dad said my arm is good enough to play outfield too," Matthew replied.

"Micah says a lot of things," Dorothy smiled, and then turned to Micah. "Micah, tell me, do you also ask questions? You know, the kind of question that the answer would involve the exchanging of something round with a stone on it?"

"Mama!" Pamela exclaimed.

"Mama nothing," Dorothy smirked. "Jessica told me what happened in the kitchen before I caught y'all."

"She told me too," Henry added, facing Micah. "But I want to hear it firsthand."

Matthew trotted off to the buffet to make his own ice-cream

cone. Pamela started to go with him, but Micah restrained her.

After clearing his throat, Micah responded. "Mr. Henry, if you're asking me if I'm in love with your daughter, the answer is yes." Micah paused and smiled at Pamela, causing her to blush once again. "Do I love Matthew? Yes. If you're asking what our future plans are, I can't discuss that with you until Pamela and I have discussed it first."

"Well, when are you going to talk?" Dorothy pressed.

Melodious laughter poured from Micah. "Mother Dorothy, you remind me of my aunt. You say exactly what's on your mind."

"Ain't that the truth?" Pamela mumbled underneath her breath.

"Son, I look forward to some good news real soon." Henry patted him on the shoulder.

Pamela shook her head in disbelief. "I can't believe you two. You're practically pushing me off. Why don't you embarrass me further by attaching a big cardboard sign around my neck that reads, TAKE HER PLEASE?"

"I will just as soon as that dry throat passes," Dorothy answered.

Pamela joined in with the group and laughed at her behavior. She remained uncomfortable, but relaxed when Micah casually placed his arm around her shoulder.

Dorothy retrieved her digital camera from her purse and shared the pictures from the birthday party with Micah. He enjoyed every one of them, but the one that captured his heart was the one with Pamela, Matthew, and himself. They looked so good together, like they belonged together. *Like a family*, he thought.

"Mother Dorothy, can you make me an enlarged copy of this one?" he asked, handing back the camera.

"I knew you would like that one." Dorothy smiled at Micah, and then asked Pamela, "Would you like some more water?"

Matthew returned with a super-sized chocolate and vanilla-swirled ice-cream cone. "Mommy, you can have my water, I'm not thirsty."

Pamela threw her hands up. "Not you too," she said before taking a sip from his glass.

Chapter 10

Pamela danced around her town house to Kirk Franklin's latest CD. She was supposed to be cleaning house, but was too excited about her date later that evening with Micah. In the month since their declarations of love, their bond had grown stronger every day, and their romance had become more intense. Daily, Micah professed his love for her. His special deeds toward her and the continuous attention caused thoughts of Micah to constantly occupy her mind. His smooth voice was the first sound she heard every morning and the last before closing her eyes at night. A couple of times she fell asleep with the phone tucked between her neck and shoulder.

The three of them had dinner together two nights a week, with Micah and Pamela taking turns cooking. Micah loved her turkey spaghetti, and she couldn't get enough of his baked chicken smothered with cream of mushroom soup. On most days after T-ball practice, Micah helped Matthew with his homework to allow Pamela time to unwind from her busy day. Some nights he read Matthew a bedtime Bible story before he tucked him in for the night. He would then sit with Pamela until she fell asleep.

Saturdays were spent outside watching T-ball games. In the beginning of the season, Pamela cheered from the stands, but then she noticed a few single moms practically throwing themselves at Micah. From that moment on, Pamela made sure every female, single or married, sitting in the stands understood that Micah Stevenson was already taken. Pamela even went as far as to bring him water and wipe the sweat from his forehead between innings. She also made a point never to address Micah as "Coach" in the ladies' presence, opting for "honey" instead.

After T-ball, Pamela and Matthew cheered from the stands while Micah coached the church's team. On Sundays, they always ate dinner together after church.

Pamela had been praying and seeking God the entire month concerning Micah, and she was as sure as she knew her name Micah was her ordained mate— her Boaz and Matthew's new father. The only thing that puzzled her was the proper timing. She desired to be married before the fall season, or else she would have to wait until next spring for her dream wedding on the beach. It was the beginning of June. She had four months to get Micah to propose and plan a wedding before the end of October.

On a daily basis, anticipation and anxiety nearly consumed her. Pamela had already experienced a bad man, now she was eager to have the love of a good one. She looked forward to sharing her life and her bed with someone who loved and cherished her. Pamela yearned to freely give her love to someone and to have that love returned. Deep down, she wanted to give her trust and not worry about it being abused. She wanted to experience the excitement of a man coming home, and then the two of them spending the night giving each other the love each needed and deserved, freely and without reservations.

Pamela knew Micah felt the same although he never came out and directly verbalized it. He had shared his plans to buy a house and even browsed housing magazines with her. Whenever Micah referenced the future, he always included the three of them. On a picnic at the beach, Pamela voiced her desire to visit the Bahamas. Later that evening, they surfed the Internet for resorts in Nassau. There wasn't anything Pamela desired that Micah didn't try to provide for her, right down to a never-ending supply of chocolate crème-filled cookies.

Micah had called this morning and told Pamela tonight he wanted to talk about the future of their relationship. Matthew's T-ball team had a "bye" in their schedule, so her parents picked Matthew up from after-school care yesterday and took him to Vallejo for the weekend. Pamela and Micah would have the town house to themselves. Pamela offered to cook, but Micah insisted on picking up takeout from PF Changs. "All I want you to do is look pretty," is what he said. That's exactly what she intended to do. She planned on wearing the ensemble he brought her for Valentine's Day, but not if she didn't make it to the cleaners on time to pick it up.

Micah arose from his knees for the second time. After fasting and praying for three days and all this morning, he still didn't have the assurance he felt he needed to tell Pamela about his past. Micah was sure of one thing, Pamela was his soul mate, but that didn't guarantee how she would react to his history. If the situation were reversed, he couldn't say for certain how he would react to this type of disclosure. In his heart, Micah knew Pamela needed to know before their relationship took them down the aisle, but fear remained. He drifted back to his earlier phone conversation with AC.

"Man, I'm not sure if it's a good idea for you to tell her," AC had admitted. "I mean, that's your past and some things need to stay in the past."

"I hear you, but I don't want to spend the rest of my life looking over my shoulder, hoping she won't accidentally find out," Micah responded. "If we do get married, I don't want any secrets from my wife. I've seen the devastating effects of that firsthand, and I don't want that."

"But that was different; you're different."

"AC, think about it this way. If you were marrying an ex-prostitute, wouldn't you want to hear it from her before you say 'I do'? Or would you rather have one of her johns tell you at the wedding reception? Wouldn't you like the decision to be married to an ex-prostitute to be yours and not someone else's?"

"I hear you, man. I just want this to work out for you. I know how much you love her and how attached you are to Matthew."

"It's supposed to be that way, she's my soul mate, remember? And with Matthew, I can enjoy the childhood I didn't have."

"Micah, you've earned my respect. Most brothers, and I'm talking about saved brothers, wouldn't admit to what you're about to for fear of backlash."

"Trust me, man, it's not easy, but I know it's the right thing to do. I am afraid, but I love Pamela too much not to tell her. I'd rather hurt her now than see her hurt later."

AC had said a brief but intense prayer before hanging up. Thinking back now, Micah had to admit he did fear being judged and ostracized. That was a chance he was willing to take to keep from hurting Pamela and Matthew.

The *Mission Impossible* ring tone on his cell phone broke Micah's concentration.

"Not now," he grumbled after he read the 773 area code. "Hello, Mother," he answered dryly.

"Hi, baby, how are you doing today?"

Micah pulled the phone away from his ear to view the number again. It was his mother's number, but the cheerful and coherent voice didn't belong to the Helen Stevenson he knew. "Mother?"

"Don't act like you don't know your mother's voice," she snapped, then softened. "I know I sound different. I ain't had a drink in thirty days."

"Mother?" he said again as he stood to his feet. He gripped the phone tighter. "Is everything all right?"

"Baby, everything is fine," Helen answered with a hearty laugh.

"Mother, did you say that you have stopped drinking? Did you just say you haven't had a drink in thirty days?" He needed clarification. In the last twenty years, the longest break Helen gave her liver was twenty-four hours.

"Yes, I did," she answered proudly.

"But how? When?" Micah was stumped.

"It all started on your birthday when you said 'I love you' before you rudely hung up in my face. After I finished cursing you out over the dead line, I sat on my bed and had a conversation with myself. I said, 'Helen, as bad of a mother as you are, your son still loves you. As messed up as you are, there's at least one person in this world who loves you. That boy has every right to hate you, but he doesn't. Now get yourself together.' I had the same conversation with myself the next day, and then finished off my last bottle of Hennessy. I haven't bought another one since."

In his heart, Micah thanked God for his mother's effort and her motive behind it; however, he found it difficult to form words. "Mother, that's wonderful!"

"Thank you, but that's not why I'm calling."

"What is it?" Micah became concerned again.

"I was talking with the ladies at church the other night after Bible Study. They were bragging about their children and showing off pictures. That's when I realized I don't have any pictures of you to show off. I was too ashamed to tell them I didn't even have a picture of your graduation from high

school. Humph, truth be told, I don't remember your graduation. Anyway, I want you to take some pictures to send me
so I can show you off. And send me some of your girlfriend
too. When I get my money together, I'm coming out there to
see you."

"What?" This time her words made him fall back down
onto the futon and grip his chest.

"Yeah, Robert told me about her, said she's pretty too."
Helen laughed. "That's good because I don't want any ugly
grandchildren."

"No, Mother, slow down. Did you just say you're attending
church now?" Micah knew his ears had deceived him.

"That's right, baby, I joined church. And I'm tired of Sister
Murphy and the pastor bragging about their children, talking
about how well they're doing and how fine they are. Humph,
they just don't know, my son is fine too and doing quite well
for himself out there in California working in the entertainment business. I didn't lie either; cable is entertainment. If
you ask me, Sister Murphy's son looks like Roger Rabbit, and
the pastor's daughter is a dead ringer for one of them hyenas
in the *The Lion King*."

Micah was too stunned to laugh at his mother's musings.
"Mother, are you saved?" he asked, his voice full of hope and
fear of the answer.

"At the moment, I am," she answered after a short pause.

"I don't understand."

"It's like this, baby. When I joined church I said the sinner's prayer, and I really meant it at the time, but you know
how things come up, and sometimes I lose my temper. So I
repeat the prayer often, you know, to make sure I'm straight.
So far I've prayed that prayer at least twenty-five times in the
past thirty days. I said it this morning, and I haven't had any
visitors yet, so I'm saved right now. But if Audrey from down

the hall doesn't pay me the five dollars she owes me today, I'm going to cuss her out."

"Mother!"

"It's okay, baby, I've memorized the sinner's prayer. I don't even wait until I get to church to say it. I say it right on the spot. Sometimes I say it beforehand, just in case I forget later."

Micah laughed so hard, tears rolled down his cheeks. "Mother, I'm so happy you're going to church."

"Me too," Helen replied seriously. "I see things a lot clearer now. Don't get me wrong, I do miss my Hennessy all day long. I have to talk myself from going to Jewel Osco's for a new bottle. But I pray and read and keep telling myself, 'My baby loves me.'"

Although Helen had never openly displayed weakness, Micah could tell she was crying along with him. "Mother, do you need anything?"

"Just some pictures, and don't think I don't know you're the one who's been sending money to the electric company, keeping my lights and gas on. That's how I know you really do love me. I left you outside in the cold and in the dark night many times, but you see to it that I always have a warm place to lay my head."

A peaceful silence rested between mother and son until Helen abruptly said, "I love you, baby, but I have to go. Audrey's at the door."

"I love you too, Mother." Micah wasn't sure she'd heard him. Helen was too busy praying.

Micah sat on the futon for a long time, just crying and thanking God for his mother's breakthrough. No matter what happened later that evening, everything would work out for the good. He checked his watch, then gathered the pictures from his birthday party and headed to Walgreens to order copies.

***

Jessica screamed so loud Pamela removed the phone away from her ear. "What's up, my almost-engaged sister?"

"I didn't say he was going to propose tonight, I said I *think* he's going to propose." Pamela was putting the finishing touches on the dinner table. On the way back from the dry cleaners she picked up a floral arrangement and a bottle of nonalcoholic champagne.

"I've got my money on it and this German chocolate cake I'm baking."

"If that happens, you'll be the first person I call right after I run around the complex," Pamela laughed.

"I'll be sure to wear my dancing shoes to church tomorrow."

The doorbell sounded. "He's here, I have to go." Pamela hung up the phone and practically ran to the door.

"Hi, beautiful," Micah said after setting the bags on the counter and taking her into an embrace.

"Hey, handsome." She returned his embrace, and then quickly stepped away. The brother was looking and smelling too good.

"I hope you're hungry. I've got everything: salt & pepper shrimp, orange chicken, Mongolian beef and pot stickers, plus rice, chow mein, and vegetables."

Listening to him rattle off the smorgasbord, Pamela surmised he was very nervous. "I'm starved," she answered, helping Micah open the containers.

Micah shared the good news about his mother, and they made small talk and ate dinner with the sounds of Ben Tankard playing in the background on the CD player.

"I still can't believe it; my mother is saved and has stopped drinking. I never thought I'd hear my mother say she's a member of any church. Whenever my uncle mentioned God to her, she'd curse him out." Micah continued rambling. "And today was the first time she ever mentioned the future. She wants to come out here." Micah paused and smiled before adding, "She's happy you're cute because she doesn't want ugly grandchildren."

Pamela laughed with him, but didn't comment. She didn't want any ugly children either.

"Dance with me," Micah said after he finished off the last shrimp.

As Micah swayed with her, Pamela fantasized about what it would be like to dance with him after they're married. Her hands would roam his chiseled body uninhibited and his hands likewise over her body. She would be able to enjoy the touch of his full lips against her neck and not just the warmth of his breath. Keeping a safe distance would be of no concern.

If Micah wasn't so worried about the rest of the evening, he would have reveled in the fact that Pamela didn't protest about giving his mother cute grandchildren. If he weren't so fearful that this might be his last time dancing with Pamela, he would have relaxed and enjoyed the dance. But he was very worried.

"Let's talk," he whispered in her ear when the CD ended. Pamela followed him over to the couch where they sat side by side.

"What do you want to talk about?" Pamela asked calmly, although her heart rate and breathing increased.

Micah gathered her right hand in his and looked deeply into her eyes. "Pamela, you have brought me more happiness these past six months than I've experienced my entire life. You've made my life so complete, it's hard for me to remember my life before you, and I don't want to think about the rest of my life without you." Pamela's eyes watered. "I love you, Pamela." Micah leaned forward and kissed her lips, and she whispered the words back. "You are my soul mate and I want you to be my wife." Her tears flowed freely now. "But first, there's something I need to share with you about my past."

"What is it?" she asked in a voice just above a whisper.

Micah released her hand, and then arose from the couch. Her eyes followed him to the window, and she tried to emotionally brace herself for what she didn't know.

"I told you before about my childhood, how hard and lonely it was. What I didn't tell you was how my environment affected me emotionally. Like I said before, I didn't receive love and affection from my mother, and my father died when I was a small child. I spent my childhood searching for love and affirmation. That's one reason I kept going back to Comisky Park. The kindness the guards showed me was the closest thing I had to love."

Micah turned and faced her, and Pamela's heart went out to him, but she didn't move to join him. "After high school I enrolled into junior college. I had this bright idea that I was going to become a high-powered lawyer or doctor, anything that could one day take me away from my surroundings." Micah paused and exhaled deeply before continuing. "In my psych class, I was befriended by my professor who kept talking to me about church and how much God loves me. He invited me to his church, and one Sunday I went. That's when I learned he was the pastor of the church and not just a member. That was the first time I ever stepped into a church and it was my first introduction to God and religion. Over the years, my uncle had mentioned God to me in brief phone conversations, but I really couldn't relate."

A smile creased Micah's face as he continued talking. "That

day my life changed. For the first time, I knew I wasn't alone in the world and that God had created me for a reason. It was like every word the pastor said was spoken directly to me. From that day, I spent as much time as I could with the pastor trying to learn as much as possible about God and the love He has for me." His smile disappeared. "We hung out after class during the week and I told him about my life and he gave me advice. He was twenty years older than I, and he soon became a father figure to me, both naturally and spiritually.

"He made sure I had food and transportation and clothes. He even gave me money so I could work part time and attend school full time. At church, he assigned me as his personal assistant, so we were always together, and I accompanied him on trips. I ate dinner at his house with his wife and kids. I was so happy because here I was, this poor fatherless kid from the south side, who now had the love and respect of a powerful man of God. I craved approval, and I tried to do everything right, so I wouldn't be alone again. I did everything to please him and to keep him in my life."

Pamela didn't understand. "Micah, I thought you said that's when you became involved in destructive behavior."

Micah breathed deeply; he couldn't stop now. He had to get it all out. If he didn't, he would have to let her go.

"It is," he answered dryly. "I learned too late that nothing in life is free and not every man wearing the title 'Man of God' is sent by God."

"Micah, I don't understand." Pamela reached out to him, and he knelt in front of her and took her hands into his. For some reason he felt the need to savor the feel of her. He closed his eyes and rubbed the back of her hands against his face, then slowly kissed them. He tried to commit her touch to memory. Finally, he opened his eyes and kissed her lips for what he hoped wasn't the final time.

Pamela didn't know what he was about to say, but the sudden knot in her stomach was an indication it wasn't something she wanted to hear, but needed to hear. "Micah, you don't have to tell me this if it's too hard for you to talk about," she offered, more for her benefit than his.

"Yes, I do. You have to make an informed decision about the future of our relationship."

Reluctantly, she nodded for him to continue.

"Pamela, you once asked me if I am a virgin. That depends on your definition of a virgin. If you mean have I had sex with a woman, no I haven't." Then he added after a pause, "But I have had sex."

Pamela's face twisted as her brain tried to decipher what Micah was trying to tell her.

"For six years, I was in a homosexual relationship with my psych professor, the pastor."

The silence that followed Micah's revelation was deadening. Micah waited for her to respond, but Pamela couldn't; not yet. She had to wait for her heart to return to its proper place. It had sunk to a place so deep she could no longer feel it beating. In her mind, she tried to remember which commercial Micah had reenacted, but couldn't think of one. As the word *homosexual* replayed over and over in her head, reality set in.

"You're gay?" It was a whisper, but a charge nonetheless.

"Pamela, I am not gay. I—"

"Oh my God." She wouldn't let him finish. "You're a fagot!" she yelled and yanked her hands away along with his heart. "I've been in a relationship with a freaking fagot! I can't believe this. I have been planning to spend the rest of my life with a pervert! That's why you're so sensitive— you're gay!" Pamela's hands instinctively went to her face. "And you kissed me, you touched me!"

Micah hung his head as she ran into the bathroom and washed her hands and face. His heart sank so low, he thought it would stop beating any second and he'd have to be carried out in a body bag.

"What kind of pervert are you?" she yelled after she returned from the bathroom and found him sitting on the couch. She didn't notice his wet face or the redness in his eyes.

"I'm not a pervert. There's no need for you worry about catching anything from me. I'm not HIV positive. I have had more HIV tests than I care to count." His voice had changed from strong and deep to weak and raspy, but she didn't notice. If she did, she didn't care.

"You are lowdown and nasty. How could you get involved with me, knowing you like men? How could you do that? How could you play with me like that?"

"Pamela, I don't like men. I am not gay. That's in my past. I've been delivered from that lifestyle," he answered calmly, although inside he felt like he was on a roller-coaster ride. His head spun and his stomach turned upside down. He felt like regurgitating. "I've never played with you. My feelings for you and Matthew have always been and still are genuine."

Fear gripped Pamela at the mention of her son's name. "Oh my God, have you touched my son? Have you been using me to gain the chance to turn my son out? Is that why you coach, so you can have free access to little boys?"

That last charge was too much for Micah. The thought of inflicting any kind of harm on Matthew was unbearable to him. He'd known pain before, but the punches coming from this woman, the woman he loved, ripped him apart. He'd known his disclosure could have a negative response, but this was more than he could handle. He had to get out of there.

"Answer me!" she screamed. Micah quietly walked toward the door to leave, but Pamela jumped in front of him. "Answer me!"

Micah was a defeated man, but held himself together long enough to say what he needed to say, that mattered most to him. "Pamela, I have never touched Matthew or any other child inappropriately. I'm not attracted to men or little boys. I am not gay. I am not a freak or a fagot. I am not nasty. I am a man with a past, just like everyone else. I've made mistakes, like everyone else. I allowed my insecurity to keep me in a dangerous and ungodly relationship." Micah didn't mean to, but out of habit he reached for her hand.

She pulled away. "Don't touch me! Don't ever touch me or my son again!"

"I'm sorry you feel that way," he said sadly with his shoulders slumped.

"And I'm sorry I ever met you!" This time when he attempted to leave, she didn't stop him.

On the long walk back to his SUV, Micah felt the same way he did the day he arrived in California: broken, bruised, wounded, and empty. He had no idea love and honesty could hurt so much. He knew the possibilities, but Micah felt he had to take the chance. He would never forget the look on the pastor's wife's face when she walked in on him and the pastor in his office. She didn't have any idea her husband had been sleeping with men since he was a teenager. Micah refused to deceive Pamela. He couldn't risk her accidentally finding out after they were married. If she couldn't accept his past, it was best he knew now and not later.

Turns out Pamela couldn't handle it. He'd heard the still small voice so clearly. Pamela was the one for him. But thanks to the freedom of choice, she chose to reject him and that hurt most. Pamela had chosen to deny them both a chance at real love.

Micah didn't make it to Interstate 80 onramp before his emotions got the best of him and he had to pull over. It was more than Pamela's rejection, it was his entire life. How many more people would reject him because of his past? Would he ever be able to share his life with someone without hiding his past? Would anyone ever love him for the person he is now? Would he ever be able to open up to someone other than his uncle and AC? As a child he'd been rejected because of where he came from, and now as an adult the same thing was happening. "Will I ever be good enough?" he moaned.

His shoulders heaved as he cried like he'd done after all of his sexual experiences. His insecurities threatened to overtake him and lead him once again into a deep depression, one he was all too familiar with. It was the same depression that nearly made him take his life two years ago.

Micah raised his head, and through blurred vision, beheld the Bay. Slow, thick waves rolled in and crashed the rocks. The longer he looked out over the water, the calmer he felt. With each soft wave he could feel God's love showering him. He heard the still small voice.

Be confident, I have begun a good work in you, and I will finish what I have started.

His spirit was too broken and his heart too wounded to receive the comforting words. Micah leaned his head on the steering wheel and wept violently.

Chapter 11

Pamela couldn't stop crying. After she soaked the bed pillows, warm pellets from the showerhead mixed with the salty drops from her eyes flowed down the drain. On the drive to church, thick droplets blurred her vision, and now seated in the church's parking lot, the sobbing continued. She'd considered not attending church service, but refused to give Micah the satisfaction of knowing just how much he'd hurt her. Besides, she needed something to help get her through the embarrassment of having to admit she'd been stupid enough to get involved with him in the first place. The rage from the previous night had dissipated only to be replaced by the hurt that came along with realizing she was in love with a homosexual.

She repeatedly asked herself how she could have let this happen. Last night, Micah was supposed to propose to her, not destroy the life she'd envisioned for them. And he did it so calmly. He was so good, the way he deceived her by convincing her that he really loved her. Pamela felt used and dirty. Micah purposely set out to make her look like a fool. Why else did he look at houses and talk about a future together when all along he knew he preferred men. Micah practically told her parents he was going to marry her. Not one time did he say, "Sorry, Mr. and Mrs. Jacobs, but your daughter has the wrong anatomy for me." Matthew often addressed him as Dad, and Micah never once corrected him.

Pamela had her own skeletons in her closet pressing against the door, but nothing nearly as bad as homosexuality. That was the ultimate sin. In her book, it was the great big sin. She didn't care how many times Micah claimed he'd been delivered. It didn't matter, he was still gay. If he slept with a man once, he'd do it again, especially after a six-year affair. Obviously, he enjoyed it.

A tap on the front passenger window distracted her. It was Jessica. She wiped her face with the back of her hand, and then pressed the automatic door control button. Jessica quickly slid into the car.

"Girl, why didn't you answer my phone calls last night and this morning? What happened last night?" When Pamela didn't match her excitement, Jessica's grin evaporated.

"I couldn't talk," Pamela answered faintly.

"Oh, Pam, please tell me that you and Micah didn't spend the night together."

Jessica had said the wrong thing. Pamela broke down again. "Oh, Pam, no!"

"We didn't spend the night together," Pamela sniffled. "We'll never spend a night together."

"What happened? You guys didn't break up, did you?" Jessica couldn't imagine that.

"Turns out, I'm not his type."

"Pam, what are you talking about? That man worships you."

Pamela shook her head. "No, he doesn't. I don't have the right equipment for him."

"You're losing me."

Pamela turned her head. She didn't want to see Jessica's facial expression when she disclosed she'd been stupid enough to get caught up with a homosexual. "Micah is gay," she said plainly.

When Jessica didn't respond, Pamela turned to face her. Jessica's hands were covering her mouth.

"I don't believe it. Micah is gay?" Jessica said without lowering her hands.

"It's true. He told me so last night." The mention of last night brought on a fresh batch of tears.

"You must have misunderstood him." Jessica refused to believe the Micah she knew was gay.

"I heard him clearly!" Pamela snapped. "He clearly said he used to be in a sexual relationship with a man."

"Oh my God," Jessica whispered.

"He said the relationship lasted six years," Pamela continued. "Can you believe him? He knew his sexual preference, but he still got involved with me. Isn't that cruel?"

"Yes, it is." Pamela words replayed in Jessica's head. "Hold on. Did Micah say he *used* to be gay or did he say that he *is* gay?"

Pamela reached across Jessica for a tissue from the glove box. "He claims he's not gay, but he spent six years sleeping with his former pastor."

"His pastor?"

"Yes," Pamela smirked.

"Wow!" was Jessica's only response.

"Wow is right."

"This happened before he came to California, right?" Pamela nodded yes. "Why do you think he told you?"

"He claimed he wanted me to know so I could make an informed decision about our future. Do you know he had the nerve to tell me that he wants to marry me?" Pamela smirked.

"Pam, wait a minute. Do I understand you correctly? Micah didn't break up with you because he's a homosexual. He wants to marry you, and because of that, he shared his past history with you?"

"Past history?" Pamela sneered. "You know as well as I do, once a homo always a homo."

Jessica flinched at her friend's derogatory remark. "Pam, I don't know that. All I know is there's not one drop of residue from that lifestyle on the Micah Stevenson I know. Trust me, if there were, I would spot it. I know several homosexuals, both conservative and the flamin' ones. I even know a few down-low brothas. Micah is not like any of them."

"And how would you know?" Pamela rolled her neck. She didn't appreciate her friend defending Micah.

"For one, Micah is saved, I mean really saved. He's not one of those saved on Sunday and half-saved on Monday brothas. Micah is truly a man of God. I bet that's the reason he told you in the first place. Second, I don't believe Pastor Jackson would have allowed the two of you to get involved if Micah wasn't completely delivered from that lifestyle."

Jessica's words made sense, but Pamela didn't want to hear that. "I'm glad you're so sure about Micah, but this is my life, and I don't trust him!"

"You're right, Pam," Jessica conceded. "This is your life, and that's exactly why you should really think this through. Don't make any hasty decisions that you'll regret."

"What do I have to regret about not wanting a fagot in my bed?"

Jessica shook her head. She was not getting through. Her friend was too hurt to think objectively. "Pam, you told me you know for certain that Micah is your ordained mate sent by God. Do you think God would have told you that if He knew Micah wasn't everything you need? Don't throw your blessing away. Come on, Pam." She tapped her shoulder. "You know you love him."

Pamela wished it wasn't true, but it was. "Why did I fall in love with a homosexual?" she cried out loud.

Jessica put her arms around her and comforted her. "You're not in love with a homosexual. You're in love with Micah Stevenson, a saved and blessed man."

***

"Son, I'm so sorry to hear that," was all Pastor Jackson could say after Micah told him about Pamela's reaction to his disclosure. "Maybe in a few days, after she's had time to think, she'll reconsider."

"I doubt that," Micah responded, thinking back to Pamela's vicious statements.

"Pray about it, son. Prayer changes things and people."

Micah leaned back in his chair. "Pastor, I don't think it's worth the effort."

"Micah, you're hurt right now, but trust me, love is always worth the effort."

"Yeah, but is love for everybody?" Micah smirked. "Or just for the select few who never sin?"

"Love is for everyone. God is love, and He sent His son to die for all of us." He couldn't sit back and allow his nephew to revert into the shell of a man he once was. He'd worked too hard to see that happen. Pastor Jackson knelt in front of his desk. Micah asked what he was doing.

"It's praying time. I refuse to allow the spirit of depression to overtake you. I don't care what it looks like now, you've got to hold on to what God has told you. Now get on your knees!" Pastor Jackson ordered.

Micah quietly obeyed.

All through service Pamela tried to ignore the inner voice telling her to talk with Micah. She needed to talk to him. Pamela needed to understand how all this happened. Why he led her on, and why he played with her emotions. Maybe he really wasn't gay. Micah didn't look gay, neither did he act gay. Based on what Pamela knew, he didn't possess any characteristics of a homosexual. Micah didn't sway his hips when he walked, nor did his wrists hang limp. He wasn't skinny and feminine, but buff and practically dripped with testosterone. If he hadn't told her, she wouldn't have guessed in a million years what it was he was trying to reveal to her. She thought he was going to tell her about a baby momma somewhere or that he'd murdered someone— anything but this.

Pamela didn't understand how he could love her and desire to marry her, and then a minute later tell her he's gay. She really didn't understand how he could praise God the way he was doing at that very moment, considering his lifestyle. Micah was dancing in the Spirit like he and Jesus really had a relationship.

"Maybe I will hear what he has to say, then again maybe I won't," she mumbled to herself. Jessica settled the debate for her. A second after the benediction, Jessica yanked her by the arm.

"You need to talk to him." Before Pamela could protest, Jessica dragged her in Micah's direction.

"Man, you did the right thing," AC said, patting Micah on the back. "It'll work out."

Micah didn't want to discuss his problems anymore. "I see it's working out for you." Micah pointed to the cake box underneath AC's arm.

"German chocolate, this time," AC smiled.

"Man, I'm going to tell my aunt I'm jealous."

"Excuse us," Jessica interrupted. "Minister Combs, may I speak to you for a moment, please?"

Micah winced at the sight of Pamela. He was not ready for a repeat of last night, especially not in public. But in no time, AC and Jessica had stepped away.

"Hello, Micah." Pamela spoke first.

"Hello, Sister Roberts." At first Pamela didn't know who he was talking to. He hadn't called her that in months. Micah turned to leave, but her voice called him back.

"Can we talk?" she asked timidly.

Micah put his hands inside his pockets. "Sister Roberts, do you want to talk, or did you remember some more names you would like to call me?"

Pamela shook her head. "I want to talk. I need to understand some things."

Her soft eyes were sincere.

"When?"

"How about now? You could stop by," Pamela suggested.

Micah didn't think he would ever be ready to step foot inside her town house again, not after last night. "That's not a good idea." Pamela looked disappointed. "I could meet you somewhere," he offered.

"Where?"

Micah racked his brain for somewhere appropriate, just in case last night's scene repeated itself. He didn't like open scenes. "I'll meet you at the San Leandro Marina in an hour."

"Okay." Pamela agreed, but then remembered her son. "Wait, I can't. I forgot I have to pick Matthew up from my parents."

"Some other time then." Micah gave her a half smile and once again turned to leave.

"Hold on!" Jessica jumped in out of nowhere. "I'll pick up Matthew and bring him home later on tonight."

"That's a forty-five minute drive in traffic from here," Pamela protested.

"I'll tag along to keep her company," AC offered. Pamela didn't miss the brief smile that almost crossed Jessica's face.

"That's a good idea," Jessica said. "With that big red shiny suit you're wearing, we'll be mistaken for an emergency vehicle. We'll get through traffic in no time."

Pamela snickered at Jessica's comment, but Micah laughed out loud.

"I'll meet you in the parking lot." AC stomped off, but held on to the cake.

Micah sobered as soon as he was alone with Pamela again. "See you in an hour." He then walked away.

The early June weather was perfect for a walk along the San Leandro Marina. The sky free of clouds and the soft breeze from the ocean cooled the temperature down to a comfortable 68 degrees. The mile-long trail offered spectacular views of the San Mateo Bridge and the brilliant blue Pacific Ocean. Today, the crystal blue waters went on forever before kissing the blue sky. To the right lay the runway for the Oakland International Airport. It was an adventure to watch the big 747s land and take off, seemingly just a short swim away.

When Pamela pulled into the parking lot, Micah was already there standing next to his SUV enjoying the view. He had changed into walking shorts, a T-shirt, and closed-toe sandals. Micah turned his back to her when she pulled into the stall beside him.

Pamela turned the engine off, and he continued staring out over the ocean. It took her a moment to realize that he wasn't going to open the door for her. Slowly, she exited the vehicle and walked over to him.

"Do you want to talk here, or do you want to walk?" he asked without facing her.

She wasn't used to him being so forward with her. "I came prepared," she said looking down at her Nikes. "We can walk."

"Let's go." Micah swiftly started for the trail without reaching for her hand.

"Ms. Roberts, what is it you would like to talk about?"

Pamela didn't like this. Yesterday he said he loved her and

wanted to marry her. Today he treated her like a stranger. This didn't feel right to her. They were walking side by side and he chose to keep his hands in his pockets. She wanted him to reach for her hand, but he didn't. "Micah, you can call me Pamela."

He shook his head. "Not anymore," he said as his eyes followed an aircraft landing on the runway a short distance away.

Pamela swallowed the lump forming in her throat. "Micah, I want to know why you entered into a relationship with me knowing you're gay."

"Not that you'll believe me, because you didn't last night, but I'll tell you again. I am not gay." This time when he said it, she almost believed it.

"Then why did you have sex with a man for six years? You wouldn't have done that if you weren't a homosexual."

Micah sighed. "Ms. Roberts, I'll tell you how it happened, that is, if you'll listen. Then you can draw your own conclusions, like I know you will."

Pamela heard the slight bitterness in his tone, but pressed forward. "I'm listening."

Micah slowed his stride before he began to open his heart once again to the woman who'd so easily broken it. "I didn't experience love, or at least what I thought was love until I met Pastor Richard Lewis. He was everything I thought a father and a friend were supposed to be. He gave me something no one had given me before— his time and attention. I didn't think anything was wrong when he first put his arm around my shoulder or rested his hand on my leg. It didn't bother me when he began hugging me. I'd seen him hug his entire congregation at one time or another. I was even cool when he started kissing me on the cheek."

The thought of a man kissing Micah made Pamela's stomach turn.

"He'd always say, 'There's nothing wrong with greeting your brother with a holy kiss'" Micah continued. "Then one day, he hugged me and wouldn't let me go, then kissed me on the mouth. I was nineteen and scared out of my mind. I didn't know what to say or do. This man was my father figure and also my pastor." Micah paused to watch another airplane land. Pamela waited for him to continue.

"I pushed away from him, and that's when the manipulation and seduction that would control my life for the next six years started."

Pamela looked puzzled. "I don't understand."

"This is how Richard used my insecurity and vulnerability to get what he wanted from me."

"Micah, come here." When Micah didn't respond Richard moved toward him. "Micah, you know I love you, don't you?" Micah was trembling, but he managed to nod. "I'm the only one who loves you. I'm the only one who looks out for you." Richard cupped Micah's face in his hands. "I'm the only one who takes care of you. I take care of you very well, better than your own mother." Richard started unbuttoning Micah's shirt.

"B-but–," Micah stammered.

"No buts, Micah. I have given you more than your own mother has or any other family member. When you didn't have anyone, I was right there. I'll always be here for you. That's because I love you, and I'm going to show you how much."

Micah trembled as Richard's fingers touched his skin and his lips brushed Micah's neck. "You do love me, don't you, Micah?"

Micah said yes, because he did, but he didn't mean it in that way.

"Then show me," Richard whispered in his ear. "Let me make love to you."

"Micah, that's enough of that!" Pamela screamed. "I don't

want to hear the gory details," she said without looking him in the face.

"Do you want me to continue?"

Pamela nodded, still looking away.

"That was my first sexual experience, and that's when my life began to spin out of control. I was so confused I nearly lost my mind. I didn't like what we were doing, and deep down I knew it was wrong. But Richard justified everything by saying, 'God is love' and there's nothing wrong with two people loving each other.' The weird thing is, every Sunday he would mount his pulpit and say how much he loved his wife, and after service in his office, he wanted me. Sometimes I'd successfully resist him, other times he would threaten to stop paying my rent or take my car. But he really kept his hold on me by threatening to walk out of my life. At the time, I really believed I needed him. I didn't have anyone else. My mother was always drunk. It took her three weeks to notice I had moved out of the apartment. I didn't have any close friends outside of Richard.

"He preached against homosexuality at least once a month, but he told me what we were doing was okay, but I knew it wasn't. I didn't want to do it. He said as long as we asked for forgiveness everything would be all right." Micah looked in her direction. "Do you want to hear something really sad?"

"Nothing could be sadder than what you've already told me," Pamela answered still looking away. She doubted if she would ever be able to look Micah in the face again.

"He would lead me in a prayer for forgiveness after we finished. Richard would be praying, and I'd be crying. Then a year before it ended, something I'll never forget happened. His wife walked in on us, and that really messed me up. His wife had been so nice to me and watching her scream and crumbling on the floor like a wounded child was too much for me. She didn't know Richard had been sleeping with men since he was a teenager. I didn't know that until I was too emotionally tied into him. I spent most of that last year in and out of the county's psych ward.

"It was a constant battle for me. I prayed and I fasted, but I just couldn't break free from the hold Richard had on me. He convinced me that without him I wouldn't be anything, and no one would ever love me. Up until that point no one had. Then two years ago I gave up. I couldn't take it anymore. I didn't want Richard, but I couldn't let him go, so I was going to remove myself from the equation. I was going to commit suicide."

Pamela stopped walking and sat down on a bench. This story was too much for her.

Micah stopped walking, but he didn't sit down. "Richard and I were secretly living together at the time. When his wife threw him out, he simply moved into the apartment he had rented for me. I went into the bathroom and emptied out a full bottle of Vicodin. Before taking the pills I decided to call my mother to tell her good-bye. Of course she was drunk, but she said the one sentence that changed my life."

"What did she say?" Pamela asked, looking in his direction, but not in his eyes.

Micah's voice quivered. "She said, 'I talked to your Uncle Robert this morning.'" Micah wiped his face. "I had only seen my uncle a handful of times my entire life, but I knew he was a preacher, and my mother always said he really knew God. That's why she didn't talk to him that often. He would preach to her, and she didn't want to hear any preaching. Anyway, I asked her for his number and what's amazing is that she was coherent enough to give me the right number. At the time, I didn't know what compelled me to call him. Today, I know it was God. When my uncle answered the phone, I couldn't help it. I poured the last six years of my life out to him. He listened quietly, then he said something I'll always love him for." Micah took a moment to steady his voice. "He told me to pack a bag and head to Midway. My uncle purchased me a one-way ticket out of Chicago. I was in California by evening, and I haven't looked back. I didn't say bye or leave a note. I came here with only the clothes on my back. I didn't want anything connected to Richard or that lifestyle."

Micah walked away to collect himself, and Pamela needed a moment to release herself. She wanted to comfort him, but she couldn't move. She closed her eyes and prayed quietly for him. When he returned, her tears were still flowing.

He picked up where he left off. "My uncle and AC helped me to see that the spirit of lust in Richard Lewis marked me from the start. I was an easy target because of my naïveté and insecurity."

"AC knows about this?" Pamela seemed surprised.

"Yes, and so does my aunt. If it weren't for my uncle, aunt, and AC, I'd probably be dead. They spent many nights praying and helping me to break free from the stronghold Richard had on my mind and spirit."

"Have you been with any other men?"

Micah shook his head. "Were you listening, Ms. Roberts? I don't like men. I've never liked men in that way. As far back as I can remember I've been attracted to women. I was with Richard because, due to my insecurity, I allowed the spirit of lust to control me. God has delivered me. I have no desire whatsoever to be touched by a man or to touch a man. The next time I have sex will be when I make love to my wife on our wedding night. That will be the first time I make love and the only time that matters."

Pamela had to walk on that statement. The only thing that disgusted her more than Micah having sex with a man was the image of him making love to a woman other than herself.

"Ms. Roberts, is there anything else you would like to discuss?" Micah asked when he caught up with her.

Pamela shook her head. They walked the last quarter mile in silence. From time to time, Micah would look over at her and try to find a glimpse of hope in her facial expression, but he couldn't.

Pamela wasn't angry anymore, but she wasn't ready for things to go back to the way they were. She also wasn't ready to remove Micah completely out of her life. What if he weren't completely through with that lifestyle? What if he weren't telling her the truth?

"It was a nice ride, wasn't it?" he asked at the end of the trail, preparing for the inevitable.

"What ride?"

"You and me; it was nice. I'll always remember our time together."

"Who says it's over?" Pamela questioned.

"You did last night."

"I also said I love you. That hasn't changed, but I need some time to figure this out." She finally looked him in the eyes. "I heard everything you said, and I think I understand, but I don't know if this is right for me. Plus, I have Matthew to think about. I have to be careful about what I expose him to. He's my son, and I have to do what I feel is best for him."

Micah braced himself for her next blow by stepping toward his vehicle.

"I don't think it's a good idea for the two of you to continue spending so much time together, at least not until I figure this out. I'm going to ask my neighbor to pick Matthew up from after-school care on the days I'm running late and also to take him to practice. I'll explain to Matthew that it's only temporary. There's only a week left in the season anyway."

Micah didn't say anything, just unlocked his SUV.

"You and I should cut back as well. You do understand, don't you?" she asked just before he started the engine.

"Ms. Roberts, I understand completely." Micah left her standing alone in the parking lot watching his taillights.

Pamela clicked her seat belt a second before her cell phone vibrated. She checked the caller ID before answering. It was her mother.

"What's the latest with you and Micah?" Dorothy asked.

"Nothing, Mama." Pamela tried to sound upbeat. She didn't want her mother to worry about her.

"Then why did you send Jessica to pick Matthew up?"

"We needed to talk, that's all." Pamela wasn't ready to share the last twenty-four hours with her family.

"Is everything all right?"

"It will be. I'll call you in a couple of days." Pamela hung up before her mother started in with her twenty questions.

That night Pamela couldn't sleep. Micah's story replayed constantly in her mind. She wanted to believe him, but it was too incredible. The pastor of the church seducing young men? Pamela couldn't believe a man of God would jeopardize his family and use the Word of God to justify it. Why would a man who likes men marry a woman and keep a boyfriend on the side in the church? Micah was lying, he had to be. That's what men do when they get caught; they lie. That's the only thing that made sense to her. She guessed this Richard Lewis character didn't even exist. But what if he did?

Pamela sat at her home workstation and turned on her computer. She opened the search engine and typed in *Pastor Richard Lewis in Chicago*. To both her surprise and relief, she found multiple articles about the Pentecostal pastor. Pamela clicked on the link to his church's Web site.

"Oh my God," she said as his image downloaded. Pastor Richard Lewis looked just as sanctimonious as any preacher she'd ever seen. He was tall and majestic in his purple and gold robe. She read his bio; single father of two adult children with a Ph.D. in psychology. One of his major accomplishments included the creation of a mentoring program for males ages sixteen to twenty-five. She clicked the icon and browsed the photo gallery. That's when she saw it.

In an old photo of the grand opening ceremony of the church's new job training center, Pastor Lewis posed with the Mayor of Chicago and several other civic leaders. In the background off to the right was a young man holding an overcoat and a briefcase. The man wore a black casual suit and white dress shirt. Every face in the picture bore a smile except his. His face looked sullen and sad. That man was Micah.

"Micah is telling the truth," she whispered. "What am I going to do?" Pamela stared mindlessly at the screen so long, the screen saver photo of her, Micah, and Matthew popped up. The content face smiling back at her was a big contrast from the gloomy guy on the Web site photo. Micah wasn't the same person he was back then, but just how different remained to be seen.

Chapter 12

Matthew skipped into the kitchen and sat down at the table for breakfast. "Good morning, Mommy."

"Hey, baby." Pamela placed a plate of pancakes with sausage and a glass of apple juice in front of him and then stood back and watched her son eat his breakfast. She didn't want to tell him that he wouldn't be spending time alone with Micah anymore, but she had to. She was his mother, and it was her job to protect him.

"Matthew," she began, "Mr. Larson is going to pick you up from after-school care and take you to practice when I'm running late." She'd spoken to her overfriendly neighbor earlier that morning, and he readily agreed.

Matthew swallowed the piece of sausage he'd been chewing, then asked, "What about Micah?"

Pamela chose her words carefully. "Mr. Larson lives closer to the practice field. He can take you without getting stuck in traffic." That didn't even make sense to her. The direction of the practice field was opposite commute traffic.

"Micah doesn't get stuck."

Pamela forgot her son was smarter than the average six-year-old. She'd have to come up with something better than that. "I know, but Mr. Larson wants to help out." That was true. He'd been offering his assistance to her for months.

"We will still have dinner together with Micah, right?"

Pamela hadn't thought about that. "I don't know."

Matthew continued eating, but Pamela could tell he wasn't happy about this new arrangement, but she wasn't going to change her mind.

"Matthew, what kinds of things do you and Micah do when I'm not around?" Pamela had to be certain Micah hadn't violated her son.

"We talk and play games."

"What do you talk about?" she pressed.

Matthew finished off his pancakes before answering. "School and baseball. We talk a lot about my homework. Sometimes we talk about you."

"Me?" Pamela seemed surprised.

"Micah says he loves you very much." Matthew giggled.

Pamela pushed that thought to the back of her mind and focused on her fact-finding mission. "What kind of games do you play?"

Matthew twisted his face as if he were trying to remember something important. He used his fingers to count. "We play catch . . . the song game . . . um, the word game, and numbers."

Pamela decided to use a direct approach. "Matthew, does Micah touch you in any way?"

"He touches me all the time." Matthew smiled, but Pamela's heart skipped a beat.

"Exactly where does he touch you?" she asked in a controlled tone.

"You know, Mommy," Matthew giggled. "He rubs my head and holds my hand. We hug. I ride his shoulders. My favorite is when he tickles me."

"Does he touch you in any other way?"

He thought for a moment. "No." Matthew then put his plate and glass into the sink and ran upstairs.

Pamela stood over the sink and said a prayer of thanks. Her

son hadn't been molested by Micah, and she would see to it that he never would be.

Micah went through his day trying unsuccessfully to keep his thoughts away from Pamela. He checked his watch for the third time in the last hour. If it were last Friday, they would have talked twice by now and it wasn't even noon. He would have told her how much he loved her, and she would have repeated the same sentiments to him. Between service calls, he would have driven by her office building and attached a love note to the windshield of her Altima. Later, Pamela would call him, giggling over the sweet written words. But it wasn't Friday, it was Monday. Just two days without Pamela and Matthew and his heart refused to stop aching for them.

Yesterday at the marina when Pamela said she still loved him, Micah had a brief surge of hope. But that spark was extinguished in the next breath when she treated him like a registered sex offender and a pedophile.

The more the weekend replayed in his mind, Micah realized Pamela really didn't know him at all. Six months of quality time together and she didn't know him. She really didn't if she honestly believed he would violate Matthew, especially after he explained how he had been taken advantage of. He also realized Pamela left him in limbo in regards to their relationship. Micah didn't know if they were still in a relationship or not. She wasn't clear about anything with him, except that he stay away from her son. Micah pondered her request out loud.

"She wants time, but she didn't say how much time. She loves me, but she wants to limit our communication." Micah didn't know if he should call her or speak to her at all. Since he didn't know what to do, he decided to do nothing.

***

Finally finished with recording multiple transactions all morning, Jessica stepped into Pamela's office and sat down. "Now we can talk. How did it go yesterday?"

Pamela shrugged her shoulders. "We talked. He explained everything to me, but nothing has changed."

"What did he say?"

Jessica listened to Pamela repeat the prevalent details of Micah's unbelievable, but apparently true story. "That's so sad," Jessica said. "What type of person would prey on innocent victims like that? What type of man would sacrifice the welfare of his family like that? What pastor would deceive God's people like that?"

"See for yourself." Pamela pulled up the Web site, and then turned the monitor so Jessica could view it.

"Girl, he looks like the devil himself!" Jessica exclaimed.

Pamela shook her head and shrugged her shoulders. "He looks normal to me."

"Girl, please. Look at those beady eyes and the way his eyebrows almost touch each other. I wouldn't trust him as far as I can throw Anthony Combs."

Pamela laughed, but she still didn't see what Jessica saw. But then again, she wasn't the best judge of character when it came to men.

"At least you know the truth. Now you and Micah can move forward." When Pamela didn't respond, Jessica asked, "You are going to move forward, aren't you?"

Pamela sighed deeply. "I don't think so," she finally answered. Since Jessica's mouth was already gaped open, she decided to just lay it all out. "I also asked him to keep his distance from Matthew."

"What?"

"Jess, I don't want to be married to a homosexual," Pamela answered honestly. "And I don't want my son molested."

Jessica planted her palms on the desk and leaned forward.

"Pam, did you hear *anything* Micah told you? He's not a homosexual or a child molester. Lust doesn't control him anymore."

"I know, but that's now. What happens two years or five years from now when his desires change? What happens when he craves a man, and Matthew is the only male around?"

"What do you mean? Micah is healed," Jessica insisted. "He's not going to crave a man, and he loves Matthew. He would never hurt him."

"But Jess, you've heard the stories. Homosexuality is a hard, if not impossible, thing to break free from."

"So is fornication, drugs, alcohol, gambling, abuse . . . shall I go on?" Jessica asked. "Everything is hard without God, but everything is possible with Him."

"Homosexuality is different," Pamela contended and threw her hands up. "It's unnatural and nasty."

Jessica refused to back down. "It's also nasty to give our bodies to everyone who comes through the drive-thru. It's unnatural to pollute our bodies with drugs and alcohol. It's very unnatural and deadly, I might add, to beat another human. But God forgives us for those sins every day."

"And every day, people fall," Pamela contended. "You remember Eugene and Cassandra. Eugene swore up and down he was free, but after Cassandra married him and had their daughter, he left her and went back to his homosexual lifestyle; even moved in with his lover."

"Pam, that's different. Pastor Jackson warned Cassandra over and over again about marrying Eugene. He even refused to officiate the wedding," Jessica explained.

"It still proves my point. He did fall, didn't he?"

"Did you fall back into *your* mess?" Jessica snapped.

"What?" Pamela didn't know what her past had to with the conversation. "What I used to do is irrelevant."

Jessica stared long and hard at her friend of twelve years.

"Pam, you know you're my girl, so I can come real with you, right?"

Pamela leaned back and folded her arms. "Go ahead."

"Pamela, you are judgmental and self-righteous."

"What?" Pamela slapped her palms onto her desk and leaned forward.

"Have you forgotten that you didn't fall out of Jesus' lap? Have you forgotten that since salvation, you've messed up in one area or another? I know you remember how God delivered you and brought you out of destructive behavior. Do I need to take you on a trip down memory lane?"

"Of course not!" Pamela snapped.

"If God can heal you and you never go back to destroying your body, why can't He heal Micah and sustain him?"

"That's different," Pamela said, and to emphasize her point, rolled her eyes. "I didn't lust after a woman!"

Jessica's next statement not only infuriated Pamela, but it pulled the scab off an old wound.

"Micah's past is no different from the lust that controlled your late husband."

Pamela's face flushed. "What are you talking about?" Her volume caught the attention of a coworker out in the hallway.

Jessica promptly went and closed the door. "Marlon slept with everything walking, and you always took him back," she clarified after she returned to the desk.

"Marlon did not sleep with a man!"

"How do you know? He wasn't sleeping with you." Pamela moved her mouth, but she couldn't deny the raw truth. Jessica continued. "How is it that you can accept the lust in a man who sleeps around and cheats constantly? You can accept a man who purposefully hurts you time and time again. You can tolerate a man who didn't care enough to show up for the birth of his own child. You can accept a man who didn't try to do right by you or by God. You can marry a man who loved himself and probably never loved you. You can accept all that, but you can't accept Micah?"

Pamela stood to her feet. "How dare you compare my late husband to Micah Stevenson?" Her voice trembled.

Jessica met her stance and locked eyes. "You're right, Pam, there is no comparison. Micah is saved, and he loves you. He cares enough about you to tell you the truth and open his heart to you and allow you to see his vulnerability and weakness. To top it off, he's a great father to Matthew. But that's not enough for you. Do you know how many women would love to have someone love them half as much as Micah loves you? I know I would. If a man like Micah wanted to marry me, I'd do it and treat him like a king." Jessica folded her arms and rolled her eyes.

"Then you can have him!" Pamela stormed out of her own office and ran down the hall into the restroom. Once secure inside the stall, she cried the tears she'd been fighting to keep at bay.

Why did Jessica have to bring up all the mess she'd been trying hard to forget? Ever since Micah left Saturday night, she'd been suppressing the feelings she'd buried deep down inside when her husband died five years ago. Marlon wasn't a good husband. He was worse than lousy and an even worse father. The one thing he did teach her was that a person's behavior is repetitive. People rarely changed.

Later that afternoon, Pamela called her mother, but that didn't yield any relief from her mental anguish. After she heard the story, her mother felt the same way as Jessica.

"Pam, he is not like that anymore," Dorothy told her. "He's free now."

"Momma, how do you know?" Without meaning to, Pamela yelled at her mother.

"Pamela Ann, I will reach through this phone and beat the devil out of you if ever raise your voice at me again! Do you understand?"

"Yes, Mama; I'm sorry," Pamela mumbled, knowing there was no possible way her mother could make good on such a threat.

"I know this is not what you expected, but it's not as bad as you think. Micah is honest, saved, and he loves you. I know that's why he told you."

Pamela was growing tired of the "Micah Stevenson Cheerleading Squad." "Mama, I don't want to be married to a down-low brother." Pamela thought that would quiet her mother, since her closest friend's husband had revealed he was sleeping with men after being married to his wife for over twenty years.

"Correct me if I wrong. I don't have junior college education like you do. Doesn't the term *down-low* in itself imply that someone's trying to *hide* something? Micah's not hiding anything from you. Micah poured his heart out to you." Pamela had to admit that was true. "Can I ask you something?"

Pamela knew her response didn't matter. Dorothy Jacobs was going to say what was on her mind. "Yes." Pamela barely got the one syllable word out before Dorothy began grilling her.

"Are *you* saved? I mean really saved and not playing around with God?"

Pamela nodded.

"I can't hear you."

She forgot her mother couldn't see her through the phone. "Yes, I'm saved."

"Do you know the voice of the Lord?"

"Yes." She knew exactly where her mother was going.

"What did He tell you about Micah?"

Pamela hung her head and massaged her temples. If she thought Dorothy Jacobs wouldn't drive all the way from Vallejo to beat her down, Pamela would have hung up in her face to keep from answering the question.

"Well, what did He say?" Dorothy pushed.

"Micah is my husband," Pamela mumbled the words so fast, Dorothy couldn't make out what she had said.

"What?"

Pamela exhaled deeply. "He said Micah is my husband."

"That's all I need to hear."

Pamela sat there in shock and listened to the flat line. Her mother had hung up in her face.

A moment after hanging up the phone, Dorothy Jacobs got on her knees alongside her bed and prayed hard. She knew her daughter well. Pamela was stubborn and hardheaded just like she used to be. Pamela's stubbornness once before had taken her to a place so desolate Dorothy thought she was going to bury her only child. Pamela refused to listen to her ten years ago and carried the scars to prove it. The problem was her daughter refused to acknowledge those scars. Marlon Roberts tricked her baby out of much more than her virginity. He also robbed her of her trust and compassion. After Pamela accepted Christ, the darkness lifted, but every so often Dorothy could see the fear and distrust in her eyes. That is, until Micah entered into the picture.

It was only with him that Pamela relaxed enough to be her real self, Dorothy estimated. Pamela laughed and blushed more since she'd been dating Micah than she'd done her entire childhood. Micah was good for her and very good for Matthew. Micah was probably unaware that he helped rebuild

Pamela's self-esteem and confidence. He made her feel special in ways her father couldn't. Micah made her feel like a woman.

Dorothy wasn't naïve. She understood very well the consequences of a homosexual lifestyle. She knew the enticement and seduction into lust was strong and powerful. But she also knew God and the power of God. Just as clear as He exposed to her the deceitfulness in the heart of Marlon Roberts, God revealed to her the purity in Micah's. She knew without question, Micah Stevenson was just what her baby and grandson needed. Dorothy stretched on the floor. There was no way she would allow Marlon to control her baby from down under without a fight.

Chapter 13

"Want some?" Jessica entered Pamela's office unannounced and offered Pamela half of her Subway sandwich. Pamela ignored her, but Jessica sat down anyway. "Girl, stop acting silly and take this." Jessica slid half of the sandwich and a bottle of water across her desk. "You know you're hungry."

Pamela looked up at her and rolled her eyes, but she took the sandwich. "Jessica, you make me sick."

"Whatever. I love you too," Jessica said before biting into the turkey club. "I just don't want you to make the biggest mistake of your life. You did say Micah's your soul mate?" Jessica reminded her with raised eyebrows.

"You sound just like my mother," Pamela smirked.

"We're only repeating what *you* said God said."

Pamela took a drink of water before responding. "God did say it, but I don't know if I can deal with this. To be honest, I don't want to deal with this again."

"Pam, he's not Marlon."

Pamela wanted to believe that, but she'd been fooled countless times before into falling for the baby-it-won't-happen-again speech. "In my heart, I know he's not, but I haven't been able to convince my mind yet."

"Pam, let me be transparent for a minute," Jessica said after swallowing a swig of water. "I'm a thirty-year-old single woman. I go to work five days a week and church on Sundays and Wednesdays. I wake up alone, and I fall asleep alone. On the weekends I dine alone or shop alone. I even go to the movies alone. I've gone to Blockbuster so much that all of the sales-people know me by name. I'm secure with myself, and I like who I am, so I don't mind dining alone. But I would love to have someone hold the door open for me as I enter the res-taurant or pull my chair out. I don't mind watching the latest big-screen release by myself, but I would love to have someone to discuss the movie with on the way to the car. If I get sick, there's no one to take care of me but me. When I'm happy, there's no one to run home to and share the good news with, neither is someone there to encourage me when I'm down."

"I'm single too, Jess," Pamela interrupted. "I understand what it's like living alone."

"But at least you have Matthew to talk to. What I desire more than anything is someone to share my life with, and I also want to be a mother. But God hasn't sent my soul mate to me yet." Jessica took another sip of water. "But He has sent yours. True, he's flawed, but we're all flawed, and even at that, he's everything you need. Would you rather be alone forever looking for someone to fill the space in your heart that can only be occupied by Micah? Or would you rather experience the love of a good man?"

Pamela didn't answer, just continued chewing very slowly.

"Do you want to hear something funny?" Jessica asked.

Pamela still didn't answer.

"Pam, if my soul mate approached me today, I'd take Anthony Combs in a minute. Shiny suits and all!" Jessica laughed. "Girl, I'd love every bit of that eight-pack."

"But that's something easy to fix . . ." Pamela stopped talk-ing and waved her hands in the air. "Hold on, did you just say Anthony Combs is your soul mate?"

"We're talking about you right now," Jessica retorted, real-izing she'd spilled what she'd known for months. "Like I was saying, you don't need to fix Micah. God has already done that. All you need to do is love him."

"This is not some simple flaw, like being color blind, this is a major issue," Pamela contended.

"It isn't any more major than the problem you had. Why is it that we want our men to be the perfect knights in shiny armor, but we want them to accept us with all of our issues and hang-ups?"

Pamela stood and walked over to the window and offered Jessica her back. "Jess, it's not that I want Micah to be perfect, I just want to be able to trust him."

"You can."

"I tried that before, and it didn't work."

Jessica walked over to her and placed her arm around her shoulder. "Not with Micah you didn't. Please don't make Micah pay for Marlon's mistakes."

Pamela pulled away from her. "That's not what I'm doing!" she barked.

"Then what do you call it?"

"I am protecting me and my son."

There wasn't any getting through to Pam, not today. Jessica collected her lunch trash, but kept talking. "I call it D-E-N-I-A-L. You're taking your unresolved issues with that overgrown boy you had for a husband out on Micah." Jessica placed her hand on the doorknob. "When you're ready to be healed, call me. I'll bring the blessed oil and a throw sheet." Jessica laughed and so did Pamela, finally.

Micah hurried into Bible Study minutes before Pastor Jackson mounted the podium. His plan was to get there early enough to sit on the front row. That way he could look straight ahead without having to see Pamela. But thanks to his last customer, the closest seat he found was three rows from the back.

"I can do this," he told himself. It had been three days since he laid eyes on the woman he loved. Three days since he'd heard her soft voice. Three days since she threw the dagger that pierced his heart almost beyond repair. Regardless of the distance and restrictions she'd put between them, if she'd just said the word, restoration would be granted.

Micah had just about convinced himself that he could get through Bible Study when Pamela and Matthew hurried into the sanctuary and took the empty seats right next to him.

"Hey, Micah." Matthew wasted no time jumping on Micah's lap and giving him a hug.

"Hey, buddy." The joy that instantaneously filled Micah's heart helped ease the sorrow that had encased him like a glove since his love pulled away from him. He guardedly made eye contact with Pamela, and surprisingly, she gave him a smile. "I miss you so much," is what he wanted to say, but what he voiced was a simple and guarded, "Hello."

"Hi, honey," she replied as she rummaged through her bag for her Bible Study journal and an ink pen. She found the journal, but didn't have any luck with the pen.

Micah didn't know what to make of her greeting. Was she softening her stance or just putting up a good front? After all, one could find Academy Award–winning performances in the church on any given day. "Here." He held out a pen with the cable company's logo on it. She smiled and accepted it just as Sister Davis came to collect Matthew for the children's Bible Study class in the fellowship hall.

With Matthew gone, there was nothing between them but space, which was normal. Not wanting to be the headline news for Praise Temple's I-got-it-and-I-got-to-report-it gossip columnists, they always made a conscious effort not sit too close to one another in church.

Pamela tried hard to decipher the words flowing from Pastor Jackson's mouth, but it was impossible. The thumping in her chest was too loud. She'd known she would see Micah, but didn't know she'd be so close to him. And what was worse, she wanted to be even closer, having realized that the second she saw him, the hardness toward him softened and all she wanted was for things to be like they were four days ago. She wanted her daily phone calls. She missed their commercial time together. She missed his smile, his eyelashes, his cologne— she missed him.

Her note taking was useless. She gave up. The only thing she could hear was her heart reminding her of how much she needed him in her life. Before her rational mind could stop her hand, she wrote the words *I miss you* repeatedly across the page of her journal.

"I miss you too," Micah whispered in her ear. Stunned, she dropped the pen and locked eyes with him.

In her eyes, Micah's could tell that she meant those three little words, but her eyes also told him she wasn't quite ready to overlook his past just yet. He broke their gaze, and she watched as he scribbled the words *I love you* in his notebook. Pamela promptly held her index finger up and stepped out. When she returned, Micah had moved his seat.

When she didn't find Matthew in the fellowship hall after Bible Study, Pamela knew exactly where to look for her young man. She suppressed her emotions, the anticipation of being close to Micah once again, and headed for the cable company van.

"Micah, are you coming for dinner after practice tomorrow?" Matthew asked, leaning against the cable company van.

"I don't know," Micah answered honestly. "I may not be able to make it."

"I like the way you help me with my homework. Mommy is always too tired."

"I know," Micah said plainly, then had a thought. "Maybe Mr. Larson can help you before practice."

"He's too old," Matthew answered. "The new stuff is too hard for him."

Micah laughed at his little friend's observation. "I'll see what I can do after practice," he promised.

As she neared the cable company van, Pamela's emotions were finally under control. That is, until she observed the way Micah interacted with her son. Normally, Micah would take him for a ride on his shoulders right there in the parking lot. Tonight, Micah made sure he kept at least an arm's distance from Matthew. With every attempt Matthew made to draw closer to him, Micah casually moved, eventually opting to sit inside the van with the door closed. From where she stood, Pamela could read his avoidance tactics. She was sure Matthew could too, and that made her regret the things she'd said. A tear slid down her cheek when she recognized she had taken away her son's friend.

"Here comes your mother." Micah pointed in Pamela's direction making sure he avoided eye contact. He couldn't look at her now. He was angry for having to push Matthew away. He hated to think Matthew was experiencing, at his hands, the same rejection he'd become accustomed to, but that was what his mother wanted.

"I'll see you tomorrow at practice." Matthew hesitated a moment not sure of what to do. Micah usually hugged him before they parted.

"Tomorrow, little buddy," Micah said, and then extended his hand out the window. "Don't forget to bring your homework." The smile that Matthew gave him while he shook his hand was missing something and that broke Micah's heart.

"Mommy, Micah's going to help me with my homework tomorrow."

The excitement in her son's voice made it impossible for Pamela to deny her son again. "All right, I'll see you tomorrow, Micah." Pamela grabbed her son by the hand. "We'll talk later."

Micah didn't even watch them walk away. He started the engine and took off faster than normal. At the moment, a conversation with Pamela was not something he looked forward to.

The second Micah stepped into his apartment, he began pulling off his work clothes and headed for the shower. The day's physical task was minor compared to the emotional tidal wave Pamela had taken him through in just two short hours. From the moment she sat next to him, his world was all right again. When her fingers penned on paper what was in her heart, he allowed his guard to lower just a little. But then she walked away from him, and the wound in his heart deepened. He wasn't naïve. He'd known there was a fifty-fifty chance of Pamela ending their relationship, and mentally, he thought he was prepared to handle it. Sadly for him, he'd underestimated the progress he'd made. Being saved gave him some security, but rejection was still hard to handle no matter how familiar it was.

The hot pellets from the Spiderman showerhead were a welcomed reprieve from his inner turmoil, but as he stepped from the steam-filled bathroom and into the bedroom, his dilemma returned. How could he help Matthew tomorrow, and how could he protect him from getting hurt in this mess? Pamela's ring tone filled his room before he could come to a resolution. "How ironic," he grumbled before he answered the call. Hearing the melody for "You Are the Sunshine of My Life" only magnified the dark clouds hanging over his life.

"You didn't have to change your seat," Pamela said softly.

"I know being in close proximity to me bothers you. I didn't want you to feel uncomfortable in church," Micah replied.

"Then you should have stayed. I meant what I said, I mean wrote; I miss you. Micah, I miss you so much."

In the prolonged silence that followed, Micah tried to find the proper way to respond. He didn't want to rush her, but he didn't want her to drag him along either.

"Matthew wants me to help him with his homework tomorrow. Is that all right with you?" Micah held his breath, once again preparing to ride out another emotional tidal wave.

"What time shall we expect you?" she asked cheerfully.

"Mr. Larson will drop Matthew at home around 7:00."

Micah wanted to tell her that it didn't make sense for her neighbor to pick Matthew up. After all, he was his coach, and they were coming from the same place, but he didn't say that. Pamela was his mother, and she could do whatever she wanted to when it came to Matthew. "I'll be there," he replied, and then waited for her to direct the rest of the conversation, if there was any.

"Micah, I . . . I'll see you tomorrow."

"Good night, Ms. Roberts." He was about to disconnect when she called out to him.

"Micah, I don't like you calling me Ms. Roberts. It's so impersonal, like what we have is nothing more than a business or professional relationship. What we have is much more than that. At least it is to me."

Micah closed his eyes and breathed deeply once again. "Pamela, what do we have?"

"Micah we love each other, don't we? I know I love you."

Micah didn't realize he was crying until he felt a tear fall onto his fingers near the receiver. Before attempting to speak, he swallowed the lump in his throat. "Pamela, I do love you, more than you know."

"I do know. Good night."

Micah wanted to be happy, but he couldn't. It was too early.

Chapter 14

Pamela moved around the kitchen quickly preparing dinner for her son and Micah. At first she tried to convince herself she wasn't cooking for Micah, then gave up trying while leaning over the sink, which was filled with potatoes. She had a vegetable peeler in hand. Micah adored her homemade garlic mashed potatoes and her sautéed green beans. She didn't have time to make meatloaf. Micah would have to settle for baked salmon instead, and he would have to wait until the weekend for some peach cobbler.

Pamela wasn't sure how the evening would go, but anything was better than the last five days. She missed him so much. The emptiness was so unbearable at times that as she lay in bed at night, she would stare at the phone, wishing it would ring. When it didn't, she would cry until sleep came.

Her stomach bubbled with joy as she approached her car in the parking lot after work today. A yellow piece of paper held in place by the wiper blade flapped against her windshield. Assuming it was a love note from Micah, she sprinted toward the vehicle in three-inch heels and snatched the paper. In her excitement she didn't notice that every car in the parking lot had the same yellow decoration. Her knees buckled, and she had to lean against the car to keep from falling as she read the flyer that announced the opening of a new Mexican restaurant at Emery Bay. Once inside the vehicle, she banged the steering wheel in frustration. The feelings she had for her late husband didn't come close to what she felt for Micah Stevenson. With Micah, she felt it all; fear, anger, hurt, disappointment, but the one emotion that always remained and overshadowed the others was love.

She'd just placed the salmon in the oven when the doorbell sounded. After washing and drying her hands, she flung the door open without looking through the peephole, assuming it was her son returning from practice.

"Micah, what are you doing here?" With her elevated tone the question sounded like an accusation.

Micah stepped backward with his hands raised. "I can leave."

"That's not what I mean," Pamela said, shaking her head. "How did you get here before Matthew?"

"I don't know. Your neighbor left the practice field before I did," Micah answered.

Pamela ignored the nagging feeling in her stomach. This was the second time in three days Mr. Larson had failed to bring Matthew directly home. Tonight when Matthew came home she would have a talk with her neighbor.

"They should be here any minute. Come in." Pamela stepped to the side to allow room for Micah to pass, but he hesitated.

"Are you sure you want me here?"

"Yes, Micah, I'm sure." This time she added the smile that she knew he couldn't resist.

Micah cautiously stepped inside, making sure he didn't brush her, but Pamela grabbed his arm. Micah slowly moved his eyes from her hand to her face. "What is it?"

Pamela tried to restrain herself, but couldn't. She didn't want to. "Can I have a hug, please?"

He gazed deeper into her eyes, and then answered with a voice that trembled. "Pamela, you can have whatever you want from me." He then opened his arms to her and immediately she melted into him. "I've missed you so much," he whispered in her ear. She was about to say the same when Matthew ran through the open door.

"Hi." Matthew giggled when he caught them hugging.

"Hello, baby." Pamela quickly broke away from Micah.

"Where's Mr. Larson?" Pamela asked, looking down the walkway.

"He went home."

Pamela walked outside and looked toward Mr. Larson's unit, but she didn't see him. She stepped back inside and closed the door. "Where did you go after practice?"

"We went to Wal-Mart. He got me this toy." Matthew held up the action figure capable of transforming into three super cosmic beasts.

"That was nice of him," she said out loud, but still thought she needed to have a talk with Mr. Larson.

Matthew turned to Micah and waited. Pamela guessed he wasn't sure if he should hug Micah or wait for him to put his hand out. "No horseback rides today?" Pamela said, then nodded at Micah to indicate it was okay for him to play with her son.

Micah swallowed hard then gave his little friend what he wanted. He'd barely squatted when Matthew's little arms and legs gripped him. The two jovially bounced around the living room and kitchen, but not without Pamela's watchful eye. She stood there watching them with her arms folded, something she'd never done before. That made Micah uncomfortable.

Abruptly, Micah ended the horseplay. "Come on, buddy, let's get started on your homework."

"Okay." Matthew started for the living room, but Pamela called him back.

"Why don't you work at the kitchen table? It's more comfortable." She meant to sound suggestive, but firmly expressed her command.

"Sure," Micah said dryly. He brushed past her without making eye contact and sat at the table. He clinched his fist and planted them firmly on the table. His jaws flexed, and he took a deep breath before he pasted a smile on his face for Matthew's sake.

"Dinner's ready," Pamela announced some time later.

"We're almost done," Micah responded. Pamela missed the irritation in his response and continued fixing his plate.

Ten minutes later Matthew was ready to eat. Pamela set three plates on the table, and Micah stood to leave.

"Don't you want to stay for dinner?" Pamela asked, oblivious to how her actions had offended him.

"No, I don't!" he answered sharply, then added, "I'm not feeling well," when Matthew looked up.

She continued talking, and he continued walking toward the door. "I can pack you a plate to take home for later or maybe for lunch tomorrow," she offered. She didn't want him to leave.

He waved back to Matthew. "See you on Saturday."

"I hope you feel better. I'll pray for you when I say my prayers," Matthew said.

Micah waited until he opened the front door before responding to Pamela's offer.

"I don't want anything from anyone who doesn't trust me." His voice was low enough where Matthew couldn't hear.

Pamela's mouth dropped as she watched Micah walk down her walkway. She called after him, but he didn't respond.

Pamela shook the red and white pom-poms and yelled from the stands. "Good hit, Number Seven!"

"Run, Matthew!" Jessica screamed. The mother and god-mother jumped and exchanged high fives, and then did a celebratory dance when Matthew made it all the way to second base.

"Girl, I'm going to miss this. Coming to Matthew's games has been the most exciting thing I've done all spring," Jessica announced after she sipped her drink.

"I'll have to do something about that." AC's voice startled both women, Jessica so much that she dropped her two-dollar drink on the bench in front of her.

"Are you serious?" Jessica asked cautiously.

"Yes, I am." AC casually propped his foot on the bench and leaned forward.

Pamela laughed as her friend lost all modesty.

Jessica leaned forward and batted her eyelashes. Her normally high-pitched voice suddenly transformed to low and sultry. "What did you have in mind?"

Pamela thought she heard a hint of seduction in her friend's voice.

AC placed her left hand in his and winked. "I thought I would ask the league to extend the season to give you something to do or maybe they can send you home with play-by-play videos."

Pamela pretended she was too engulfed in the game to notice her friend had just received a double serving of her own medicine.

Jessica snatched her hand away from AC and then stomped from the bleachers. As soon as she was out of earshot, AC and Pamela laughed so hard, they almost missed Matthew coming home to score.

Pamela slapped AC on the arm. "Why did you do that? You know my girl likes you."

"I know." AC smiled. "I like her too, and if she ever stops making fun of me, I'll tell her."

AC followed Pamela's eyes to the coach's box where Micah stood. The entire game Micah had avoided looking in her direction. Actually, he had been avoiding her since he left her house two days ago. Pamela repeatedly left messages on both his home and cell phones without any response from him.

"You know my boy loves you." AC interrupted her thoughts. Pamela sighed. "I know he does. I love him too, but sometimes love is not enough." Pamela was thinking more of her marriage to Marlon than her relationship with Micah. There wasn't any amount of love she could have given Marlon that would have kept him faithful to her.

"I wouldn't know about that. I'm still waiting for love," AC answered. "What I do know is this: Micah Stevenson has earned my unwavering respect. He loves God, he's honest and has more integrity than most people I know. One day he's going to make someone a great husband." AC looked Pamela dead in the eyes before adding, "Wouldn't it be a shame if that person is not you?"

Pamela followed Jessica's earlier lead and stomped from the bleachers.

Micah's interaction with the team and their families after the game made Pamela both jealous and furious. It wasn't any one particular thing he did. It was the way the single women hovered over him and his apparent enjoyment. Normally, Pamela would have been standing next to him and the lionesses would have held their paws at bay, but now he was fair game.

Today was the last game, and most of the parents brought thank-you gifts for Micah and the assistant coach. They weren't big gifts. Most of them were baked goods or a gift card, but Pamela didn't care. She knew with every gift came an invitation for Micah to satisfy more than his sweet tooth. It wouldn't have bothered her so much if AC hadn't said what he said earlier. His question brought home the reality of Micah with someone else, especially since now he wasn't speaking to her. Pamela would have made it through the female parade if Tamara hadn't approached Micah showing more than enough cleavage and running her hands all over him.

Tamara, the first baseman's mother, made known her attraction to Micah at the first practice. She always leaned a certain way or said little things that made her intentions known. Of course, Micah never encouraged her, but today, he didn't discourage her either. After Tamara whispered something in Micah's ear and he laughed, Pamela stomped over.

"Excuse me, Micah, may I speak to you for a moment," Pamela asked with a smile that was friendlier than her tone.

Both Tamara and Micah stared at Pamela as if she were an intruder. Tamara then rolled her eyes. Micah didn't respond.

"Tamara, I'll call you later," Micah said without addressing Pamela's question.

"I can't wait," Tamara purred, then sashayed away. When Micah finally turned his attention to Pamela, her smile was gone.

"Call her and die!" Pamela snarled.

"Pamela, this little show of jealousy is cute, but I have to call her and tell her how wonderful her peach cobbler is," Micah said, holding up the aluminum pan. "You know it's my favorite."

"Whatever, Micah." Pamela rolled her eyes. She didn't see the point in fighting over something that wasn't going to happen. "Would you join Matthew and me for dinner? I'm making turkey spaghetti."

"Pamela, I don't think that's a good idea. You don't trust me, remember? And I don't like being in the company with people who don't trust me." Micah turned and started toward his SUV.

"Micah, wait!" she called after him. This time he stopped. "I'm sorry about the other night." Micah didn't say anything, just gazed at her. "Come on, it would mean a lot to Matthew." Pamela couldn't believe she was desperate enough to use her son as a pawn. "It would mean a lot to me too." She lowered her lashes. "I miss your company."

Micah smiled and gave in as always. "Why not? I'll bring dessert," he added with the aluminum pan held high.

Pamela didn't say a word.

Later, after devouring turkey spaghetti, salad, and garlic bread, Micah and Matthew remained at the table and enjoyed warm peach cobbler with vanilla ice cream.

"Mommy, this is good." Matthew held his spoon in the air.

"Pamela, I think you have some real competition here," Micah agreed with Matthew. "Tamara's peach cobbler is just as good as yours, if not better. This is the best cobbler I have ever tasted."

"Is that right?" Pamela was calm.

"Without a doubt," Micah said honestly.

"That's because I made it," Pamela announced then stood and collected her dirty dishes.

Micah was confused. "What happened to the one Tamara made?"

"It's in the garbage with the rest of the trash," Pamela answered sharply, then whispered in his ear. "Don't ever bring another woman's food into my house."

Micah laughed out loud. Having Pamela this jealous was hilarious, especially since he wasn't interested in Tamara at all.

Matthew laughed also. He thought his mother had whispered something funny like she always did.

"What about my aunt?" Micah asked. "Or one of the church mothers? Can I at least enjoy some old-school cooking?"

She conceded and rewarded him with the smile he loved so much. "All right, no one under age sixty."

Micah finished off his dessert, then he and Matthew cleared the table. He would have left right after, but Matthew asked him to watch a DVD with him. Micah agreed, but only because he knew Matthew would fall asleep within minutes like he always did after a full meal. Sure enough, *Willie Wonka & the Chocolate Factory* wasn't halfway through when Micah carried him upstairs to his bedroom. Pamela followed behind.

He placed Matthew on the bed, and then rubbed his head. "See you later, buddy." In times past, he would have kissed his forehead, but not tonight. He started for the door.

Pamela dropped the shoe she'd just removed from her son's foot and grabbed Micah's arm. "Don't leave. I want to talk to you. Please," she pleaded when Micah didn't respond.

"Five minutes, and then I'm out." He left the room before she agreed to his time restraints.

Pamela returned downstairs to find Micah seated on the couch with his eyes closed and his hands stuffed into the front pockets of his jacket.

"I don't have all night. What do you want to talk about?" His eyes remained closed.

She sat next to him. "I really am sorry about the other night. I'm trying, but this is hard for me."

"It's hard for me too, but I never would make you feel as dirty as you made me feel." Micah still kept his eyes closed. "I know what I told you is hard to digest, but you could still treat me with respect. Don't you know me at all?"

Pamela reached out to him and instinctively, he moved his arm away. "Micah, please look at me. I really am sorry."

Prepared to accept defeat, Pamela lowered her head. Then AC's and Jessica's words crossed her mind. They were two people searching for the love that was right in front of them, but they didn't know it. Pamela knew without a doubt that Micah loved her. That was enough to give it another try.

"I saw him," she said softly. "I wanted to know if—"

"You saw who?" he interrupted.

"Richard Lewis."

Micah's eyes bucked open, and his head jolted forward. "Where?"

"I found his church's Web site." Micah leaned back against the couch, but didn't say anything. "He wasn't what I expected. Then again, I don't know what I expected. I think I wanted him to be a fictitious person and for your story to be the product of a vivid imagination."

"It's not. Pamela, it's very real. So is my love for you."

Pamela broke his gaze and lowered her head before stating the questions she felt she needed to know the answers to. "Did you love him?" Micah closed his eyes and exhaled as he shook his head. "Micah, I want to know if you loved him the same way you love me. Did you share romantic meals with him? Did you write him love letters like the ones you've written to me? Did you share a favorite song? Did you think about him all day, like you used to think about me? Do you miss him? Do you ever think about him when we're together? Did you enjoy sleeping with him?"

Micah massaged his temples, something he'd been doing a lot lately. Stress headaches were becoming synonymous with being in Pamela's presence. "I thought you didn't want to know the gory details."

"Please tell me. I think the answers will help me to understand."

Micah laced his fingers together underneath his chin and exhaled deeply again.

"Yes, Pamela, I did love him. But not like you think. I wasn't romantically in love with him. What I felt for Richard derived from the respect I had for him. As I said before, I considered him to be my natural as well as my spiritual father.

For me, there wasn't anything romantic about our distorted relationship. I honestly didn't want to have sex with him, but to say I never enjoyed it would be a lie. That was part of the stronghold and confusion. My flesh did respond to him in the way flesh is supposed to respond when stimulated. Before and after each encounter I was miserable and swore never to do it again. I guess in a sense it's the same with a man and woman practicing fornication. Before the act, you tell yourself you're not going to do it. Then it starts to feel good and you push back the severity of your actions. Afterward, you feel guilty and vow it will never happen again."

Micah stopped talking, but Pamela motioned with her hand for him to continue. "Do I miss him? Not at all. I do think about him. I don't think about the times we had sex, but I do think about the lies he told me. I think about the manipulation he used to control me. I don't ever want to forget that. I need to remember that, so I'll never fall into that trap again.

"I think about his wife, Brenda. To this day, I regret hurting her. She didn't deserve the betrayal she received at our hands. Brenda had a nervous breakdown after learning I was just one of her husband's *friends*. Like I said before, he'd been sleeping with men for years. Turns out, he only married Brenda so he could be elected pastor of his first church. I wrote her a letter last year apologizing, but Brenda never responded."

Thinking that she didn't want to be another Brenda, Pamela turned her head away from him.

Micah gently turned her face back to him. "I never think about him when you and I are together. Every word I have ever written to you was straight from my heart for you only. You're the only person who has ever filled my heart and occupied my mind constantly. You're the only person I have been *in* love with, and you're the only person I want to love."

Micah cupped her face and used his thumbs to wipe the tears streaming down her cheeks. She accepted his touch, but when he leaned in to kiss her, she pulled away and turned her head. Micah left without saying another word.

Chapter 15

Matthew vigorously shook Pamela for the third time. Being stuck in the house on a Saturday watching his mother sleep was not on his list of fun things to do. "Mommy, can I go outside? Please?"

Pamela turned over on the couch. "We'll go to the movies later, but now Mommy's tired." Physically, she was tired, having worked long hours at the title company all week. Mentally, she was drained. She and Micah hadn't spoken since his last visit seven days ago, and she was miserable. Pamela couldn't eat, and sound sleep hadn't paid her a visit in days.

"Can I play inside the patio then?"

Pamela hated to keep Matthew cooped up inside on the weekend, but she was too fatigued to move. She missed Micah's help now more than ever. "Sure, Matthew, just make sure you stay inside the gate," she ordered, then pulled the blanket over her head.

"Thanks, Mommy." Matthew trotted away, and Pamela dozed off.

Pamela finally awakened from the dream she was enjoying of her and Micah walking along the beach. They were holding hands and making plans for their future. "Lord, that was not funny," she mumbled while looking upward at the ceiling.

After a good stretch, she sat up on the couch and called for Matthew to come inside. When he hadn't responded by the time she'd finished folding her blanket, she called again. Still no answer. Pamela looked over at the clock on the stove and gasped. She'd been asleep for over two hours.

"Matthew!" she yelled as she stepped out into the small enclosed area outside the patio door. His toys were there, but Matthew wasn't. Pamela fought back the panic that suddenly welled inside of her and ran upstairs. "Matthew!" She pushed his bedroom door open. He wasn't there. She ran through every room in the house. She checked underneath the beds, inside the closets; even the shower stalls. Still no Matthew. With every empty room her heart sank deeper and fear overtook her. "Matthew! Matthew!" She ran downstairs and checked the garage; nothing. She checked the walkway out front; nothing. She ran through the complex without any shoes on calling for her son. "Matthew! Matthew!"

"Oh God, where's my son?" she cried after she ran the length of the complex and didn't find him. She didn't find him or anyone else. The complex was unusually empty for a Saturday afternoon.

"Maybe he's at Shondra's playing with Tyson." She spoke the thought out loud, although no one was around. That had to be it. Matthew and Tyson played together often. Tyson had even slept over a couple of times. "That's it," she reasoned. She ran up the stairs to her neighbor's unit. "Matthew got tired of playing alone and went to Tyson's house for company." Her theory proved wrong when no one answered unit number five. Pamela proceeded to knock on every door in the complex. No one had seen Matthew. *Maybe he's back at home by now,* she thought as she ran back to her unit.

"Matthew!" she screamed upon entering. Silence answered. Matthew still wasn't there. Pamela picked up the phone to call the police, but then thought of Jessica. "She has a key to the house. Maybe Jessica came by and picked Matthew up. She has done that before. She'd always ask first, but maybe she didn't want to awake me." Once again, Pamela convinced herself of an explanation for her son's absence as she punched Jessica's phone number.

"Is Matthew with you?" she yelled into the phone when Jessica answered on the first ring.

"No, isn't he with you?" Jessica responded in a voice that matched Pamela's.

The negative answer unleashed Pamela's pent up emotions. "Jess, I can't find him," she cried. "I fell asleep, and now I can't find him! I can't find my son!"

"Pam, calm down!"

"I can't calm down. I don't know where my son is!"

"Stay with me, Pam. We're going to find him." Jessica paused. "Have you talked to Micah? Maybe he picked him up."

Pamela's hard tears softened a little. "I didn't think about that, but it does make sense." Pamela disconnected before Jessica could tell her that she was on her way over.

Pamela punched Micah's cell number, and for the first time in days wished Matthew was with him. She prayed Micah had picked him up so she could rest, like he'd done many times before when she endured a hard week. But how would Micah know what type of week she'd endured? They hadn't talked in seven long days.

"Hello." Micah sounded like he was still in bed. But that couldn't be, it was two o'clock in the afternoon.

"Do you have my son?" Pamela yelled into the phone.

Micah took a deep breath before answering. "Pamela, what are you talking about? You told me to stay away from your son, remember?"

"Micah, please tell me you have my son," she begged. "I know what I said was wrong, but just please tell me Matthew is with you."

On the other end of the phone, Micah sat up and tried to focus on what she was saying. "Pamela, what's going on? Where's Matthew?"

"I don't know!" she cried.

Micah was wide awake now. "What do you mean you don't know?"

Pamela cried so hard, he barely understood her. "I fell asleep, and when I woke up, he was gone. I can't find my son. He's not here. I have checked everywhere. Please tell me he's with you."

"Pamela, listen to me!" Micah ordered. "Hang up and call the police." Pamela nodded like he could see her consenting to his command. "Do you hear me?"

She disconnected his call without another word and dialed 911.

Waiting for the police to arrive was torture for Pamela. Sweat dripped from her pores. This had to be what burning in hell's fire felt like. It had been over two hours since she had laid eyes on her son, heard his whining, or been embarrassed by one of his inquisitive questions. She was afraid and lonely, and the darkness that covered her at the thought of not knowing where her only child was threatened to swallow her. If anything happened to Matthew, that's exactly what would happen— she would die, and she knew it. Pamela couldn't stand the loneliness any longer; she picked up the phone and called her parents.

"Oh Jesus!" Dorothy cried and immediately went into prayer. Pamela listened until the police knocked on her door.

Jessica arrived with the police. That was a good thing, because Pamela couldn't speak clearly. Between wiping her friend's nose and trying to comfort her, Jessica told the officers what Pamela had told her, then handed Matthew's current school picture from the mantle to the police for an adequate description. She couldn't tell them what Matthew was wearing. Unfortunately for Pamela, she couldn't remember what her son had on that morning. She'd been too sleepy to take note.

"Where's my son?" Pamela cried continually. Jessica tried to comfort her, but it was useless. Pamela was inconsolable.

"Ms. Roberts," the female officer started, "what about your son's father? Would he have taken him?"

"He's dead."

"What about his family?" the officer continued. "How's your relationship with them?"

"I haven't talked to them in years. They live out of state. They have never shown any interest in my son," Pamela answered sadly. Her former in-laws hadn't laid eyes on Matthew since he was in diapers at his father's funeral.

"Did you find him yet?" Micah entered the town house with AC. At the sound of his voice, everyone turned and gave him a brief glance, but Pamela jumped from the couch and ran to him.

At first, Micah didn't return her embrace, but she held on to him so tightly. He had to grip her to keep from losing his balance. Pamela cried so hard and loud, the officers stepped outside to give her a moment to collect herself.

Jessica answered for Pamela. "They're interviewing the neighbors now to see if anyone saw him leave the complex."

"How long has he been gone?" AC wanted to know.

"Almost three hours," Jessica answered again.

"Oh God, please let my baby be okay," Pamela cried, still clinging to Micah.

"Pamela, what's going on?" It was her neighbor, Shondra.

Everyone, including the police officers, turned and inspected the woman sporting a fresh set of gold acrylic nails. By now, the entire complex knew what was going on; why didn't Shondra?

"We're looking for Matthew. He appears to be missing," the female officer answered from behind her. "Have you seen him?"

"Have you checked with Mr. Larson?" Shondra asked. "I saw Matthew in his car when I left for the nail shop."

Pamela's body relaxed a bit and thought that if Matthew was with Mr. Larson, everything was fine. She would definitely have that discussion with him this time about taking her son places without her permission.

After Shondra gave the officers her account of what she witnessed, Micah shook his head. The story didn't sound right.

"What's Larson's first name?" the male officer asked.

"Steve or Steven," Pamela answered. "He could be home. His car is not parked outside, but he normally parks in his garage."

"Let's go and have a talk with him," the officer said after speaking codes the civilians didn't understand into the two-way radio.

Pamela and Micah started to follow the officers to Mr. Larson's unit, but were instructed to remain in Pamela's unit. They did watch from Pamela's front door. The spark of hope Pamela had moments earlier quickly flickered when her neighbor didn't respond to the officer's persistent banging.

"What's his number?" Micah asked Pamela from the doorway, then used his cell phone to call both Larson's home and cell numbers, but didn't get an answer from either number. The knot in his stomach suddenly became worse than the pain in his right ankle from the injury he sustained the day before.

From where they stood, they could see the female officer say something into the two-way radio, then the male officer kicked Mr. Larson's door open.

"Oh no," Micah moaned. He figured the police must have

had probable cause for them to enter Larson's place without a warrant. A few minutes later, Micah's fears were validated when the officers unwound yellow tape and declared Larson's unit a crime scene.

Pamela took off running and screaming toward Larson's unit. She made it inside before the officers could stop her. Micah, AC, and Jessica were just a step behind. The sight before her brought Pamela to her knees.

Numerous stacks of pornography magazines lined the floor of the living room. The walls were covered with pictures of men and boys of various ages, sizes, and nationalities, all with little or no clothing and all in compromising positions. On the coffee table, it appeared Larson was making a magazine of his own. He had pictures of boys Matthew's age or younger, all nude. In some pictures, he fondled the boys, and in others, Larson guided the little hands over his own body parts.

"Oh God, no!" Pamela screamed. Micah picked her up and carried her out of the unit and out into the common area. "Oh God, please!" Pamela's cries were so loud they were heard throughout the entire complex. Micah kept his emotions bottled up. Jessica cried along with Pamela while AC held her.

"Ms. Roberts, were you aware that Steven Larson is a registered sex offender in the Megan's Law database?" the female officer asked, standing on the lawn next to them.

Pamela was too dazed to answer. "He preys on little boys Matthew's age and younger. He's a pedophile. We're treating this as child abduction and have activated an Amber Alert."

The officer's words were too much for Pamela. Her body went limp in Micah's arms, and then everything went black.

Chapter 16

Pamela finally regained consciousness while she rested in her bed with Dorothy snuggled against her, praying hard for her. Pamela's back faced her bedroom door so she didn't see Micah leaning against the door frame. He had been there the entire time, praying for her and for Matthew.

If anything happened to Matthew, Micah felt he would never forgive himself for not protecting him from the hands of a predator. As for Pamela, she would literally go crazy without Matthew. He was her world.

"Oh God, I'm sorry. Please have mercy and help me," Pamela said out loud, then looked up at her mother. The last four hours were not part of some crazy dream. It was real, all of it. Her son had been abducted by a pedophile.

"Pam, this is not your fault." Her mother comforted her by rubbing her head and rocking her.

"It is my fault, Mama. It's entirely my fault. I created this mess," Pamela whined.

"How were you supposed to know the man is possessed by a lust demon?" Dorothy tried to hold Pamela's chin up so she could make eye contact with her, but Pamela wouldn't allow it.

"Mama, I really didn't know the man," Pamela answered sadly. "I'd only spoken to him in passing since he moved here last year. He seemed so nice, and he always offered to assist me with Matthew. He said he'd grown up in a single-parent home and understood how hard it is to raise a child alone."

"I still don't see how this is your fault. You didn't know he was only being nice to you just to get his hands on my grand-baby. You just needed the help he provided."

"No, Mama." Pamela's body trembled as a new batch of tears fell. "I didn't need his help. I had all the help I needed in Micah. I trusted Micah, but after he told me about his past, I was afraid to leave him alone with Matthew. I was afraid he would abuse Matthew, if he already hadn't."

Dorothy looked over her shoulder to the doorway at Micah. His back now faced the room.

"I know Micah loves him and would never hurt him, but I got scared, and I handed my baby over to a child molester. I watched Micah like a hawk, but I gave Steve Larson free access to my baby."

Dorothy didn't know what to say, so she didn't say any-thing, just prayed harder. When she checked the doorway again, Micah was gone.

Outside on Pamela's porch, Micah allowed himself to re-lease his pent-up frustration by throwing blows at the air. Surprisingly, he didn't cry. He was too angry to cry. His anger toward Pamela mounted by the second. How could she be so naïve and callous at the same time? Steve Larson's unsolicited offers were the classic method of operation for a pedophile, and Pamela couldn't see that. "All she saw was my past!" he grunted. After all he'd done for her and Matthew, Pamela pre-ferred a child molester over him. "I'll never be good enough for her," he grumbled and slapped at the juniper bush. "After Matthew is back, I'm out of here!" he declared. "She's not worth it."

Pamela and Dorothy joined the others downstairs about an hour later. To Pamela, her town house resembled a police precinct more than a single-family residence. Officers, both uniformed and plainclothed, were taking pictures, writing notes, or talking on phones in codes she didn't understand. Pamela asked the female officer for an update, and just as Pamela feared, there wasn't one.

Pamela frantically scanned the room. In addition to the police, Pastor Jackson and the first lady were also present. She decided not to interrupt the conversation they were having with her father. Henry's face was covered with worry.

Pamela did a double take when she saw AC and Jessica holding hands. She assumed they were praying, although their heads weren't bowed and their eyes were wide open.

Dorothy placed a cup of tea on the counter. Pamela climbed on the bar stool and hoped the warm liquid would stop her body from shaking. She was blowing the steam when Micah walked in the door from outside. For the first time, Pamela noticed that he was limping and his right ankle and part of his foot was bandaged.

"Micah, what's wrong with your foot?"

Micah didn't answer her. He didn't even look at her.

AC noticed his hardened expression and answered for him. "My boy fell off a roof yesterday and broke his foot. We were in the emergency room half the night waiting on X-rays."

"Oh my goodness." Pamela couldn't believe it. Micah had carried her around on a broken foot.

"Are you in any pain? Do you need anything?" She walked toward him.

This time he answered, not because he wanted to, but because they had an audience and what he felt or didn't feel for Pamela right now was irrelevant. His main concern was Matthew. "It's just a hairline fracture. I just took another dose of pain medicine. I'll be fine once it kicks in." Instead of looking her in the face, he looked over her head at the kitchen clock. "Any news?"

"No," Pamela whispered, then laid her head against his chest. He didn't embrace her.

"You should really get off of that foot," his aunt ordered.

Micah started for the recliner with Pamela clinging to him. Before he had the opportunity to release Pamela and position himself over the chair, his cell phone blared. He didn't recognize the number, but with Matthew missing, he felt he needed to answer the call. "This is Micah Stevenson," he said after the caller asked to speak to him.

"Yes, I know Matthew Roberts."

At the sound of Matthew's name, the entire room quieted down except Pamela.

"Who is it?"

The caller's next statement caused Micah to fall back into the chair, taking Pamela with him.

"What is it?" Pamela asked. Dread gripped her once again.

"I'm on my way." Micah threw the phone to the officer closest to him, and after rising to his feet, set Pamela on her feet. "They found him, and he's all right!" he yelled. "He's at the Albany Police Station on San Pablo Avenue."

Everyone cheered and Pamela fell to her knees, but this time her tears were happy. Micah had stepped out into the walkway when Pamela realized he was going to leave without her. She quickly pulled herself together and ran after him and AC.

On the way to the police station, Pamela never questioned why the police called Micah and not her. She simply thanked God for her baby being alive.

Chapter 17

AC let Pamela and Micah out in front of the police station, and then went to find a place to park. Pamela ran into the three-story building, leaving the impaired Micah behind, to find her son. Micah made it just in time for the elevator that would take them to the third floor. Once inside the elevator, Pamela nervously grabbed at Micah's arm, then once the doors opened on the third floor, she practically dragged him down the hall. Micah didn't say anything, just limped behind.

"Where's my son?" Pamela barked at the first officer she saw.

"Excuse me?" the officer replied.

"I said, where's my son?"

Micah jumped in before Pamela caught a case for assaulting an officer for being non-responsive. "Officer, my name is Micah Stevenson, and I'm here to see Officer Townes."

No sooner had Micah said his name, Matthew came running from nowhere, yelling, "Micah! Micah!"

Micah thought his heart would burst at the sight of his little buddy. Micah ignored the throbbing in his foot and squatted to Matthew's level. He embraced the child so tightly, he was afraid he would break something. Matthew returned his embrace and laid his head on his shoulder.

"Are you all right?" Micah asked him. Matthew was smiling, but Micah could see the fear in his little brown eyes.

"I'm okay now," Matthew nodded. "What happened to your foot?"

"I'll tell you about that later." Micah looked up at the shocked expression on Pamela's face. He guessed she was stunned that her son, the child she birthed, came to him first and not her. "Your mother and I were very worried about you."

Matthew finally looked up at his mother and saw her tears. He reached for her.

"I'm okay, Mommy." Matthew hugged her around the legs. "I'm not scared anymore."

"Mr. Stevenson, Ms. Roberts, follow me," Officer Townes offered. Neither had seen him walk up. "I'll fill you in on the details. Matthew can wait out here with one of the other officers."

"No!" Matthew screamedx and shook his head vigorously. "I want to stay with my dad."

Officer Townes glanced from Pamela to Micah. "Normally, I wouldn't allow this, but since Larson has confessed, Matthew won't be asked to testify."

Micah gritted his teeth and stood upright. Matthew released Pamela and leaned against Micah's leg. They held hands as they slowly followed the officer down the long, carpeted hallway. Pamela dragged behind. Once inside the stale-smelling consultation room, Matthew sat on Micah's lap with his head resting on Micah's shoulder.

Pamela's worry turned into hurt. She couldn't understand why Matthew wouldn't come to her and let her comfort him. Matthew loved Micah, but she's the woman who suffered through long hours of hard labor to give him life, not Micah.

"Mr. Stevenson, you have a very special little boy," Officer Townes began. "You have done a wonderful job with training him."

Micah squeezed Matthew. "Thank you."

"Officer, what happened today?" Pamela asked. She felt like an outsider and didn't like it.

Officer Townes opened the manila folder in front of him and cleared his throat.

"According to Matthew, your neighbor, Steven Larson, approached him while he was playing outside on the patio. When asked where you were," the officer pointed at Pamela, "Matthew told him you were asleep. Larson left, but returned a short while later to say you called and asked if he could take Matthew to the movies because you were too tired."

"What?" Pamela said. "How did he know I was planning on taking Matthew to the movies later?"

"Lucky guess, I suppose. Anyway," Officer Townes continued, "Larson took Matthew to the movie theater on Solano Avenue. Matthew wanted to sit in the middle of the theater, but Larson said he would be able to see better from the balcony. They sat up there alone. At the end of the movie, Larson asked Matthew to play a game with him. If he played the game, Larson promised he would take him to a baseball game. But first Matthew had to promise to keep the game their little secret."

Pamela laid her head on the table and cried as Officer Townes explained how Larson fondled Matthew. Micah didn't say anything; he was too angry and hurt. His grip on Matthew tightened, and his jaw flinched.

Officer Townes continued. "Then Larson made the perfect mistake by asking Matthew to touch him." Pamela sobbed louder. "Matthew told him he needed some more popcorn first, and Larson bought it. According to witnesses, as soon as they stepped into the concession area, Matthew started pointing and screaming, 'Help, help, he touched my private!' He caught the attention of everyone. Larson didn't know what to do. Matthew screamed until Larson finally took off running. Some movie patrons caught him at the exit door and pinned him down until we arrived."

Matthew lifted his head from Micah's shoulder. "See, Dad, I was listening. I did just like you told us to."

Pamela was confused. She stopped crying. "Us? Were there other children involved?"

"He means the T-ball team," Micah clarified for Pamela. "I try to teach all of my players how to look out for and how to respond to sexual predators."

"Oh." Pamela couldn't think of anything else to say. At the moment she felt like a fool. The man she tried to keep away from her son turned out to be the one who saved Matthew from the man she gave him to.

Officer Townes turned to Micah. "You're doing a good job, Mr. Stevenson. This could have been much worse and could have gone on for a longer period of time. From the moment we picked him up, Matthew insisted that we call you. He said that was what he was supposed to do if anything like this ever happened."

"I also gave the kids my cell number," Micah explained for Pamela who was still speechless.

Officer Townes stood. "We'll be working with the Berkeley Police Department on this. If we need to talk to Matthew again, we'll be in touch. I strongly suggest that you get Matthew some counseling. He appears to be fine, but you never can tell how something like this can affect a child emotionally."

"I will." From an unknown source Pamela found the strength to stand. She saw the grimace on Micah's face as he tried to keep his weight off his right foot and stand while holding Matthew. "I can carry him." Pamela offered, but Matthew wouldn't loosen his grip on Micah's neck.

Back inside the elevator, Pamela, with grief, observed how Matthew clung to Micah and wondered if her son still loved her. Did her son blame her? Outside of the brief hug, he hadn't touched her. Once inside AC's Explorer, Matthew sat in the backseat with Micah. From the front seat, Pamela silently prayed that both her son and Micah would one day forgive her for her futility. Steve Larson may have violated her son, but she committed the biggest monstrosity of all. She opened the door that gave him free access.

She thought back to an earlier conversation with Micah about his mother. At the time, Pamela swore she would never put her son in danger the way Micah's mother had done with him. Pamela looked down on Helen Stevenson, whom she had never met, because Micah had to rely on others for his basic needs. Today, Pamela learned she wasn't any different from Helen. They both were controlled by something. Helen, alcohol, and Pamela, fear. Pamela's fear drove her to make a bad decision that could scar her son for life, just like Helen had done to Micah.

Judge not, that ye be not judged. For with what judgment ye judge, ye shall be judged: and with what measure ye mete, it shall be measured to you again. Those two verses rang loudly in her head all the way home.

The gearshift hardly rested in the park position before Matthew was bombarded with hugs and kisses from his grandparents and godmother, along with Pastor Jackson and the first lady. The group had been waiting outside for AC's SUV to drive into the complex. Matthew joyfully received the affection, but kept Micah in view at all times.

Jessica prepared a celebratory dinner, courtesy of the local favorite BBQ spot. Just before everyone sat down to eat, the group held hands in a circle, and Pastor Jackson prayed until he was sweating. He thanked God for bringing Matthew back safely and for the predator to be freed from his demons. It was during the prayer that Micah was finally able to release the emotions he'd been holding in since first receiving Pamela's call. Micah cried, and so did everyone else, including Matthew.

After dinner, with Matthew sitting between them, Pamela and Micah recapped the details of Matthew's ordeal.

"That was a very smart thing you did," Pastor Jackson told Matthew.

"That's what my dad told me to do," Matthew said, smiling back at Micah.

An uncomfortable quietness filled the room until Pamela said, "You have a very good dad." She said the words to her son, but looked at Micah.

Pastor Jackson sat straight up. Dorothy and Jessica both prayed Pamela really meant what she was implying.

Micah refused to get his hopes up; his heart was still bleeding from her earlier stabs. He focused his attention back to Matthew. He was the only person that mattered to him. Today had proven to him that no matter how things worked out between him and Pamela, Matthew would always be a son to him. "It's time for you to take a bath."

"Okay," Matthew said. "But can you stay with me tonight?"

Micah was taken by surprise at Matthew's request. He didn't know how to answer him.

Dorothy offered assistance. "Grandpa and I are staying over tonight."

"Okay, but I want Micah to stay too," Matthew insisted.

Pastor Jackson cleared his throat. "Sister Dorothy, can you take Matthew upstairs? I want to talk to Micah and Pamela."

"Come on, baby; let's take a bath." Dorothy quickly took her grandson by the hand, but before they made it to the staircase, Matthew called over his shoulder to Micah, "I'll be right back, Dad. Don't leave."

"There's nothing to talk about," First Lady said once Matthew reached the top step. "That baby has made up his mind."

"Normally, I wouldn't say this," Pastor Jackson began, "but

under the circumstances, I think what Matthew suggested is a good idea."

"So do I," Henry added.

"Matthew has been violated by a male, and he needs to be with a male he trusts so he can feel safe again," Pastor Jackson explained.

"Matthew doesn't trust anyone more than he trusts Micah. You heard for yourself. In his eyes, Micah is his father, and tonight he needs his father," Jessica added.

"You noticed that child hasn't left Micah's side since you picked him up?" First Lady jumped in.

"How can I not notice?" A touch of jealousy laced Pamela's words, but no one in the room seemed to care.

"Won't nothing that ain't supposed to happen go on with me and Dorothy here, anyhow." Henry stared hard at Micah.

"Micah, I'll pick you up after service tomorrow," AC offered.

Pamela blew the stray hair strands that dangled in her face. They had everything figured out. "Is that all right with you?" Pamela finally asked Micah. "My son needs you."

"I'll do anything for Matthew, but are *you* okay with this? Do *you* mind me being here with Matthew?"

Pamela could hear the pleading in his voice. Micah wanted to stay, and she wanted him to stay. Matthew wasn't the only one who needed the presence of a man in their life. Of course, she couldn't admit that with everyone staring at her mouth. "Would you like one pillow or two?" she asked with a smile as if everything were perfect.

"One is fine." Micah didn't grin or blink.

Pastor Jackson slapped his knees. "Good. Now that everything is under control, we should go home and let them spend some quality time together." Everyone agreed and stood for one more prayer circle, and then said good-bye.

Matthew returned downstairs after his bath, slightly damp, with a book in his hand. He positioned himself under Micah's arm and listened attentively as Micah brought the words on the pages to life. Before sending him back upstairs, Micah prayed with Matthew. Pamela followed him upstairs. It was then Matthew finally allowed his mother to hold him for a while.

With Henry and Dorothy retired to the extra bedroom upstairs, Micah assumed he had the living room all to himself for the rest of the night. He removed his pants and button down shirt, then stretched his long body over the couch. He covered himself with the blanket Pamela had left for him and waited for sleep to come. Startled, he gasped when Pamela lifted his right leg. He hadn't heard her enter the room.

"This should be elevated," she said and placed a pillow underneath his foot. Pamela got on her knees in front of him to inspect the foot more closely. "I'll rewrap this for you tomorrow."

"Sure. Whatever," he said and closed his eyes.

Pamela moved upward near his face and stared at him lying there, big, yet gentle. The eyelashes she loved so much concealed the eyes that revealed the depth of the pain her irresponsible actions inflicted on him. Her heart ached for him, and her soul longed for the contentment his presence once gave her. Pamela made a decision. She wanted Micah, flaws and all. Pamela didn't know how, but she was going to try to move past his history. Jessica and her mother were right; the Micah she loved was not the same man who engaged in those illicit acts. The man she loved was kind, considerate, sensitive, compassionate, and God-fearing.

"Thank you. Micah, thank you for everything, especially for being here today when I . . . when we needed you. Thank you for teaching Matthew what to do and for loving me even though I blatantly distrusted you." She whispered the words as she traced his cheek with her fingertip.

Her touch shocked him, and his eyes popped open. "I love you," she said softly.

"Is that enough?" he questioned. He was a long way from being over his hurt. "Are you really *in* love with me? Or are you just happy because your son is home?"

That wasn't the reaction she expected, but figured she deserved as much. She continued to stroke his cheek. "I am happy Matthew is safe, but I've been in love with you long before today."

Micah remained cautious. Pamela had taught him not to assume anything. "But is that love enough for us to move forward?"

"I want it to be," she answered honestly.

Micah reached for her, but she pulled away. He sighed deeply and closed his eyes again. "Good night, Pamela."

Pamela arose to her feet and stood over him. "Micah, I have to pull back this time. The way I feel right now makes it unsafe for me to be this close to you, especially with you being impaired." She took a step backward.

His eyes opened in time to watch her retreat another step. He smiled and nodded his understanding, but didn't verbally respond. He watched her walk backward halfway up the stairs. Then she turned and ran the rest of the way.

Here we go again, he thought while lying on his back.

Pamela awoke in the middle of the night and went to check on Matthew. When she didn't find him in his bed, she ran downstairs only to find him cuddled under Micah's arm. Pamela turned out the light and went back to bed.

Chapter 18

"Father, I thank you because on this morning I know where my son is. I thank you because even when I make mistakes you still love me. Father, forgive me for putting my son in danger. Show me the people and the things I need to protect him from. Then show me how to trust the people you have placed in his life. And Father, please show me how to accept the man you have sent to me. In your son Jesus' name I pray. Amen."

After her morning prayer, Pamela showered and prepared herself for the day. It was only 8:30 A.M., but already her day felt strange. She hadn't spent a Sunday morning at home in a very long time. The last Sunday she remembered spending at home, she was too high to go to church, couldn't even point in the direction of any church. Today, she planned to stay home to look after her men. The opportunity brought a smile to her face. Matthew needed to be around family, and Micah needed to stay off his foot so it could heal properly. She was certain the stress he placed on it yesterday had set back the healing process.

Pamela intended to be at his beck and call all day long. Micah deserved that and so much more. He deserved her love.

Pamela bounced down the stairs, and then trotted into the kitchen. She stopped when she didn't see anyone but Dorothy. "Where is everybody?"

"Good morning to you too," Dorothy snapped.

"Sorry, Mama. I expected to find my men waiting anxiously for me to feed them."

Dorothy raised an eyebrow. "Your men?"

Pamela blushed. "Yes, my men."

"Henry and Micah are watching Matthew outside. Breakfast will be ready soon. You can help me finish."

Pamela looked toward the patio. "Micah needs to stay off his foot."

"I know," Dorothy agreed, "but he said he needed some fresh air, and you know wherever he goes, Matthew follows."

Pamela smiled. "It's amazing, isn't it? How close they are?"

"I want to hear how close you and Micah are." Dorothy handed Pamela five plates from the cabinet. "Are you ready to accept him?"

Pamela walked to the table and began to arrange the setting. "Mama, I love Micah. He's my soul mate, of that I'm certain."

"But . . ."

"There are no buts, Mama," Pamela said. "If I can get past his history, I'm going to marry him."

"I hope you can." Dorothy passed her five glasses. "Micah is a good man. I watched him yesterday. He put Matthew and your needs before his own and didn't complain one time, and he had plenty right to, but he didn't. He hobbled around carrying both you and Matthew on a broken foot."

"I know he's a good man, but I'm afraid he'll keep going back to his old lifestyle, like before," Pamela admitted. "If that happens, then what?"

"Baby, don't let a bad, dead man keep you from the love of a good living one."

Micah's *Mission Impossible* ringtone prevented Pamela from responding. She hurried into the living room and pulled the phone from his jacket pocket just before the call went to voice mail. "Hello, Micah Stevenson's phone."

"Pamela, is that you?" the female caller asked, then added, "It better be you. Shouldn't no other woman be answering my son's phone this time of morning." The caller paused. "It's not even ten o'clock in California. *You* shouldn't be answering his phone this time of morning either."

Pamela laughed. "Hello, Mrs. Stevenson; it's me, Pamela. It's nice to finally speak to you."

"I'll tell you how nice it is. What are you doing with Micah this early in the morning? I talked with my brother this morning, and he didn't tell me y'all got married."

"No, Mrs. Stevenson, we didn't. Micah spent the night at my place last night."

"Oh Jesus!" Helen exclaimed. "Go get Micah. I want y'all to repeat this prayer after me."

Pamela laughed out loud. She remembered what Micah had told her about his mother and her daily recital of the sinner's prayer. Pamela went on to explain that her parents also spent the night and that Micah had slept on the couch.

"Now that we got that out of the way, I'm glad you answered the phone. Now I don't have to wait until I see you to say what's on my mind," Helen said.

"What is it, Mrs. Stevenson?"

"Please, call me Helen. Anyway, I was looking at those pictures Micah sent me from his birthday, and I had a conversation with myself. I said, 'Helen, that's a nice girl there. She loves your son. She must really love him to go through all that trouble.' Then I said, 'Thanks to her, these are the only birthday pictures I have of my baby in the last twenty-four years. You need to thank her.' That's exactly what I was going to do when I get there. But since you answered his phone, I'll do it now. Thank you for putting a smile on my baby's face. He deserves that."

Helen's gratitude brought a wave of shame crashing down on Pamela after the way Pamela had judged her.

"You're welcome, Ms. Helen."

"Now I know I haven't been much of a mother, but I still have the right to tell you not to mess over my son. Micah's a good man. I don't know *how* he turned out so good, because all he ever saw me do was act a fool. But that's another story. Like I said, you better be good to my son, or else you'll have to deal with me."

"Yes, ma'am."

Micah limped through the patio door followed by Henry and Matthew.

Pamela walked over to Micah and hugged him, then made him sit down. "Ms. Helen, you're right, Micah is a good man, and he deserves a good woman. He deserves me."

Micah was more surprised that Pamela was speaking with his mother than by the words she used.

"Here he is now. It was nice talking to you, Ms. Helen." Pamela handed Micah his phone, then kissed his cheek. Micah watched her walk into the kitchen, his face filled with apprehension about their relationship.

"Hello, Mother. This is a surprise," he said after he positioned himself on the couch.

"Hi, baby. If you think my call is a surprise, wait until you hear what I have to tell you."

"What is it?" Micah wasn't used to her calling him baby, but thought he liked it.

"I'll tell you in a minute, but first let me tell you something good. I haven't had any Hennessy in fifty-eight days!"

"Wow, Mother, that's wonderful," Micah cheered.

"I haven't had to recite the prayer in two days," Helen said proudly. "I took those pictures you sent me to church, and honey, I showed them off!" Helen hollered. "I know Sister Murphy thought I was lying about having a son. You should've seen her face. She looked as ugly as her son. Then the pastor had the nerve to ask me for your information, talking about you're a good-looking man, and he thinks you would make a good catch for his daughter. Humph, *Homer Simpson* may make a great catch for that hyena, but not my baby." Micah laughed at his mother; he didn't remember her being this funny when she was drunk. "I told him you were already taken. I even showed him the picture of the three of y'all together."

"Mother, you are too much."

"Wait until you hear this." Helen's voice turned serious. "I look at your pictures every day, and every day I see more of your father in you. Now that I'm sober, I can allow myself to think about him. I think about him a lot now. I miss my husband. You know, he's the only man I ever loved. Otis Stevenson was a good man; a real good man." Helen cleared her throat, then continued. "Anyway, I had a conversation with myself. I said, 'Helen, why are you living here in Chicago all by yourself, when you have a fine son who loves you in California?' Then I thought to myself, when Micah gets married I could be a grandmother and never get to see my grandbabies because I'm way out here."

Micah held his breath wondering if his mother was about to say what he thought she was about to say.

"Then I told myself, I said, 'Helen, you've missed enough of your son's life. You need to move out to California and build a relationship with your son.'"

"Mother, are you serious?"

"Don't worry. I'm not going to live with you. I was talking to Robert this morning, and he told me I can live with him since it's just him and Faye in that four bedroom house. I told him it was all right if he talks about God since I'm saved now, and I told him if he doesn't hold service longer than two hours, I'll join his church."

Everyone in the room stopped what they were doing and

listened to the roar of Micah's laughter. "Mother, I think you may have to look for another church."

"We'll see about that, but I really want to be close to you, if you don't mind. I know I haven't shown it to you because I didn't show it to myself, but I really do love you, and I'm very proud of you."

"I love you too, Mother," Micah managed to say without getting choked up. "This sure is some surprise. When are you coming?"

"I'm leaving when my lease is up next month. That way, I can get my deposit back. You know me, I never turn down money. I've already started packing; even told my pastor I'm leaving."

"Mother, in all the times you've mentioned your church, you've never told me the name of the church or your pastor's name."

"I'm sorry, baby, I thought I told you. The name of the church is Life Changing Ministries, and my pastor's name is Reverend Richard Lewis."

"Honey, what's wrong?" Pamela had asked Micah that question at least five times since he hung up the phone from speaking with his mother hours ago. The only thing he would tell her is that they'd talk later.

Now that her parents were gone, she hoped he would talk before AC came to pick him up. AC was due two hours ago, but called to say he suddenly had dinner plans, but would be by as soon as he could. Pamela figured those sudden plans included Jessica, since she also phoned to say she wasn't coming by. Matthew was upstairs asleep, and now that her desires were calm, she planned to spend some quality time with Micah.

Micah adjusted his position on the couch to allow space for Pamela to sit next to him. Miraculously, his foot felt better, and he hadn't required any pain medication in over eight hours. As promised, earlier that afternoon, Pamela gently washed and massaged his foot, then rewrapped his bandages. She also treated him to a neck and shoulder massage that yielded moans of satisfaction.

Once she settled on the couch, he covered her hand with his. "Did you mean what you told my mother? Do really you believe that I deserve you?"

"Yes." Pamela smiled. "And I deserve you."

"Are you saying that you're ready for our relationship to move forward to permanent status?"

"I'm saying that I'm ready to resume our relationship." Pamela wanted to say she was ready to be his wife, but as much as she loved him, she couldn't say that just yet.

"I'll take that, for now." He half grinned. "Is it all right if I put my arm around you?"

Pamela leaned into him and rested her head against his chest. Micah squeezed her lightly and brushed her hair with his free hand.

"Micah," she whispered, "what's really bothering you?"

Micah stopped his soft strokes and sighed. "Today, my mother told me the name of the church she attends and the name of her pastor." Micah paused. "She attends Richard's church. Richard Lewis is her pastor."

Pamela moved from Micah's embrace and sat straight up. "What?"

Micah shook his head from side to side. "All this time she's been attending Richard's church, and I didn't know it."

Pamela didn't understand. "Why would your mother want to attend his church after the relationship he had with you? Why would she trust him as her pastor?"

"My mother doesn't know about our relationship. She doesn't even know that I know Richard." Micah threw his hands into the air. "And I can't tell her now."

"Why not? She has the right to know what type of man she's sitting under," Pamela insisted. "She needs to know the man who's supposed to watch over her soul needs someone to watch over his."

"I agree, but my mother has been trying to live a saved life for less than two months. If I tell her that her pastor is a bi-sexual who slept with her son for six years, it will devastate her. She might give up and start drinking again."

Pamela wasn't convinced. "What if he tells her? Did you think about that? Don't you think she should hear it from you?"

"Richard's not going to tell her. If he were, he wouldn't have tried to get my contact information by lying about want-ing to fix me up with his daughter," Micah reasoned.

Pamela jumped to her feet. "Richard wants to get in touch with you? If they never met, how does he know Helen is your mother?"

"My mother showed the pictures from my birthday party to him. If he were going to tell her, he would have told her then. But as always, Reverend Lewis chose the back door." It wasn't until he saw the disgust on Pamela's face that Micah realized he'd used a bad choice of words. "What I mean is Richard was trying to manipulate my mother."

Pamela softened her expression. "I know what you meant, but don't you think that's more of a reason to tell her? He'll probably try again."

"If she were staying in Chicago, I would, but she'll be here in a less than a month. I don't want to disrupt her new life. For the first time in almost twenty-five years, my mother feels good about life and about herself. Strange as this may sound,

Richard is responsible for some of the changes she's made in her life. Despite what he does behind closed doors, whatever he's saying from the pulpit is helping my mother turn her life around."

"That's what I don't understand." Pamela shook her head and sat back down next to him. "How can he think that it's okay to sleep with men and still preach the Word of God every Sunday, and how are the people blessed?"

"That was confusing to me also," Micah admitted. "Richard is a very gifted preacher. He knows how to make words that were written thousands of years ago sound like they were designed just for you today. People joined the church just about every Sunday. Richard would say, 'If God wasn't pleased with me, He would not continue to add to the church.' What I had to learn was the Word of God is powerful no matter who's preaching it. It's not the messenger that saves people and changes their lives; it's the Word of God itself. And no matter how Richard justifies it, homosexuality is wrong."

Micah watched her slowly withdrawing from him. Pamela remained in the same spot, but her thoughts were someplace else. He attempted to pull her closer to him, but she resisted.

"I don't want to see him, nor do I want to talk with Richard." Micah assumed her thoughts. "If I wanted Richard, I would have called him a long time ago. You don't have to worry about me going back to him. If Richard walked in here right now, I would still sit here with you."

"Are you sure?" She looked deep into his eyes and tried to read his soul.

"Positive." He reached for her again, and this time she didn't resist. "Richard is my past. You're my future," he assured her.

"Okay," Pamela whispered, and then leaned back against his chest.

He stroked her hair once again and wondered how many more times he would have to reassure her before she would believe him.

Chapter 19

Without knocking, Jessica floated into Pamela's office and plopped in a chair. "How's my godson?"

Pamela pressed the last Post-it onto the document before she answered her extraperky friend. "He slept in my bed last night, but this morning he was fine. When I called to check on him, he and Micah were surfing the net for summer day camps."

Jessica picked up the framed picture of Matthew that Pamela kept on her desk. "When is his first counseling appointment?"

Pamela was glad her friend didn't decipher from her previous statement that she'd left Matthew with Micah. Jessica would never tire of singing, 'I told you so.' It made sense since he was off from work for his foot, and she wanted to keep Matthew home for a few days.

"Tomorrow," Pamela answered.

Jessica replaced the frame. After interlocking her fingers on Pamela's desk she asked, "How are you doing, really?"

Pamela propped her elbows on her desk and rested her face in the palm of her right hand. "I'm so angry at myself for putting my baby in contact with that crazy man. I can't believe I did that."

"Why do you think you did it?" Jessica asked in a way that let Pamela know it didn't matter what answer she gave, her friend was going to tell her the real reason. "Did you honestly believe Micah was going to violate Matthew?"

Pamela leaned back in her chair. "No," she admitted. "I just wanted to make sure Matthew didn't receive a repeat of the mistreatment he'd received from his worthless father. I felt like the biggest fool while I listened to the officer sing Micah's praises for teaching my son how to deal with sexual predators. And an even bigger fool for passing judgment on Micah's mother."

"I told you once before that you're judgmental and self-righteous," Jessica said after Pamela explained how Helen neglected Micah.

"I didn't agree before, but you may be on to something." Pamela still wasn't ready to take full ownership of that assessment.

"Do you want to know what else I'm on to, aside from knowing that you dropped Matthew off at Micah's this morning?" Jessica smiled mischievously. "I did catch that."

"I caught one of your secrets too," Pamela smiled.

Jessica dismissed Pamela with a wave of her hand. "So what? I had dinner with Anthony Combs on yesterday and talked to him this morning. We're talking about you right now."

"What about me?" Pamela rolled her eyes at her best friend. She detested the way Jessica always managed to keep her at the center of conversation.

"I want you to seriously think about this before you answer." Jessica waited for Pamela to nod her head in consent. "Pam, why do you think it's so easy for you to compare Micah to Marlon?"

Pamela thought long and hard before coming up with an answer. "I guess because Marlon was my first. He was the first man I gave my heart and my body to. Ours was the first real relationship I experienced." Pamela frowned. "Actually, that is the only experience I have. That being the case, it's only normal that I compare Micah to him."

Jessica reached across the desk and took Pamela's hand. "Pam, all of that may be true, but the truth is, you haven't forgiven Marlon for all the pain he caused you. You haven't forgiven him for manipulating your virginity from you, and then marrying you when he knew he wasn't ready to be faithful." Pamela tried to pull her hand back, but Jessica tightened her grip. "You haven't forgiven him for taking advantage of your love."

Pamela shook her head in disagreement. "What are you talking about? Marlon has been dead for five years, and I've moved on."

"No, you haven't." Jessica's voice was filled with compassion. "Five years ago, you buried the pain deep down inside and focused on making a life for yourself and Matthew. But you never acknowledged the hurt or the scars Marlon left on your heart. That's why in the beginning you denied your feelings for Micah. You were afraid he would hurt you the way Marlon had. It's hard for you to trust Micah because Marlon abused your trust. It's hard for you to believe Micah won't revert to his old lifestyle because Marlon always reverted back to his."

Pamela yanked her hand back. No matter how soft Jessica had spoken those words, they cut like a knife and burned her like fire. "Jess, I don't think that's the case."

"Then why do you always compare Micah to Marlon?" Jessica persisted.

Pamela couldn't answer. It just came natural to her, perhaps because their names started with the same letter. It was a lame excuse, but that's all she had.

Jessica checked her watch. "I have an eleven o'clock signing." She stood to her feet. "Pam, just think about it. Once you forgive Marlon, you'll be able to move forward with your life and in your relationship with Micah."

"Marlon is dead, what difference does it make now if I forgive him? I'm not saying that I haven't, but he's gone. He can't right his wrongs now."

"No, he can't, but you can release the hold he has on you," Jessica responded, and then left her alone.

Pamela pondered Jessica's words all day long. She still didn't agree, at least not completely, but her words did have some validity. Marlon had left her with deep wounds. It was those wounds that made her join the church after his death. When she got saved, she believed Jesus took all the hurt away. In any case, she wasn't ready to revisit the darkness her late husband had not only taken her to, but left her there, alone and battered.

"I'm not going there," she mumbled as the image of Marlon in bed with one of their neighbors flashed before her. She pushed the picture from her mind and dove deep into her work. Marlon was her past, and she was determined not to let him into her present.

Chapter 20

Helen shook her head as she struggled to keep from laughing out loud. Watching Sister Murphy maneuver to squeeze her hips into the little space on the end of the pew was hilarious. Lula Murphy's backside reminded her of those trucks with the black and yellow WIDE LOAD signs. Big hips and all, Lula had proven to be a good friend to Helen in the past seventy-nine days. Helen had called her many times when she felt like reuniting with her old friend, Mr. Hennessy. Lula would pray hard until Helen felt strong again and encouraged her to fight on.

"Sister Stevenson, today is your big day!" Lula exclaimed after she settled and caught her breath.

"Yes, Lord." Helen's smile showed all of her remaining teeth. "I can't wait to see my baby. It'll be nice to see my brother and his wife, but what I really want is to hold my son. Just three days, and I'll be with my baby." Helen raised both hands in the air. "I am so thankful to God for giving me another chance with my baby. I just know he's going to marry that Pamela. I'm going to have me a real family!" Helen was so excited she didn't bother to wipe the tears that trickled down her cheeks.

"I'll be sure to take you directly to the train station as soon as service is over. I don't want you to miss your train." Sister Murphy tapped her leg. "You do have your ticket, don't you?"

Helen knew she had the ticket. She'd been double-and triple-checking her purse all morning. One more time wouldn't hurt. She opened her purse and pulled out the envelope that contained the pictures Micah had sent her and the one-way train ticket her brother sent her for Chicago to Emeryville, California.

"I got everything right here." Helen smiled and held on to the envelope with all of her strength.

"Don't forget to call me when you get to Hollywood, and send me some pictures of movie stars."

Helen shook her head and smacked her lips. "Lula, how many times do I have to tell you? I'm going to Northern California, near San Francisco; not Los Angeles. And movie stars don't just hang out in the street waiting for somebody to walk up and take their picture."

Lula frowned. "Oh well, but don't forget to write me some-time, and you can call me or I'll call you collect. Since you'll be living in a mansion and all, you can afford the call."

Helen laughed and started to tell her friend that a four-bedroom house was not a mansion, but figured Lula, who she considered a country bumpkin, wouldn't understand.

"Don't you get out west and forget your friends in the Windy City," Lula told her.

Helen placed her arm around Lula. "You're the only real friend I got here. That's why I gave you my brother's address and phone number. I want you to keep in touch, just in case I need you to pray."

Lula returned her hug. "Anytime, anytime."

Helen arose to her feet for praise and worship. Lula tapped her on the arm and asked, "What are you doing? I ain't never seen you stand and praise the Lord."

"This is my last day here, and I'm going to give it all I got!" Helen yelled over the praise and worship singers. She then fixed her eyes on the big screen containing the words to the song, and for the first time, she sung along. She became so caught up with the song, Helen started dancing in the Spirit.

"Yes, Lord! Thank you, Jesus! I love you, Lord!" Helen shouted as she danced across the front of the sanctuary with her hands raised.

Lula was so happy for her friend that she jumped up and danced with her. She tried to keep up with Helen's pace, but Helen was moving to a beat no one could grasp but her.

Helen danced until she was tired, then fell to her knees at the end of the front pew.

"Thank you, Father!" she cried and gripped her chest. She repeated those words until the pain in her chest stopped and she reached total peace.

"Are you going to dance today?" Matthew asked Micah right before the start of Sunday service.

"I might." Micah squeezed his shoulder. Since his ordeal, Matthew made a habit of sitting next to Micah during service.

"If you do, I'm going to dance too." Matthew smiled and showed the empty space in his mouth from his missing baby tooth.

Micah certainly felt like dancing, and he had many reasons to celebrate. First and foremost, he was saved. His relationship with Pamela was moving along slowly, but moving nonetheless. There were moments when he thought Pamela was ready to make a permanent commitment. Then there were those times when she was distant and would pull away from him. He constantly had to reassure her that it was she he desired and not Richard.

The three of them had fallen back into their weekly routine of dinner together three times a week and Saturday afternoon outings. Matthew's counseling sessions were going better than expected. The therapist planned to end the sessions at the end of the month. Micah's foot healed sooner than expected, and he was back at work. But what filled his heart with unexplainable joy was his mother's anticipated arrival in three days.

Micah never thought he could feel so happy about seeing his mother. He planned to pick her up and spin her around the moment he saw her. God certainly worked a miracle; Helen Stevenson was a changed woman. Every time he thought about how his mother was motivated to stop drinking simply because he told her that he loved her, he had to choke back tears. Thinking back to his birthday, he reasoned it must have been the Holy Spirit that made him utter those three words on that day. He remembered vividly that he didn't want to speak to her at all. That was all in the past. He now looked forward to their weekly chats.

Last night they talked for over an hour. Helen went on and on about how she couldn't wait to see him and how she was going to make him a big dinner when she got there, even gave him a grocery list. What she didn't know was that Micah had AC call in a favor from a buddy of his. Pastor Jackson and Micah were going to pick up Helen from the train station in a white stretch limousine, and then whisk her off to dinner at Fisherman's Wharf in San Francisco. Helen loved seafood, and Micah was going to make sure she had all that she could handle. For the following evening, Pamela and his aunt had arranged a "Welcome to California" dinner with family and close friends. Micah knew she would like that too since Helen hadn't seen some of her relatives in over twenty years. He also knew she would like Pamela and Matthew.

Praise and worship was just about over when Micah noticed that Pastor Jackson hadn't made his arrival to the pulpit. This was unusual for him. Pastor Jackson liked to take part in as much of the service as possible.

"Go sit with your mother; I'm going to check on Pastor Jackson," Micah instructed Matthew who readily obeyed.

No sooner had Matthew made it across the sanctuary to Pamela, the first lady beckoned for Pamela to join her in the pastor's office. Micah stepped from his row to find AC in the aisle motioning for him to follow.

"Pastor needs to see you in his office," AC said somberly.

"Is he all right?" Micah asked, but AC didn't answer, just turned and started toward the pastor's office.

From her seat, Jessica prayed. She didn't know what was going on, but whatever it was it had to be major for both Pastor Jackson and First Lady to be out of service on Sunday morning.

Cautiously, Micah stepped inside Pastor Jackson's office and into the eerie atmosphere. Pastor Jackson sat at his desk and his wife stood next to him with her arm around him, comforting him. Pamela moved beside Micah and intertwined her arm with his. Micah recognized the sadness in her eyes, but couldn't identify the source.

He looked back at his uncle and asked, "What's going on?"

Pastor Jackson propped his elbows on the desk, and then laced his fingers together underneath his chin. "Son, I am so sorry to have to tell you this," he began, then paused to gain control of his emotions.

"What's going on?" Micah asked for the second time, this time more urgent than the first.

Pastor Jackson sighed. "I received a call from Cook County Hospital." He paused again. "Your mother, my baby sister, died this morning."

Micah completely blocked the words from penetrating his brain. "So what's the problem?" He shrugged his shoulders.

His nonchalant response only made it harder for Pastor Jackson to repeat the dreaded words. "I'm sorry, but Helen died of an apparent heart attack," Pastor Jackson repeated somberly.

Micah shook his head. "They're mistaken. My mother is on a train at this very moment headed to California."

Pastor Jackson sadly shook his head. "No, she's not. She suffered a heart attack in service this morning and died," he stated for the third time, then pulled a handkerchief from his pocket and wiped his face.

"I just talked to her last night." Micah refused to accept his uncle's words. "She's coming to see me. We're taking her to dinner on Wednesday, and we have the party on Thursday." Micah looked at his aunt. His eyes pleaded with her to confirm their plans.

"I'm sorry, baby," First Lady whispered. "Your mother is gone."

Micah turned to his right to Pamela, and she nodded in confirmation. "Honey, it's true." He looked back at AC who also nodded affirmatively. Micah's eyes slammed shut as excruciating pain filled his chest cavity. He thought he was having a heart attack and gripped his chest with both hands. The ache in his heart was so strong that he fell to his knees and wept violently. If the choir had not been in full swing, Micah's cries would have been heard throughout the sanctuary.

"Oh God, why? Why now? Why my mother?" Micah cried out between sobs.

Pastor Jackson lowered his head and wept on his desk.

"My mother is gone!" Micah wailed repeatedly as he lay in the fetal position on the floor. He cried so hard and so long that his breathing became labored, and AC had to prop him upright in a chair so air could circulate through his lungs. Pamela loosed his tie and unbuttoned the top button on his shirt. As he lay limp, She wiped his nose and dried his chin.

"Ever since she told me she was coming, I could hardly

think of anything else. I was so happy that she was moving here. I wanted to sit beside my mother in church and talk with her about the Lord. Now that will never happen. She will never have the cute grandchildren she talked so much about," Micah rambled.

"She didn't suffer," Pastor Jackson said after the room quieted again. "Her friend, Lula Murphy, said she went praising God. She said she'd never seen Helen so happy."

Except for frequent sniffles the room grew silent again.

"I want to see her," Micah said weakly.

"I have Sister Davis checking with the airlines as we speak. More than likely, we'll be on the first plane in the morning," Pastor Jackson answered.

"Thank you," Micah whispered, not because his uncle was taking care of his travel arrangements, but because he was going to accompany him back to Chicago.

"I have to stop at my safe deposit box first and get her life insurance policy before we leave."

That was news to Micah. "My mother has an insurance policy?"

"She sure does. Helen took out a policy for $250,000 right after your father died. Your mother wanted to make sure you would be taken care of just in case she drunk herself to death. She made you the beneficiary, but sent the policy to me for safekeeping since you were underage," Pastor Jackson explained.

"That was a long time ago. More than likely the policy lapsed years ago for nonpayment. We barely had money for food. I'm sure she wasn't able to keep up with the premiums," Micah surmised after blowing his nose.

"Oh, this policy is good," Pastor Jackson said with surety. "Your mother may have spent most of her fixed income on alcohol, but she made sure she paid the insurance every month.

When she didn't have the money, she called and had me pay it. In fact, that was about the only time she would let me minister to her about Jesus, when she needed money for her insurance."

"Baby, even after you turned eighteen, Helen kept up with that policy. Helen said that policy was the only thing she had of value to leave you and for us to make sure you get your money," his aunt added.

Micah closed his eyes and recalled his mother's instructions. If anything were to happen to her, he was to look in her phone book and call Uncle Robert and Aunt Faye. Micah bent over with his face in his hands and wept some more. He had no idea his mother had left him anything. He didn't know all those years his mother neglected him that she was really looking out for him in the best way she knew how. Micah longed for his mother even more now. He would give anything, including the money, to have his mother on that train coming to see him.

Pamela wrapped her arms around him in an effort to comfort him.

Sister Davis stepped into the office. "Pastor, I can get you on a 6:00 A.M. flight to Midway."

"The bank doesn't open until nine," Pastor Jackson responded.

"I can take First Lady to the bank first thing in the morning, then fax you the information," AC suggested. "I'm sure whatever mortuary you choose will have a fax machine."

"If not, the hotel will have one," Sister Davis added.

"All right." Pastor Jackson nodded his approval. Micah's head was still in his hands, but he nodded his approval of the arrangements also.

Sister Davis opened the door to leave just as Jessica was about to knock.

"Is everything all right?" Jessica noticed the gloomy expressions on everyone's face and heard Micah's soft cries.

"No." AC stepped back into the hallway with her and closed the door behind him. When he reentered the office a few minutes later, Jessica informed Pamela she'd take Matthew home with her tonight and drop him off at summer day camp in the morning.

Pamela acknowledged the offer with a nod, but kept her attention on Micah.

After Jessica left, Pastor Jackson suggested that Pamela take Micah home. Pamela thought that was a good idea, but Micah refused to move, refused to lift his head.

"I'll bring your vehicle home when Pastor and I pick you up in the morning." AC lifted Micah to his feet. When Micah reached his full height, he slumped onto AC and embraced him hard. He lost control of his emotions again.

"I got you, man," AC said as he choked back his own tears. "We're friends, remember?" Micah nodded against his shoulder and reached for Pamela. She encircled Micah with her arms and proceeded to pray for him. Pastor Jackson and the first lady joined in. They prayed until Micah's tears ceased and he was composed enough to walk to the car.

Micah relaxed in the reclined front passenger seat of Pamela's Altima. No words left his mouth during the entire ride to his apartment.

The inside of the small outdated elevator in the apartment complex felt more like a coffin to Micah than a vehicle used to take him from one level to another. He'd never been claustrophobic before, but today, the tight, cold, slow-moving boxcar made him sweat and nearly hyperventilate.

"We're almost there." Pamela squeezed his hand. She looked over at him and thought in his grief-stricken state he was still handsome. Allowing her to see him in this vulnerable state made her love him even more. She moved her mouth to tell him what was in her heart, but couldn't find her voice soon enough. The car stopped, and the moment passed. The doors opened about the same time Micah completely removed his dress shirt, revealing his soaked T-shirt.

Once inside his apartment, Micah broke down again when the gift basket he had Pamela create for Helen's arrival came into view. When he finished crying, Pamela talked him into taking a shower. She took advantage of the time and placed the basket in her car, and then ordered him some chicken wonton soup from the Chinese restaurant around the corner.

Pamela returned to find Micah sitting on the futon in navy sweats and a white T-shirt, his face void of expression. She started to ask how he felt, but remembered how much she hated that question when Marlon died. People constantly asked, "How do you feel? Are you all right? Do you need anything?" She wanted to scream, "I feel horrible, and I'm not all right. I need my husband."

Pamela imagined that's exactly how Micah felt right now, so she didn't ask him anything. She opted to feed him some of the soup instead. Pamela figured he'd talk when he was ready. He accepted the soup she quietly spoon-fed him. About a fourth of the way through, he shook his head, indicating he didn't want any more, then leaned his head back so that it rested against the wall. Pamela covered the round Styrofoam container and set it on the glass coffee table.

"Do you want something else?"

"No," he answered without opening his eyes. Pamela scooted to the opposite end of the futon.

"Come here." She patted her lap. The apprehension he felt showed on his face.

"It's all right." She invited him again.

Micah laid his head in her lap and relaxed to the soft feel of her fingertips as she massaged his head. In no time, he drifted off to sleep.

Pamela awakened a few hours later just as the sun was setting. She yawned and stretched her arms, then surveyed the small living room. She didn't see Micah. She stood and followed the movements she heard coming from his bedroom. The open door offered an unobstructed view. She didn't make her presence known but stood quietly in the doorway observing. Micah busied himself with packing a suitcase and a garment bag.

Pamela blinked her eyes repeatedly. She lowered her head into her hands, then looked up again and tried to focus on the present and not the past. Watching Micah pack his clothes sent her mind reeling back to the day before her husband died. The incident resurfaced so strong that she heard the conversation in her head verbatim and smelled Marlon's cologne.

"Marlon, please don't go!" Pamela begged "Why can't you stay here with me and Matthew?"

"Look, Pam, I told you, I'll be back." Marlon continued to get dressed. "I always come back, don't I?"

"Why do you want to be with her in the first place? I'm your wife, and that's your son." She pointed at Matthew sleeping in his crib. "You're supposed to be here with us, not running the streets with your girlfriend!"

"How many times do I have to tell you I'll be back? The boy is too young to miss me anyway." He raised his voice, and Pamela started crying.

"What's wrong with me? Why don't you want to be with me? Why do you always push me away?"

Marlon hated to see her cry. After splashing on cologne, he sat down on the bed next to her and held her, then lifted her chin and kissed her so deeply she stopped crying and moaned with pleasure. Marlon held her face in his hands as he voiced the words, "Pamela Roberts, I love you. You are my wife. If I didn't want to be with you, you wouldn't be wearing my ring and carrying my last name. Do you understand that?"

"Yes," Pamela said faintly.

"What I do with Angie or anyone else doesn't mean anything. It's just fun. Tonight I'm going to have some fun, then I'm coming back home to you."

This time when Marlon kissed her, she felt like regurgitating on him. Pamela hated herself for being so weak and gullible. She pushed away from him.

"Marlon, if you leave this time, don't come back. I'm tired of this!"

He threw his hands in the air and just that fast, the gentleness was gone. "Whatever, Pam. I am not changing. You knew how l liked to live before you married me. If you can't accept me the way I am, then maybe I should leave you." Marlon's pager went off; he looked down at the number. Pamela sat disheartened by his ultimatum while he answered the page. "Sorry . . . I know . . . I can't wait to see you either . . . I'm on my way."

Marlon stopped before walking out of their bedroom and turned back to her. "Tomorrow, you, me, and the kid can have a picnic in the park," he said, then left. That was the last time she saw him alive.

Pamela closed her eyes and shook her head. "Why am I thinking about that now?" she mumbled. "Why am I thinking about Marlon when I'm here with Micah?"

Suddenly, she understood why. Watching Micah pack his toiletries brought the realization that he was leaving in a few hours for Chicago. She panicked as the past and present collided with an explosive bang and distorted her reality. Marlon had left, her and now Micah was going to Chicago. Marlon left her to be with other women, and now Micah was leaving her to see Richard Lewis, his former lover. Once again, Pamela was being left behind and tossed aside for someone else.

"Are you going to sleep with Richard?" she asked before she could stop the words from rolling off her tongue.

At first, Pamela's voice startled him, and Micah stopped what he was doing. But as he digested her words, anger overtook him, and for the first time, he allowed his anger to flow freely against her. "What did you just ask me?" he yelled.

Pamela wished she could take back those seven words, but it was too late. "I mean, are you ready to see him?" she asked nervously.

"You meant what you said the first time!" Micah snapped.

"But I didn't mean it that way." Pamela wrapped her arms around herself in attempt to shield herself from his wrath.

Micah shook his head. "You are amazing! My mother just died. I'm going to Chicago to bury my mother. I can't believe you have the audacity to ask me if I'm going to have sex with Richard!" He couldn't stand to look at her. Micah brushed past her and went into the living room. She followed a step behind him.

He stopped abruptly and turned, causing her to bump into him. "What is it going to take for you? When are you going to let my past go?"

"Micah, I didn't mean to say it like that." She tried to explain again. "I—"

He cut her off. "Just how did you mean to tell me that you still don't trust me? How did you mean to tell me that you think I've been lying to you all this time? How did you mean to tell me that you can't let go of my past? And exactly how did you mean to tell me that I have been wasting my time with you?"

Pamela had seen Micah sad and hurt before, but this was the first time she experienced his anger. She knew she deserved it, but begged for mercy anyway. "Please just listen to me. I—"

"No, Pamela!" He cut her off again. "I've seen it in your eyes since the first night I told you my complete history. When you said you wanted to resume our relationship, I tried to ignore it, but it was still there. That look that says, 'I want to accept you, but I just can't.' I have done everything possible to make this relationship work, but that's still not enough for you. You don't want me." He pointed at himself. "You want someone perfect."

"No, I do want you." Pamela grabbed his arm. "I just have a hard time separating the past from the present," she tried to explain. Pamela knew he didn't understand because she didn't quite understand her rationale.

Micah exhaled deeply, then turned his back to her. His heart had never ached as much as it did at this moment. The loss of his mother and now Pamela was unbearable. He felt like taking a running start and jumping from the third-floor balcony. "Devil, you are a liar!" he yelled.

Deep down he knew this pain would never completely go away, but he would survive. He would survive this just like he'd survived his father's death, his mother's neglect, and Richard's trickery. Knowing that did nothing to dull the pain. Micah had opened himself up completely to her. He loved Pamela with everything he had in him—only to be rewarded with rejection again. It was time to let her go and move on.

He turned back to face her. "When I come back, I'll have a talk with Matthew."

Pamela leaned against the wall and wrapped her arms around her body. "What will you tell him?"

"That you've decided to return your present."

The finality in his tone caused Pamela to shake and gasp for air. "Why would you tell him that?" she asked nervously.

"Because it's the truth," Micah answered matter-of-factly. He tried to sound strong although his insides were shattered. "Of course, I won't use those words. I'll explain it to him where he can understand."

Pamela's knees grew weak, and she had to grip the wall to keep from falling. This is not what she wanted. It really wasn't. "Micah, you don't have to do that now." Her voice was so low, she barely heard herself speak.

"Yes, I do. I have to do what's best for me, not you." Micah closed his eyes and massaged his temples. "Pamela, let me explain something to you. Seven weeks ago, my mother called out of the blue just to say that she loved me and wanted pictures so she could show me off to her new church members. She apologized for being a bad mother and told me that she was proud of me. I hadn't heard my mother in a sound frame of mind in years, but then seven weeks ago, she told me I was the only good thing in her life. She said she was turning her life around and wanted to come out here to be close to me. After neglecting me for most of my life, she wanted to be a part of my world." Micah swallowed hard. "That was seven weeks ago, and today my mother is dead. Her experience has taught me that life is too short to waste time on destructive behavior and relationships that aren't going anywhere."

Pamela blinked back the tears threatening to gush through and slide down her cheeks. "You think our relationship is destructive?"

"The way it is now, yes." Micah answered plainly. "To be honest, we haven't had a relationship since that awful night I made the mistake of trusting you with my indiscretions. Since that time, no matter how hard you try, you haven't been able to get close to me. You can barely look me in the face any-more. No matter how much we talk or how much I reassure you, it's not enough for you. No matter how hard you try, you can't open yourself up to be with me. Over all that, what hurts the most is that you really believed I would violate Matthew." Micah felt the hurt and frustration he'd been holding in since Matthew's ordeal resurface, and this time, he didn't suppress it. Tears flowed down his cheeks. "How many times and in how many ways do I have to prove to you that I love Matthew like a son? God knows I love you. I would never do anything to hurt either of you. I would give my life for both of you." By the last sentence, Micah's voice trembled.

His words broke the dam. Thick tears clouded Pamela's vi-sion. "I love you too," she whimpered and slid down the wall.

"But you can't get past my past, and that's destroying me. That's what destroyed us, your unwillingness to love me in spite of my faults."

Micah waited for her to contest, but she didn't. He watched her slide down the wall until she sat on the floor. Pamela low-ered her head and cried hard, hot tears, but unlike before, her sorrow didn't stimulate his compassion. Micah sat on the futon with his elbows perched on his legs and his fingers laced underneath his chin.

"Pamela, life is too short for me to stay in a relationship that isn't going anywhere. And it's too short for you to stay in one just because you don't know how to fully let go."

"What if I don't want to let go?" She finally gave him the eye contact he'd been longing for, but it was too late. Micah pressed on as if she weren't crying, as if her tears didn't move him.

"I know without a doubt that you, Pamela Roberts, are the woman God created for me. I love you so much it scares me, but I have to let you go. I don't believe I'll ever love anyone as much as I love you, but that's a moot point. It's not healthy for me stay in a relationship with someone who doesn't really want me, so I'm ending this charade now. For the most part, it was a nice ride, but here's where I get off. It's over, Pamela, and that's final."

She maneuvered to her knees and crawled to him and leaned back on her legs in front of him. "Micah, please don't say that. We can work this out."

Micah ignored her outstretched hand. "Pamela, I gave you the best I have to offer. I gave you me, but you can't accept me. I told you about my past, not to hurt you, but because I didn't want any secrets between us. I wanted to be honest with you. I didn't want you to accidentally find out later from someone else. I trusted you, Pamela, and I thought you loved me for the person I am now." Micah placed his hand on his chest. "I opened myself up and let you into my heart, and you broke it. In every way I could think of, I expressed my love for you. If you wanted something, I got it for you. When you were sad, I made you laugh. When you were tired, I allowed you to rest. When you were afraid, I comforted you. I did everything for you, but for some reason, that wasn't good enough for you. You insist on judging me by my past. Doesn't my present count for anything?" Micah questioned. "Doesn't all the time we spent together show you that who I am today is not the person I was in my past?"

"Micah, I'm afraid," Pamela admitted for the first time. She was afraid of being hurt again, but Micah didn't know that. She'd never shared that part of her life with him.

Micah stood and threw his hands in the air. "You don't think I am scared?" he asked incredulously. "Pamela, no matter how wonderful I am, or how great of a person I am, or how many times I testify how God has delivered me and turned my life around, people still hold my past against me,

just like you do. I'm afraid to start friendships in and out of
the church because I know as soon as I say I slept with a man,
people will ostracize me. It doesn't matter that I was seduced
into the lifestyle by my pastor. The only thing people will see
is that I yielded. Do you think it's easy for me to listen to
drug dealers, prostitutes, alcoholics, adulterers, and even mur-
derers declare their deliverance and everyone celebrates with
them? Everybody accepts them. But if I stand up and say I've
been delivered from homosexuality, I'll be treated like dirt.
How do you think I feel knowing that no matter how clean I
am, I'm still unclean in the eyes of people? Even through your
eyes, I'm dirty and nasty."

The hurt in Micah's eyes was more than she could bear.
The hurt in his tone was more than she could stand to hear.
Pamela closed her eyes and shook her head and tried to block
out the evidence of the pain she'd caused the man God sent
to her.

"Micah, I don't think you're nasty. I just—" Pamela started.

His anger returned, and he wouldn't allow her to finish the
statement. "You called me a fagot! You scrubbed your face
after I kissed you that night! And let's not forget, you chose to
leave Matthew in the care of a child molester over me!"

Pamela didn't have any words. Micah had said everything,
and it was all true. There was no rebuttal, no closing argument to persuade the jury. Pamela did the only thing she
could do— cry.

Micah's jaw flinched as he tried to hold back his own tears.
He couldn't cry, not now and not for her. His mother was
lying on a cold metal slab somewhere on the south side of
Chicago. Putting her to rest in peace was his first priority.
Grieving over what could have been with Pamela would have
to wait.

"Pamela, it's late, and I have to finish packing. You should
leave now."

She wanted to stay, but Micah walked briskly past her and opened the front door signaling her dismissal.

Pamela remained quiet except for her labored sniffles. Silently, she stood to her feet and collected her purse from the kitchen. Then slowly she moved toward the door. She tried one last time to make eye contact with Micah, but he refused to look at her. Before clearing the door, she made one last attempt to say everything that was in her heart, but he wasn't having it. Before she got the first word out, Micah held up his opened-palm hand.

"Pamela, it's over," were the last words she heard before he closed the door on her.

Chapter 21

Pamela's vision was so blurred that she could barely see directly in front of her. She didn't bother waiting for the elevator. Needing to distance herself from the reality of what had just happened, she headed straight for the stairs. Pamela had to hold on to the rail to keep from tumbling down the three flights of stairs at Micah's apartment building. Her reckless movements nearly knocked down a young child, but she refused to stop. She had to get away from Micah's rejection.

Once inside the confines of her car, Pamela cried loud sobs and unleashed hot tears that soaked her blouse. The same blouse Micah's tears had soaked hours earlier. This official breakup with Micah was more than she could handle. Micah was right, she needed to let go. But it wasn't him she needed to let go of; it was the darkness of her own past that snared her, not his. Micah Stevenson was her love, but then so was Marlon Roberts. And no matter how many promises he made to her, Marlon always reverted back to his old self. Micah could do the same thing to her one day. She could compete with Marlon's women, but she was no match for a man.

Her late husband paraded his infidelity like a badge of honor. Micah had never given her any indication that his heart wasn't sincere. She realized that now, but it was too late.

She merged onto Interstate 880 with questions pounding the inside of her head. Was Jessica right? Was she judging Micah by Marlon's actions? Was she sitting in the seat of God, saying who can be delivered and who can't? Had she become a self-appointed judge? The true answers to those questions were more than she could stand. The answer to every question was a resounding yes. Pamela pulled over to the shoulder and wept violently. Her body shook, and her shoulders heaved. The pain in her abdomen intensified and caused her to hunch forward.

She needed something to take the pain of her reality away and to give her back the temporary peace of her perfect world. The world before Micah dismissed her. She wanted to laugh at commercials and tell jokes with him again. She wanted to make a peach cobbler for him and listen to him moan his appreciation as he savored every bite. She wanted to feel the curl of his eyelashes brush against her forehead when he held her.

"Oh God!" she screamed out loud and swerved to miss hitting a car as she merged back into traffic without signaling. "I can't stand this. Please make this pain go away!"

The pain not only continued, but grew worse. By the time she exited on Ashby Avenue, Pamela couldn't stand the heartache and the throbbing migraine anymore. It only took seconds for her to remember how she numbed the afflictions caused by Marlon. She would do that this time. It worked then, and she knew it would work now.

Pamela became antsy with the thought of having it. She knew it would make her feel better if only for a short time. She had to have it, and right now she needed its calming therapy. She needed something to help her stop missing Micah. Instead of going to an empty house, Pamela went in search of an old friend.

She found a bag of her former grass companion on a corner not too far from her town house complex. When the guy without a name or a face walked over to her window, she had second thoughts, but Micah's words continued to replay over and over in her head like a scratched record. "You called me a fagot! You're not good for me! You gave me back! It's over!" She had to make the cold hard truth go away, it hurt too much. Besides, if God didn't want her to use marijuana for its therapeutic effects, He wouldn't have created the herb, she reasoned. Pamela handed the twenty-dollar bill over, took the plastic bag, and then sped to her town house. The gearshift was barely in park before she opened the car door and ran to her front door.

"God, help me to understand why I pushed Micah away." Pamela was so disorientated, she didn't realize she was praying to God and preparing to smoke a blunt at the same time. "Lord, I need you to show what's wrong with me." She continued talking to God while she searched the kitchen drawers.

The more she prayed and the longer it took for Pamela to find something to roll her friend in, the more she didn't want the false comfort, and the more she comprehended she was making a big mistake. She looked down at the plastic bag and started crying. She couldn't do this. She couldn't destroy her relationship with God; it was too important. It wasn't God's fault she pushed Micah away. It was hers and the state of denial she had allowed to rule her life.

"Why did you allow me to fall in love with a homosexual?" she cried after she dumped the green leaves down the garbage disposal.

The same reason I allowed Micah to love a drug user, the still voice answered.

"I am not a drug user," she yelled at the ceiling. "You delivered me from this a long time ago; I just got weak. You know I didn't mean to buy this. I love you too much to choose this over you." Pamela threw the little plastic bag unto the floor, and then leaned over the sink.

Micah is not a homosexual. I delivered him from that just like I delivered you from your habit. If I can deliver you, why can't I deliver him? Are you better than he? Is my power not strong enough for him? If I can take the taste of marijuana from you, can I not heal him and change his life?

Pamela argued with the voice. "But God, Marlon—"

If any man be in me, he is a new creature. Old things are passed away and behold I make all things new. Marlon was never in me; you can't compare the two. Micah is my servant. You don't have the right to judge my servant by someone who was never mine. Whom I call clean, you don't have the right to call dirty. Whom I call holy, is holy. Whom I have freed, you don't have the right to keep in bondage.

Pamela dropped to her knees right there in the kitchen and cried out, this time for forgiveness. Jessica and her mother were right. Since the night Micah confided in her, she'd directed the anger she felt for her late husband at Micah. She hadn't forgiven Marlon and had judged Micah by Marlon's actions. She allowed her baggage from the past to slowly eat away her future until there was nothing left but her wounded heart.

"God, please help me so I can move forward," she cried.

Chapter 22

Micah stared out the small window of the 747 aircraft as he waited for push off from Gate 22 at the Oakland Airport. The last time he sat in the small confines of an airplane was on his ride into California two and a half years ago aboard the same carrier. That day when the plane started down the short runway at Midway, Micah said good-bye to Chicago. He never imagined he'd be back so soon and certainly not for this reason.

Five days in Chicago would be challenging for him. He didn't have a clue as to how to plan a funeral. Helen never expressed what her final wishes were, but he believed his mother would want to be buried close to his father. He was going to try to make that happen. He knew her favorite color was pink; therefore, Micah was going to find a nice pink dress or suit for her to wear. He guessed she would like a white casket. He still couldn't think of a picture nice enough to use for her obituary. What would the obituary say? How long should the service be? Should there even be a service, considering his mother didn't have many friends outside of her three-story apartment building? All these thoughts kept him from sleeping last night.

"Son, I brought this picture of your mother. It was taken years ago, before you were born." Pastor Jackson held the faded colored photo out to Micah. "She said this was her favorite picture."

Micah took the picture he'd never seen before. His eyes watered at the sight of her. Helen was beautiful in the pink chiffon prom dress and tiara. Her chocolate skin was smooth and flawless, not the blotchy skin he was accustomed to seeing. Her ebony eyes were happy and bright, almost like they were dancing.

Micah wiped his eyes. "I can't believe this is my mother."

"That's Helen all right. The family was so happy when she won prom queen. The next day, we threw a big BBQ to celebrate. That was a big thing for us Jacksons back then." Pastor Jackson smiled, recalling the fond memory. "She met your father and had you two years later."

"My mother didn't even make it to fifty," Micah said sadly.

"No, but at least she was saved when she went."

Micah pondered his uncle's statement. It comforted him to know that his mother's eternal life would be more peaceful than her natural one. Helen received salvation, and in the end, that's all that mattered. "Did she ever say what type of service she wanted?"

"No, but I know one thing, Richard Lewis will not preach her eulogy," Pastor Jackson stated plainly. Micah agreed. In fact, he preferred to have his mother's funeral at the mortuary than at Life Changing Ministries. Micah had told his uncle about Helen attending Richard's church. Pastor Jackson agreed with Micah on not telling Helen about his relationship with Reverend. Lewis.

"Son, how do you feel about seeing him?" Pastor Jackson asked after he adjusted his seat to the upright position. "He tried to use your mother to get in touch with you. That right there tells me he hasn't changed, and in his mind, he's still connected to you."

"I don't care what he thinks. I have moved on. If I do see Richard, it will only be to discuss the funeral service, that's all." The conversation was interrupted by the overhead instructions to watch the airline attendants demonstrate the emergency procedures.

Micah's cell phone sounded. He quickly retrieved it from his jacket pocket and after he checked the caller ID, he turned the phone off. But not before his uncle read Pamela's name across the screen.

Pastor Jackson fastened his seat belt before he asked, "Is everything good between you and Pamela?"

"Everything is perfect. I ended our relationship last night," Micah answered quickly, and then grabbed the magazine from the seat pocket in front of him.

Pastor Jackson took the magazine from him and placed it back in the seat pocket. "Why did you do that? I thought things were better between the two of you after that incident with her neighbor."

"I wanted them to be," Micah admitted. "But my past is too much for Pamela to handle." Micah didn't mention she accused him of wanting to sleep with Richard.

"I am so sorry to hear that," Pastor Jackson mumbled. "I thought for sure she was the one."

"Yeah, so did I," Micah leaned his head against the headrest with his eyes closed. He hoped his actions relayed to his uncle that he didn't want to continue the conversation.

Pastor Jackson bowed his head in prayer as the aircraft pushed away from the gate. Traveling mercies weren't the only thing he was praying for. Micah was too vulnerable. He'd just lost his mother, and now the woman he loved was no longer in his life. Sudden and unfortunate events were the catalysts leading Micah back in the same direction of the man who had preyed on him before when he was in a low state. For the endurance of the four-hour flight, Pastor Jackson prayed fervently that Micah would be able to overcome the attack he was sure the enemy would launch through Richard Lewis.

***

Without knocking, Pamela stumbled into Jessica's office and collapsed in the blue chair in front of her desk. "You were right, Jess, about everything. I messed up." Before Jessica could ask her what was wrong, Pamela leaned on the desk and cried with her head in her hands.

"Would you mind telling me what you did before you ruin my desk calendar?"

"Micah's gone," Pamela managed between sobs.

Jessica laughed at her friend. "That man has you twisted inside out. He's only been gone for a few hours, and you're already crying. Girl, he'll be back." Jessica leaned back in her chair and reached for her mouse.

"He's not coming back, at least not to me," Pamela said before Jessica could click the print icon on her flat screen.

"Pam, what are you talking about? Micah is only going to bury his mother. After that, he's coming back to Cali, and when he does, he'll be at your beck and call like always."

"No, he won't. He ended our relationship last night." Pamela barely got the words out before a fresh batch of tears escaped.

Jessica pushed the mouse away and stood straight up. "Pamela, what did you do to him? I know you did or said something really crazy. Micah loves you way too much to just end your relationship."

"You were right, I'm self-righteous and judgmental, and I've been in denial about forgiving Marlon."

Jessica slid the entire box of tissue across the desk to her. "You must have really blown it to finally be willing to admit all that." Jessica's voice softened, and she sat back down. "Pam, tell me what happened."

Between shedding more tears and blowing her nose, it took Pamela ten whole minutes to convey the events of her breakup with Micah.

"Oh, Jess, what am I going to do? He wouldn't answer my calls last night or this morning. You should have seen the disgust in his eyes when he slammed the door on me. He hates me."

Jessica sighed deeply. "Pam, I really wish you would have listened to me earlier, but you didn't. Now all you can do is pray Micah has a change of heart. But in the meantime, you need to deal with your unresolved issues."

"I can't," Pamela whimpered.

"You have to. If you don't, every time Micah or anyone else does something that resembles Marlon's actions, you're going to find yourself in this same situation over and over again."

"How do I do that? How do I forgive a person who's dead?" Pamela sincerely asked.

"Start by accepting your true feelings. Let go of the façade and the fairytale you've created and deal with what's really going on inside. After that, the rest will come."

Jessica's words made sense to Pamela, but it wasn't going to be easy. For five years she worked relentlessly to portray a man Matthew would be proud of. Pamela played the part so well before her son, even she believed the fantasy at times.

"What if Micah doesn't change his mind?" Pamela whined. "What if he doesn't love me anymore?"

Jessica sighed. "Pam, of course Micah still loves you; probably always will. But even if you and Micah never reunite, you need to do this one for yourself. You need to heal from the wounds Marlon inflicted so *you* can be free." Jessica paused. "I know you're not going to like what I'm about to say, but I have to say it because it's crucial that you understand how important it is for you to be healed. You being whole and complete will be worth it, even if you have to watch Micah marry someone else."

Jessica was right again. Pamela didn't like that at all. "Micah is not marrying anyone but me!" she yelled. Pamela stood to her feet with renewed determination. Her neck rolled as she spoke. "God told me that Micah is my husband, and once God tells you something, He doesn't take it back. He knows what's best for me. That's why after I prayed, He sent me Micah. He sent Micah to me, not someone else!" Pamela poked herself in the chest.

Jessica didn't have to say one word; she just leaned back in her chair and observed Pamela's animation. This was the first time Pamela really listened to her own words and applied them to herself. Jessica watched Pamela fall back into the chair only to start crying again. "Oh, Jess, God did send me Micah. Why did I run him away? He was so good to me. How could I have treated him so callously?"

"Because you haven't freed yourself from your past," Jessica answered softly. "You were so busy worrying about how Micah's past would hurt you, and you never considered how your past and present state of mind could hurt *him*."

"Jess, I hurt him in so many ways, but this time, I went too far."

Jessica stood and walked around the desk to the door. "Let's pray," she said, and then took Jessica's hands into hers after locking the office door.

Chapter 23

Micah waited impatiently for the elevator that would take him and Pastor Jackson to the rental car garage. Chicago's Midway Airport had undergone a total makeover since his departure over two years ago. "Where did the elevator and garage come from?" he grumbled. He didn't appreciate the slowness of what should have been a convenience.

During the four-hour flight, Micah had convinced himself that the person lying in the morgue at Cook County Hospital was not his mother. This was all a mistake, and his mother was on a train headed to California. As soon as he cleared up the mistaken identity, he would head back home and await her arrival.

With contract and keys in hand, Micah sat in the driver's seat of the rented Chevrolet and turned his cell phone back on. He checked his messages in hopes of a call from his mother. She'd told him she would call him and share the interesting sites along her journey. His heart sank and reality once again returned. There weren't any messages from Helen, and there never would be. Micah was too distracted to drive and handed Pastor Jackson the keys. While he walked around to the passenger side, Micah removed his Nike sweat jacket. The late August heat and humidity nearly caused him to suffocate. He'd only been away from his native town two years, but the Bay Area's moderate weather had spoiled him.

Pastor Jackson looked down at the time on the console.

"We can't check into the hotel for another two hours." Micah waited for what he knew was coming next. "We should stop by the hospital first, then contact a mortuary," Pastor Jackson suggested. "Your mother's friend, Lula Murphy, has Helen's suitcases at her house. She wants us to stop by for dinner later on this evening, if you're up to it."

Viewing his mother's cold body through a glass window was not something Micah wanted to do. Not today, not ever, but he had to. He nodded and gave his uncle the directions to Cook County Hospital.

Micah reclined the passenger seat and took in South Cicero Avenue. Not much had changed in the two years he'd been away. More hotels and businesses were added, and of course, the ever-present Citgo gas stations and Currency Exchanges were everywhere. Pastor Jackson merged onto I-55, and Micah's heart skipped a beat. Off to the far left standing tall in all of its glory was the magnificent Chicago skyline.

In Micah's opinion, nothing was more breathtaking than the Chicago skyline. When he was a kid, he used to dream about living in a high-rise overlooking Lake Michigan and running the city from an office at the top of the John Hancock Center or the Sears Tower. From the south side of Chicago, where he lived, downtown was always a far-off dream. He didn't experience the heartbeat of downtown Chicago until he enrolled in Malcolm X City College and met Richard Lewis.

The congested traffic merging on the Dan Ryan brought with it thoughts of Richard and the mess he allowed Richard to make of his life. After all, it was Richard who introduced him to the world outside of the south side. In the courting stages, Richard had taken him to fine restaurants, plays, sporting events, even shopping on the Magnificent Mile and dinner in the John Hancock Center's Signature Room on the 95th floor. Richard took him places he probably would have never seen until years later, if ever. In the beginning, Richard made Micah think he could do anything and be anything. Thinking back now, Micah realized it was all part of the scheme to get him so wrapped up into Richard that he'd do anything he wanted him to, including sleep with him. Proof of that was how Richard always regurgitated in Micah's face everything he'd ever done for him whenever Micah refused his advances. Richard never failed to remind him that he was the only person who cared anything about his welfare.

Micah shook the thoughts of Richard away as his uncle took the Morgan Street exit off I-290. His chest tightened as the mass of brick that was known as Cook County Hospital came into view, and he was quickly reminded of the purpose of his visit.

Viewing his mother's lifeless body through the morgue window was harder than he thought. That ended all hope of this being a terrible mistake. It wasn't a mistake; his mother was dead. Micah's only consolation was that aside from being a shade darker than normal, Helen looked peaceful, like she was simply taking a nap. Pastor Jackson said a brief prayer, and Micah signed for her personal belongings.

The rest of the afternoon Micah was distant, and for the most part, quiet. Every so often, Pastor Jackson would hear him sniffle or moan the words, "My mother is gone" or "I don't have anyone now." Pastor Jackson reminded Micah that he would always have God, and for as long as the Lord saw fit, Micah would have his uncle too.

The visit to the funeral home left Micah feeling not only destitute, but also confused. He had no idea how many details went into planning a funeral. There were so many things to decide on, about most of which he was clueless. Micah sat in the morbid office and slowly turned the pages of a catalog filled with caskets. He decided on a rose-colored one with soft pink interior. He and Pastor Jackson agreed Helen would be pleased. After deciding that the service should be held in the mortuary's chapel on Friday, Micah left the rest of the details to his uncle. He sat outside in the car.

"I contacted the cemetery. Looks like they can lay Helen next to your father," Pastor Jackson informed Micah when he finally joined him in the car. "We have to work on the obituary and find Helen something to wear, but everything else is planned."

"I'll work on the obituary tonight, and I'll go downtown to Macy's first thing tomorrow," Micah calmly responded. He lay almost flat with the seat reclined all the way back with his hands laced across his chest. His eyes were closed.

"Do you want to head to the hotel now to check in, or are you up to dinner with your mother's friend?"

What Micah wanted more than anything was a scorching hot shower, and then to collapse on a firm bed, but that would only delay the inevitable. In addition, he wanted to hear how his mother spent her last moments. "I can handle dinner," he finally answered. Pastor Jackson called out Lula Murphy's address, and Micah mumbled the directions without ever opening his eyes.

Pastor Jackson parked the Chevrolet in front of the brick house on South Hamilton Street. It was an average-looking house, Pastor Jackson thought. But then, so were most of the houses he'd seen so far. To him,, all the brick houses had the basic square design, unlike the contemporary models in the Bay Area.

Micah adjusted his seat upright and pulled the latch, but stopped short of opening the door. He knew he would see Richard at some point with him being Helen's pastor. Micah just didn't know it would be this soon. Physically, Micah was prepared for whatever Richard would throw at him. If Richard so much as put a finger on him, Micah was prepared to lay hands on him. But emotionally, he was way too weak to deal with the mind games that came along with Pastor Richard Lewis.

"What's the matter, son?" Pastor Jackson asked, discerning Micah's hesitation.

"He's here." Micah pointed to the white Lincoln Town Car with license plates reading *PTR RTL*.

"Humph, the devil always knows when to show up," Pastor Jackson replied. "Are you sure you're ready for this now?"

Micah looked his uncle in the eyes. "I wasn't ready for my mother to die, but that didn't stop her from dying. It doesn't matter if I'm ready to see him or not; he's here."

Pastor Jackson didn't like the sarcasm in his nephew's voice. "Son, your mother's passing was in God's will, not ours. I like to think that He took your mother because at that moment she was ready. Whatever the reason, it was His choice; not yours, and not mine. But you have a choice on seeing Richard Lewis or not. If you're not up to it, we can visit Sister Murphy tomorrow."

"I don't want to see him, but I do want to hear about my mother's last moments. Unfortunately, Richard played a role in her new life." Micah pushed the door open and exited the vehicle. He stretched his long frame, and then headed for the steps. Pastor Jackson followed behind, praying. Micah waited until he joined him on the porch before knocking. The door flung open before he had the chance to knock twice.

"Good evening, I'm Pastor—"

"God bless you!" Pastor Jackson didn't have a chance to finish introducing himself before Lula grabbed his hand and shook it vigorously. "I know who you are; Helen looked just like you." Lula then turned to Micah. "Baby, you look as good as your pictures." Lula grabbed Micah's hand. "Come on in-side. I told Pastor Lewis y'all were coming by for dinner, and he stopped by to help you arrange the home going celebra-tion. He's in the kitchen."

Pastor Jackson and Micah exchanged glances before fol-lowing Lula through the moderate-sized living room and into the kitchen. Richard Lewis and a much-younger male were already seated at the table. Lula made the introductions.

"Pastor," she began, "this is Sister Helen's brother, Pastor Jackson, from California." She then pointed to Micah. "And this is her son, Micah. I'm sure you remember him from the pictures." She then introduced the young man. "Pastor Jackson, Micah, this is David. He's one of the students in the mentoring program at the church."

Richard hadn't changed at all, Micah thought. He dressed the same way as he did years ago: in dress slacks and designer sweaters. Micah always thought the sweaters Richard wore re-sembled those worn by Cliff Huxtable from *The Cosby Show*. His hair and mustache were the same, except now the wavy black hair was also sprinkled with gray strands. Richard's right index finger was adorned with the same twenty-four-carat ring Micah helped him select over five years ago. He'd purchased a similar one for Micah and said the jewelry was a symbol of their commitment to one another.

Micah studied the young man seated beside his former mentor. Richard still liked younger men. The kid didn't look a day over eighteen, if that. The smile on Richard's face was all the evidence Micah needed. This kid was his next victim.

Richard stood to his full six foot three inch height and greeted them. "Welcome to Chicago, Pastor Jackson. Sorry your trip couldn't have been under better circumstances," Richard said, then addressed Micah. "I've heard a lot about you. Sister Helen talked about you all the time." Richard then extended his hand to the out of town guests.

Pastor Jackson lightly shook his hand, but Micah sat down without acknowledging him.

The surprised look on Richard's face gave Micah some satisfaction. Richard was caught off guard. The old Micah would have never disrespected him openly. When Richard smirked at him, it occurred to Micah that Richard thought he was jealous of David. He sat down next to David and wondered if he should tell the young boy to head for the river and don't look back. His thoughts were interrupted when Lula asked Pastor Jackson to say grace since he was from out of town.

During grace, which sounded more like a plea for peace, Micah opened his eyes and found Richard staring hard at him. Richard had that very same look in his eyes right before every sexual encounter. In times past, Richard's burning gaze would have melted Micah's resolve, and he would have lowered his head and surrendered. Today, Micah returned Richard's intent look with one of his own. Richard's lips moved to mouth something to Micah just as Pastor Jackson said, "Amen."

"I know y'all hungry, so eat up," Lula stated. "I made plenty of food."

"Thank you, Ms. Lula," Micah responded, although he doubted he'd eat much. He hadn't eaten anything since Pamela fed him soup over twenty-four hours ago. Being in Richard's presence made his stomach uneasy. That and just having viewed his mother's lifeless body practically tarnished his appetite.

Pastor Jackson, Richard, and David busied themselves with piling their plates with cabbage, yams, rice, and pot roast.

"So, Micah, what part of California are you from?" David asked excitedly, much to Richard's dislike.

Richard attempted to run interference. "David, I'm sure Micah doesn't feel like talking right now."

Micah ignored Richard. "San Francisco Bay Area," he answered.

"Really? I want to attend Cal Berkeley, and then Stanford for medical school. Pastor Lewis is going to help me get in after I finish undergrad." The smile on David's face confirmed to Micah that this kid didn't have a clue as to what he was getting into.

"Is that right?" Pastor Jackson asked. "How do your parents feel about you going so far away for school?"

David swallowed his food before answering. "My father's in jail, and I haven't seen my mother in years. Next month, I'll be eighteen and out of foster care. Pastor Lewis said I can go wherever I want and be whatever I want and that he will help me." By his smile, Micah could tell David really believed in Pastor Lewis the same way he had.

Pastor Jackson and Micah exchanged glances and Richard shifted in his seat.

"If there is anything I can help you with, let me know. I'll leave you my number," Micah offered to David.

"Cool." David helped himself to a second serving of yams. "Hey, do you know Beyoncé or Ciara? I would *love* to meet them. Those sisters are F-I-N-E!"

Micah smiled in agreement. "Sorry, but I haven't had the privilege of meeting either of those beautiful women. But if I do, you'll be the first to know."

Micah didn't look in his direction, but he could feel Richard's dark eyes penetrating his skin. In the past, Richard became irate to the extreme of yelling and screaming, when Micah expressed interest in women.

"Have you made any funeral plans yet?" Lula's question brought the reason for his trip to Chicago back to the forefront of Micah's mind.

"The funeral will be Friday," Micah answered, then lifted his glass of iced tea. "At the mortuary," he added after he took a long swig.

"You're more than welcome to have the service at the church," Richard offered. "Your mother was a member. She may have only been with us a short while, but I'd still be happy to officiate her home going."

Micah addressed Richard for the first time. "That won't be necessary."

"I will be giving my sister's eulogy," Pastor Jackson spoke up.

"I can understand that, but you're still welcome to use the church."

"I don't think so," Micah responded abruptly.

Richard pressed harder. "If you're concerned about money, I don't charge the members for use of the facility. In fact, I'm personally prepared to help with the cost of Sister Stevenson's final arrangements." Richard set his fork down and continued talking after Micah stopped chewing, and he interpreted Micah's smirk for a smile. "I'm sure the unexpected cost of this trip has set you back some. I'd like to help you."

Pastor Jackson cleared his throat, prompting Micah to be careful of what he said in front of Ms. Lula and David.

Micah shook his head. It amazed him that Richard still thought he could use money to control people. "No, thank you. I am well able to handle my mother's final arrangements." That was true. In addition to the unexpected insurance policy, Micah had the money he'd been saving for a house. Now that he wouldn't be getting married anytime soon, he could use that money and save the money from the policy. "I don't need your kind of help."

Richard's gaze hardened on Micah. "The offer is on the table just in case things change," Richard said, then continued eating.

Not wanting to be in the same room with Richard any longer than he had to, Micah directed his next comment to his mother's friend. "Ms. Lula, dinner is wonderful, but I really can't eat right now. I'd like to hear what happened to my mother."

"Well, baby," Lula started after she finished off her cabbage, "your mother was so happy that she was on her way to California. That's all she talked about; you and her big brother, Robert. She liked your fiancée too, and she was already making plans for grandchildren."

Micah ignored her reference to Pamela. "What happened yesterday? How did my mother die?"

"Baby, I tell you, it was the most beautiful thing I have ever seen." Lula paused to grab a clean paper towel for her eyes. "I helped her finish moving out of her apartment on Saturday. She stayed the night with me so I could take her straight to the train station after service. That's how I ended up with her luggage. There we were waiting for service to start, and she was carrying on as usual about you and how happy she was for the chance to be part of your life. Then praise service started, and Helen just went crazy." Lula smiled and cried as she told them how Helen danced and danced. "I thought she was slain in the Spirit, but she wasn't; she was with the Lord. Strange as this is, before she started dancing, Helen said this was her last day here. I thought she meant in Chicago, not her last day on earth."

Micah lowered his head, and Pastor Jackson rubbed his back.

"Baby," Lula continued, "from what Helen told me, she wasn't a very good mother to you, but I'll tell you one thing. Helen loved you, and she was very proud of you. Her main goal in life was to make up for being a drunk for most of your life. She didn't get a chance to do that, but she did leave here happy."

"How did my mother end up at your church?" Micah wanted to know.

"That's the funny part." Lula laughed. "I was in Jewel Osco's one day picking up a few items when I overheard your mother arguing with the store manager because the store didn't carry the patch to help you stop drinking. The middle-aged man tried to explain to Helen that no such thing existed, and she cursed him out."

Micah chuckled. "That sounds like my mother."

"The security guard jumped in and tried to tell her that the patch was to help you stop smoking, not drinking. She didn't like that and cursed him out too. It took your mother all of five minutes to curse out everyone in store, including me, and I was an innocent bystander! When Helen finished calling me things I can't even spell, let alone pronounce, I told her I knew who could help her with her drinking problem. She told me it better work or else she was going to curse me out again, right before she beat my behind up and down State Street!"

"That's my baby sister, always ready to fight," Pastor Jackson laughed. "She was good at it too."

"I could tell she was; that's why I prayed so hard for the Lord to help her. I prayed until I was dripping with sweat, right in the middle of State Street. I didn't care who was laughing at me, my life was at stake. I called on the God of Abraham, Isaac, Jacob, Daniel, the three Hebrew boys, and a few other folks that may not even be in the Bible. After that, I invited her to church, and we were inseparable."

Micah allowed himself to relax a little; hearing about his mother this way was therapeutic for him.

"Baby," Lula said and gently touched Micah's hand, "Helen was saved when she left here, but she would have passed up heaven in a minute, if anybody ever tried to mess over you. Of that, I am certain." Lula looked over at Richard. "Isn't that right, Pastor?"

Richard nodded, but didn't verbally respond.

Lula continued. "When she first showed them pictures to us, she said, 'That's my only child, and I'll cut a Negro, a Mexican, a Chinese, a Filipino, a Jamaican, and a white man's throat if they ever hurt my baby!' Tell them, Pastor; she sure did say that, and she meant it too."

Again, Richard didn't voice a word, but he did nod his head in agreement.

"It seems as though I just saved someone's life." Micah looked over at Richard.

Before leaving, Micah gave David his cell number. He didn't know what he was going to say to the young man. He just knew he had to do something to keep him from making the same mistakes he had. Micah also knew there was a good chance of Richard manipulating the unsuspecting child into giving him his number. That was a chance Micah was willing to take. David didn't deserve the kind of manipulation and human degradation that came along with Pastor Richard Lewis. David deserved a chance to live his life free from the control of a hypocritical preacher with a fetish for young men.

Except for Pastor Jackson's snoring, the hotel room was quiet. Micah sat up on his bed and stared amazingly at his sleeping uncle. He couldn't understand how such horrific sounds could come from a human being. His uncle gave new meaning to the term "calling the hogs." He was calling the hogs, cows, chickens, and the goats.

The noise and thoughts of his mother prevented Micah from falling asleep. Finally, he gave up and pressed the light switch on the lamp next to the bed. He stretched and walked over to the table that contained the bag from the morgue. With caution, he went through his mother's belongings. He wanted to hold on to a little piece of her forever.

The only items in her purse were five twenty dollar bills, her ID, some mints, her unused train ticket, and the pictures he'd sent her. He could tell by the worn envelope that Helen looked at those pictures often. Micah's eyes watered and his heart ached as he looked at his favorite picture. It was the one with him, Pamela, and Matthew at his birthday party. He remembered the first time he saw that photo, and he referred to them as his family. He traced Pamela's smile with his fingertip. "How do I stop loving you?" he whispered. "And how do I get you out of my heart?" The pictures weren't offering any solutions to his dilemma, so Micah put them away. The longer he gazed her image, the more he wanted to hold her. The more he wanted to hear her laugh.

Micah turned his cell phone on and checked his voice mail. AC had called and so had Jessica and his aunt. The message that touched him the most was the one left by Matthew. He said he was sorry that his mother had died and that he would pray for him when he said his prayers. Micah waited for Pamela's voice, but it never came. At first he was disappointed, but then decided it was best that he didn't hear her voice or talk to her. The breakup would be easier that way.

Micah climbed back into bed, closed his eyes, and just as he began to finally doze off, his cell phone rang.

"What do you want?" Micah said after he recognized Richard's voice.

"You," Richard answered frankly.

Micah responded with frankness. "You can't have me. You can never have me."

"I've already had you, remember?" Richard gloated. "I know being with a woman hasn't made you forget about me."

Micah's jaws flinched, and he fought to keep from yelling and waking his uncle.

"Richard, I haven't forgotten at all. I remember everything. That's exactly why I don't want anything to do with you."

There was a brief silence before Richard replied. "Micah, I really would like to talk to you. I need to talk to you. I want to know why you left without telling me. Did you know that I spent nearly a year looking for you? I didn't know if you were dead or alive until your mother showed me those pictures. How do you think I felt learning you were alive and well and hadn't bothered to contact me after all we'd shared?"

Micah was familiar with the game now, and he knew better than to enter into a conversation with Richard. "We don't have anything to talk about," Micah replied, then pushed the red END CALL button.

Chapter 24

Pamela sat on her bed with pen and pad in hand. She'd been in that same position for nearly thirty minutes thinking about what to write. "Where should I start?" she mumbled to herself. "Where do I start to heal?" She set the pad and pen down and walked over to her bedroom window. From her second-level sanctuary, she had an unobstructed view of the miniplayground in the middle of the complex. She eyed her son playing with Tyson. He looked so happy. She looked over to the right at what used to be Steve Larson's unit. He was back in jail and would be locked away for a long time under the three strikes rule.

A lone tear ran down Pamela's cheek as she thought about how she allowed her unresolved feelings for her late husband to motivate her to make the decision that could have ruined her son's life. But thanks to God and Micah, her son had recovered remarkably well and the bond between the two had grown even stronger, unbreakable.

Matthew prayed for Micah every night along with the rest of his family members. To Matthew, Micah was family; he was his father. Pamela had to admit that Micah, in their court-ship, had been better to her than Marlon had ever been, and she was crazy for pushing him away.

Pamela's heart yearned and new tears flowed every time she thought of Micah. It had been only three days since the breakup, but the emptiness she felt inside made it feel more like an eternity. Every day, she fought the urge to call him. She figured he wouldn't accept her calls if she did, so she didn't bother. Pamela wondered if he were thinking of her, if he still loved her. She wanted to talk to him so badly, but she couldn't, not until she freed herself from the bondage she'd allowed to hold her captive for far too long. She walked back to her bed and sat down. After staring at the silver urn on her dresser for a few moments, Pamela picked up the pen and began writing.

Dear Marlon,

I should have said these words to you a long time ago, while you were alive, but I couldn't. I didn't have the courage then to face the truth, but now I do. Marlon, you were a lot of things to me, but good wasn't one of them. You were the first and only man I gave myself to. And I mean really gave myself to. I lost myself in you and allowed you to abuse me and take advantage of me. I lost sight of reality. The reality being, you never really loved me; you only loved yourself. You never truly cared about my well-being. All you cared about was self-gratification. To this day, I don't understand why you married me. It certainly wasn't to have sex, because you had plenty of that without me.

You stripped me of my self-esteem to keep me dependant on you and introduced me to marijuana. You watched me change from a free-spirited, trusting individual to a fearful and paranoid woman. You didn't care if I or your son had food or shelter. All you cared about was what you wanted. What hurt most was when you questioned Matthew's paternity. How could you do that? You knew I loved you and was always faithful to you, despite your unfaithfulness. Despite your selfishness, I always gave you all of me. I had this crazy idea that one day you would realize that I was the one who loved you, not the women you constantly played with. But you died before that happened. Looking back now, it wouldn't have made a difference if you had lived. You wouldn't have changed because you didn't want to change. You liked the way you were; you told me so all the time. You did everything you wanted to do and didn't care who you hurt in the process, including me.

Pamela stopped writing long enough to wipe her eyes and blow her nose.

Thinking back now, the one good thing that came from having known you is Matthew. For giving me him, I say, thank you. He's a wonderful child who has given me blessings in more ways than I could have imagined. Marlon, he's nothing like you, and for that, I'm thankful. Even at his young age, Matthew knew you weren't much of a father. He put your picture away a long time ago. He never asks about you, and I'm glad. I don't know how to tell him his own father didn't want him. It's all right because God has sent him a wonderful man who's teaching him and giving him all the love of a father.

This same man has shown me what real love feels like, but I don't know how to receive it because of the wounds and scars you left in my heart. For five years, I suppressed how deeply you hurt me. I have subconsciously used those scars to mistrust everyone around me and to run off the man who really loves me. From the grave, I have allowed you to have the same control you had over me when you were alive. I have allowed you to control the way I think and how I see people. I couldn't fully trust the man God sent me because of how you treated me. I wasn't fair to him just like you weren't fair to me. I didn't accept his unconditional love, just like you wouldn't accept mine. I hurt the one who loves me, just like you hurt me.

Pamela waited for the paper to dry from the tears she cried.

Marlon, I have come to understand that you were who you were. I'm not making excuses for you, but you did what you did because you wanted to. There is nothing I could have done differently to change you. The truth is, I married you, but you were not my husband. Everyone saw that including me. I thought I could change you, but there was no changing you, then or now.

Now, I have to change myself. I have to move on with my life. To do that, I have to forgive you and let you go. I have to let go of all the anger, pain, mistrust, humiliation, insecurity, and the rejection. Marlon, I forgive you for everything you did to me and for the things I allowed you to do to me. That's right; you don't hold the entire blame. I opened the door and allowed you to stay too long, way too long. As of today, I am releasing myself from you. I am letting go of the pain and the memories. I'm moving on so I can be free. I deserve that. I deserve a real husband, and my son deserves a father. You deserve to rest in peace.

Good-bye, Marlon.

After rereading the letter and gaining the strength to walk, Pamela went downstairs and threw the letter into the fireplace, and then struck a match and threw it in. The orange flames brought down more tears. Drops that were heaving and hot, but she waited until the tears stopped and the tension in her chest dissipated. When nothing but ashes remained, peace settled in her heart, and a smile rested on her face.

Pamela then placed the silver urn and the photo from Matthew's drawer into the special shipping box, sealed it, and addressed it to Marlon's mother without a return address.

Chapter 25

From the moment he stepped inside the purple and white sanctuary, memories flooded Micah's mind. There were some pleasant memories, like the day he accepted salvation and the day he was baptized. The mothers of the church were always extra nice to him, and most of them tried to convince him to date a daughter or granddaughter.

Life Changing Ministries hadn't changed much at all. The purple pews with wooded ends were still stationed across the sanctuary in three rows of ten. The carpet was still purple with tiny gold specks. The ten six-foot windows, five on each side, were still covered with purple drapes that contained the similar gold specks as the carpet. From the vaulted ceiling emerged a tremendous brass chandelier with at least fifty candlestick lightbulbs.

On the podium sat eight purple chairs, four on each side of what Micah nicknamed "the throne." Richard's chair always reminded him of the throne Pharaoh sat on in the movie *The Ten Commandments*. The top of the chair was two feet higher than the other chairs, and it wasn't purple; it was gold. Richard always said purple and gold were colors of royalty, and that he was God's royal servant. Next to Richard's chair was a brass glass top table adorned with a gold water goblet and a bowl filled with fruit. Just in case the throne didn't make it clear who the pastor was, there was an almost life-sized picture of him mounted on the front right side of the church. Micah remembered when a picture of Richard and his wife hung there. Now, it was replaced with one of just Richard. Of course, in it, he wore a purple cassock with gold braiding.

"That's some shrine," Pastor Jackson said after he sat next to Micah on the third row for Bible Study.

"You're not going to the pulpit?" Micah questioned.

Pastor Jackson shook his head. "Under no circumstances will I sit on the devil's platform."

Micah sat upright and thought back to his stay at LCM. While members were added to the church on a regular basis, members also left on a regular basis. It appeared Richard had enough charisma to get them in the door, but not enough to keep people longer than two years. After his wife left him, the people still kept coming although most of the strong members left when she did. Richard's wife never came out and declared the reason she left him. Micah assumed her silence was mainly out of concern for the baby Christians and not to save Richard's reputation. That's why he was able to keep his job as pastor and his children were still speaking to him.

Micah surveyed the sanctuary. Out of the hundred-plus crowd, he only recognized about ten people, and they were probably still there because of their positions as board members.

Micah really didn't want to be there, but he wanted to see David. He hadn't heard from him, but the kid had been on his mind for two days. Actually, David was a good distraction from planning his mother's funeral. For two days, Micah and his uncle had done everything from shopping for Helen's clothing to printing her obituary, paying for the cemetery plot, and ordering flowers. Now he needed a break, and he needed to warn David about the predator on the prowl.

Richard called Micah nonstop for two days and left messages about how much he missed him and wanted to see him. Richard even had the nerve to offer to take him to the Signature Room for dinner followed by dessert at his house in his Jacuzzi. Micah didn't return any of his calls, but he knew Richard wasn't going to go away. The chase thrilled Richard more than the catch.

"Do you see him?" Micah asked, referring to David.

Pastor Jackson pointed to the left side. "Over there."

Micah stood and waved to catch David's attention. In no time, the youngster was on the third row next to Micah.

"Hey, Micah." David shook his hand. "I'm glad you came. I lost your number. It must have fallen out of my pocket the other night."

"No problem." Micah asked his uncle for a pen and issued his number to David again. "What are you doing tomorrow? I'd like to hang out with you if you're not busy."

David seemed pleased with the offer, but hesitated to accept. "I have to check with Pastor Lewis first to make sure he doesn't need me for anything."

"Sure," Micah responded. He knew Richard would come up with something to prevent David from seeing him. *God, show me how to save this kid,* Micah prayed inwardly.

Lula Murphy made it to her front-row seat just before Richard mounted his throne. She waved at both Pastor Jackson and Micah before opening her Bible.

Micah closed his eyes as Richard began to speak, but Richard's opening statement made him jolt forward.

"Tonight, I'm delighted to have one of the sons of this church in our midst. Unfortunately, the circumstance that has brought him back home is a sad one, but I'm happy he's here, nonetheless," Richard began. "Our beloved Sister Helen Stevenson's home going service will be this Friday. Her son, Micah, was a very devoted member here before moving out to California to pursue his career. He worked hard in this church and helped to mentor a lot of young men through the mentoring program. Brother Micah, please stand."

Micah looked at his uncle who was just as outdone as he before slowly rising to his feet. Micah wanted to strangle Richard. If he weren't in the house of the Lord, he would have punched him in the face.

"Please join me in welcoming Brother Micah back home to his roots. Let's give him our support during this time of bereavement." Richard then conveyed an open, but private message to him. "Brother Micah, for whatever you need, I'm here for you along with the rest of the congregation."

Micah forced a nod of appreciation to the congregation. Before sitting down, he caught a glimpse of Lula Murphy. From her facial expression, Micah knew they would have a heart-to-heart talk real soon. David looked at Micah strangely also, but he didn't say anything.

"That's what I want to talk to you about," Micah whispered to David. He still didn't say anything, just nodded.

The next sixty minutes were actually quite enjoyable. Richard knew the Bible and how to teach it well. He didn't practice all of its principles, but he was a profound teacher. No one could take that away from him.

"He's truly gifted," Pastor Jackson said after it was over. "Now I understand why Helen liked it here so much. I also understand how you ended up so confused. It's hard not to trust a man who can teach like that."

Micah was nearing the door when a young man approached him indicating Pastor Lewis wanted to see him in his office.

"Tell Pastor Lewis that I decline." Micah turned to leave before the young man could object, but Lula Murphy came from behind and pulled him out the door. Pastor Jackson followed close behind.

"Micah, what's going on?" Lula asked after they cleared the steps.

"Ms. Lula, what exactly are you referring to?" Micah stalled.

Lula narrowed her eyes, and then Micah understood how she and his mother became so close. He could tell that Lula Murphy was just as feisty as Helen.

"I'm not playing, Micah." And she wasn't. Lula didn't smile, laugh, or blink. "I thought it was strange the way you interacted with pastor the other night. I assumed it was because you'd just met him and because you are grieving, but there's more to this story, isn't it? You didn't just meet him the other night. And why didn't he tell your mother you were once a member here? He acted as if he didn't know you when she showed him those pictures."

He was right; Lula Murphy didn't miss a thing, and she wasn't going to stop until she got some answers. Micah looked over at his uncle for assistance.

"How long have you been a member here?" Pastor Jackson asked Lula.

"About eighteen months, why?" she replied.

"How much of Pastor Lewis's history do you know?" Micah asked.

"Apparently not enough," she answered sharply.

Micah didn't feel comfortable about divulging his personal business to this woman he'd just met two days prior. He folded his arms across his chest and debated what he should share. Then out of the corner of his eye, he saw David getting into Richard's Town Car.

"Micah, you'd better tell me what's going on before I take a belt to you in the name of your dearly departed mother, my friend," Lula threatened.

"Lord Jesus!" were the only words that Ms. Lula could articulate after Micah gave her the details of his relationship with Richard.

Micah didn't know if he felt worse for putting himself in the position of being ridiculed, or for tarnishing the image Lula had of her pastor. "Ms. Lula, I'm sorry."

"Are you telling me the truth?" she asked. Micah could see she hoped he was lying, that it was all a bad practical joke.

"It's the truth, all right," Pastor Jackson affirmed.

"If you want, I can let you listen to proof, right now," Micah offered.

"Prove it!" she ordered.

Micah removed his cell phone from the clip on his waist. He had planned to replay the message Richard had left earlier in the day for David, but this was just as good. He had a feeling Ms. Lula wouldn't turn her head and look the other way. No, Lula Murphy struck him as a woman who liked to get results.

The phone fell from Lula's hands. Micah caught it just before it hit the ground. "That dirty devil!" she screamed. "How can that man say those things, then get up and teach Bible Study? I knew something was wrong with him always wanting young boys around him. I felt it in my spirit." Lula paced back and forth. "He ain't getting away with this! No way!" she said, shaking her head. "I'm not going to sit by and let him spread that filth throughout God's house. Ain't no telling how many others he has violated and they just didn't say anything." Lula looked upward into the night sky. "Helen, I'm so glad you ain't here for this. You'd cut Richard Thomas Lewis to the white meat for sure!"

Chapter 26

Friday, Micah arose from bed at 6:00 A.M. He actually hadn't slept all night. The final viewing at the mortuary the night before had drained him emotionally. Helen looked so peaceful in the pink suit and white gloves he'd selected for her. Today, he was going to bury his mother. The last time he would look at her and the last time he would touch her.

Since leaving the mortuary he felt alone and desolate. Even with his uncle present, the emptiness he felt overwhelmed him. His circumstances were bleak from his prospective. He didn't have a mother or father, a sister or brother. There was no one but him. No one to love him and no one for him to love. Pastor Jackson said love was for everyone, but where was his portion? Micah fell to his knees and tried to pray, but he couldn't. He lay there frozen.

Pamela's hands shook as she punched in Micah's cell number. Chances were he wouldn't answer her call since he hadn't returned any of the messages she'd left yesterday. Why should today be any different? But today was different. Micah was burying his mother today and that would be hard on him. That's the reason she'd set her alarm for 4:00 A.M.; to offer him her support. She wanted him to know that she cared and that he wasn't alone. That he would always have her and Matthew. But Micah didn't answer the phone. She sighed and left a voice message.

"Hello, Micah. I just wanted you to know that I'm praying for you today. I'm here if you want to talk. You may not want to hear this, but I do love you, and I miss you."

Pamela hung up the phone and knelt beside her bed and prayed fervently for Micah's strength.

Micah felt the dread leave and arose from his knees and fell onto the bed. In no time, he was sound asleep.

After a brief scan of the chapel, Micah adjusted the black, gray, and pink tie that accompanied his black suit. To both his surprise and delight, the chapel was nearly full. Just about everyone in his old apartment building had come out to pay their last respects to Helen. In attendance were a couple of employees from Jewel Osco's in their work uniforms. *Mother must not have cursed them out,* he thought. Including members from church, about one hundred people attended Helen Stevenson's funeral.

"Son, are you ready?" Pastor Jackson asked, looking back at him. Micah nodded and slowly followed behind the clergy with Pastor Jackson reading the traditional ceremonial scriptures. Included with clergy were, of course, Richard and two ministers from the church.

Seated with him on the front row were Lula Murphy and a few relatives Micah hadn't seen in years, of whom his mother said wasn't worth a dime in Monopoly money.

Micah listened attentively and laughed as neighbors shared fond memories of his mother. Most of the memories revolved around Helen telling them off or cursing them out for one reason or another. Not one failed to mention how proud Helen was of her son. Micah would've given anything for her to get up out of the casket and tell him herself and give him a hug.

When Pastor Jackson began the eulogy, Micah donned his sunglasses, mainly to stop Richard from watching his eyes. Pastor Lewis had been attempting telepathic messages the entire service. Every time Micah looked up, Richard was zeroed in on him like he was some sort of specimen under a microscopic lens. When Richard's eyes traveled down to and lingered on Micah's midsection, Micah made up his mind. He was going to see Richard. He had to. This chance may never come again. No matter the outcome, he had to do his part, even if no action was taken.

Micah couldn't leave Chicago on his 6:00 A.M. return flight with a clear conscience unless he did everything he possibly could to help David. Just as Micah knew he would, Richard made sure David stayed far away from Micah. Richard had left him no choice.

At the appointed time, Micah gave his mother one last kiss and words of love. He then quickly left the chapel and waited outside for the trip to the cemetery. Lula Murphy followed behind him to offer comfort.

"You're going to be all right," she started to say, but didn't complete her thought. Like a vulture, Richard appeared out of nowhere beside Micah.

"Hang in there." Richard placed his arm around him. Micah instantly tensed at the familiar touch, then allowed himself to relax enough to hold a conversation.

"I'll go get your uncle," Lula said and took off.

"Micah," Richard began. "You don't have to deal with this by yourself. I'm here for you now, just as I have always been."

Micah thought the look on Richard's face almost looked sincere. He stepped out of the embrace. "I'm leaving in the morning, but I need to see you tonight."

The smile that cracked Richard's face almost made Micah gag. "I knew you would come around. I'll expect you around eight. Who knows, maybe after some TLC, you'll decide to postpone your trip permanently." Richard had the bravado to wink.

"See you at eight." Micah turned and walked toward the waiting limo.

"How's it going?" Jessica plopped down in one of the chairs in front of Pamela's desk.

"I don't know." Pamela looked down at her watch. "It's one o'clock there; the funeral should be over by now. I hope he's okay."

"All you can do is pray for him."

"I've been praying for my baby all day," Pamela said softly with a blank stare on her face.

Jessica's eyebrows shot up. "I was talking about Micah, not Matthew," she teased.

Pamela caught the pun, but remained serious. "Jess, I don't know what I'm going to do. I called him repeatedly yesterday, but he won't answer or return my calls. I'm so worried about him."

Jessica leaned forward on her elbows. "Are you really worried about him, or are you worried he's rekindling his relationship with his old lover?"

Normally, Pamela hated it when Jessica was so frank, but today it didn't bother her. Pamela looked her friend dead in the eyes and spoke the truth. "I am not worried at all about Micah rekindling anything with Richard Lewis. Micah is healed and delivered. Micah is a strong and powerful man of God. I'm worried because he's grieving and I'm not there to comfort him."

"Hallelujah!" Jessica shouted. "Girl, you have finally got it! I should have told Micah to break up with you a long time ago."

"Whatever." Pamela shrugged her shoulders. "I've finally got it, but now I don't have him."

"You will, but you're going to have to work hard to convince him to open up to you again. But it's nothing a lot of knee-ology can't fix."

"I have the praying part covered, but how do I get him to talk to me?"

Jessica picked up Pamela's phone and began dialing.

"Who are you calling?"

"Someone who knows how to get a lot more than talk from a man," Jessica replied.

Chapter 27

Richard fingered his hair in the mirror. He smiled at his reflection. By his estimation, he looked good for his forty-nine years. Life had treated him well. He pastored a growing church, had money, all the material possessions he desired, and tonight, he would have Micah again.

Richard grinned at that thought. He'd been with many men, but Micah had always been his favorite. If Richard believed in falling in love, he would argue that he loved Micah. But Richard didn't believe in loving anyone other than himself. He did harbor a strong emotional tie to Micah. That was probably why he still wore that ring on his right index finger. That could be the reason he searched relentlessly for Micah after his disappearance. There was even a soft moment when Richard gave up and cried, fearing Micah was dead. But now, Micah was back.

Richard couldn't explain the euphoria he felt when Micah stepped into Lula Murphy's kitchen. He had to hold on to his chair to keep from jumping up and embracing him. Tonight, he wouldn't hold back. Tonight, he would make up for the two lost years.

Micah dreaded stepping into Richard's house, but he didn't have a choice. He was certainly a creature of habit, Micah thought as he scanned his surroundings. Like the man himself, the house hadn't changed. The paint and the furniture were the same. Richard's house even smelled the same and sounded the same. Richard always kept jazz playing somewhere in his home, and tonight was no exception. He also loved black silk pajamas, which was what he was wearing when he answered the door.

At the sight of his former lover, Richard reached for Micah and attempted to embrace him, but Micah quickly moved to the right and stepped around him. Richard didn't take offense to the maneuver; he knew he'd get what he wanted before the night was over.

Richard offered him something to drink, but Micah refused. He offered him some food, and Micah refused again. Then Richard offered him a seat next to him on the couch. Micah accepted the offer, but chose to sit in the chair five feet away from Richard.

"Micah, why do you insist on running from me? You know that's what you're doing, don't you? You're not really free of our bond; if you were, you wouldn't mind being close to me. You wouldn't mind me touching you," Richard stated in that familiar calm voice.

Micah sighed. "Richard, I'm not afraid of you. I don't have any reason to run from you. It doesn't matter what you think; unlike you, I am free."

Richard leaned his arm on the couch rest and smirked. "You're confusing freedom with fear. You're scared, Micah. I can see it in your eyes. You're scared of how I make you feel. You're scared that one night with me and you won't go back to that woman. I believe her name is Pamela?"

Micah lowered his head, not because Richard was right, but because his heart had been longing for Pamela all day. At times, he even thought he felt her presence.

Richard continued. "Tell me, does she make you feel half

as good as I made you feel? Do her kisses feel like mine, and does she touch you like I can?" Micah remained quiet. "Of course not, I was your first, and I'll be your last." Richard leaned forward and whispered as if telling a secret. "I bet when you're having sex with her, you're thinking about me. I know I was thinking about you when I was with my wife. Sex with a woman is good, but it's nothing compared to what we had."

Micah shook his head but didn't voice any words. Richard didn't need to know he and Pamela were not having sex or that they were no longer together.

"How is Brenda?" Micah needed to take control of the conversation, but he also wanted to know if she had recovered.

Richard shrugged his shoulders. "She must be doing fine since she cashes my alimony checks every month. I haven't seen her since she moved back to North Carolina. The kids say she's doing okay," he lied. Richard was a professional and a certified liar. He lied all the time to get what he wanted, and he was lying now. Truth was, Brenda never fully recovered from her breakdown. She only moved back to North Carolina so her sister could look after her. After the divorce, Brenda would be seen walking up and down the streets of Chicago talking to herself at all times of night and day.

"Micah, I don't want to talk about Brenda or Pamela. I want to talk about us. Why did you leave without telling me?"

Micah allowed himself to relax in the chair. Richard took that as a sign of him weakening his position and moved to the opposite end of the couch.

"The only way I could leave was without you knowing. You would have never allowed me to freely walk away."

Richard's face attempted to portray innocence. "Micah, I didn't physically hold you here against your will."

"No, you didn't, but you did an outstanding job of keeping my mind so twisted I couldn't decipher right from wrong."

Richard seemed to like that analysis and stood to his full height. "Why are you here now? Is your mind still bound, or do you physically want me like I want you?" He walked over and stood over Micah and placed his hands on Micah's shoulders. "It's meant for us to be together. Why else would God send your mother to my church, and then before she could move away, He took her to heaven, thus, sending you back to me?"

A few years ago, that type of warped thinking would have worked on Micah, but not today. Micah removed Richard's hands from his shoulders and leaned forward with his elbows resting on his knees and spoke as clearly as possible.

"Richard, I don't want you. I didn't want you back then, and I definitely don't want you now. I'm only here now because of David."

Richard stepped back, confused. "What does David have to do with anything?"

Micah stood to his feet before making his demand. "I want you to leave him alone."

Richard laughed uncontrollably, almost hysterically. He leaned against the side of the couch and held his stomach. Micah didn't know what to expect next.

"Let me get this straight," Richard started once his laughter subsided. "You don't want me, but you don't want anyone else to have me? If this is not a relationship, I don't know what is. It's all right though, a little jealousy makes it all the more fun."

Micah threw his hands up. There was no way of getting through to him. "He's just a kid, leave him alone. If you want to practice homosexuality, then do it with a consenting adult, but leave that innocent kid alone."

"I bet you would like to be that consenting adult." This time when Richard winked, Micah became angry.

"Richard, keep your dirty hands off that kid!" Micah yelled.

Richard quickly sobered. This was the first time Micah threw a demand at him with such force. Now he didn't know what might happen next.

"He's an innocent kid with his whole life ahead of him, and that life includes women, not a nasty old man pretending to be a man of God!" Micah knew he struck a nerve. Richard's eyes darkened, and his nostrils flared.

"Who do you think you are? How dare you question my relationship with God. I am His servant!"

"Richard, you don't *know* God!" Micah answered. "Sure, you know what His Word says, but you don't do the things it takes to get to know *Him*, like living His Word. If you really knew Him, you wouldn't feel comfortable preaching and turning out young men at the same time!"

"Don't act like you didn't get anything out of it!" Richard didn't even try to deny it. "I took care of you very well!" he sneered.

"You almost caused me to take my life! If I hadn't called my mother that morning, I would be dead right now! That's how much I hated myself for being with you! Don't drag David into that hell!"

It was then Richard realized his memories with Micah were just that, memories. The control he once had over Micah was gone. But he wasn't going to grant Micah anything. No, if Richard couldn't get what he wanted, then neither would anyone else.

"I'm going to have some fun with David. He reminds me of you in so many ways— young, stupid, and ripe for the popping."

Micah shook his head. "You're sick!"

"Then why don't you lay hands on me and heal me," Richard mocked.

Micah walked over to the fireplace and stared up at the

portrait of Richard in his ministerial robe with Bible in hand. He lowered his head as if he were praying. "I'm not going to let you ruin that kid," Micah stated when he finally turned around to face his enemy.

"You don't have to let me do anything. David's not the second, fifth, or even tenth young male I've broken in, and he won't be the last."

For the first time, Micah saw that Richard got a thrill from destroying the innocent. It was to him what gasoline was to a car. Micah thanked God once again for protecting him from HIV. Despite his perversion, Richard always had enough sense to practice "safe sex."

"Richard, I'll stop you."

"And just how do you plan on stopping me?" Richard questioned with a smirk.

"I'll tell everyone what you're doing, including the church."

The hysterical laughter returned, but this time, it carried with it superciliousness.

"Who do you think they're going to believe— the son of a drunk, or me, their beloved pastor?"

Micah flinched at his words, but held his ground. "They'll believe the truth."

"They'll believe the truth I tell them, just like they believed me when Brenda left. I had the entire board convinced she had committed adultery. After all, I am a man of God, and people believe what I say. You'd be surprised at how much influence I have once I place that collar around my neck and don a robe."

"You're not a man of God; you are a confused man who needs God," Micah said sadly. "You're a forty-nine-year-old man who's so insecure with himself that you have to manipulate and seduce young men to feel good about yourself. What's really sad is, you're not happy with who you are. You

hide behind a robe and a Bible. You've lost your wife and destroyed people with your own lust, and the saddest part is you
don't even care." Micah started for the door, then stopped.
"Richard, I do want to thank you. Seeing someone as sad as
you gives me a greater determination to live my life right. I
refuse to end up like you." Micah continued walking.

"My life is fine!" Richard barked. "I'm in control! I can do
whatever I want! I can have whomever I want!"

Micah shook his head and grabbed the doorknob. "That's
not true anymore. You can't have me, and you can't have
David."

Micah slammed the door closed behind him and quickly
walked down the steps. He walked down to the next block
and climbed into the waiting van carrying his uncle, Ms. Lula,
and her son.

"Did you get that?" Micah asked while removing the camera and microphone disguised as buttons from his shirt.

"Sure did," Ms. Lula's son, the former military surveillance
specialist, answered. "We saw and heard everything."

"How soon can we get copies of the tape?" Lula asked her
son.

"Is now soon enough?" he answered and pressed the record
button.

Chapter 28

"AC, man, where are we going?" Micah asked. "You just missed my exit." AC and Pastor Jackson exchanged nervous glances. AC had picked them up from the airport and was supposed to be taking Micah to his apartment.

"I know, man, but First Lady cooked lunch and told me to bring you by before I take you home," AC finally answered.

"Yeah, you know how your aunt can get after she's spent all day cooking," Pastor Jackson added without looking over his shoulder at his nephew.

Micah appreciated his aunt for wanting to make sure he ate a balanced meal, but all he wanted right now was a hot shower and his warm bed. The four-hour flight from Midway left him stiff and irritable, thanks to the crammed seats of the economy aircraft carrier and a crying infant on each side of him. "Man, take me home. I'll stop by the house later."

AC and Pastor Jackson looked at each other, then back at Micah.

"Son, why don't you stop in and say hello. I'll have your aunt pack you some food to take home with you. Then Anthony can drive you home," Pastor Jackson suggested.

"Fine," Micah conceded. He knew it was a lost cause. AC would do whatever Pastor Jackson wanted. Micah closed his eyes and tried to prepare his mind for a long afternoon. His eyes were still closed when AC pulled into the garage.

"Wake up, man." AC reached over the seat and shook Micah.

Without so much as a mumbling word, Micah stepped from the car and walked through the garage and into his aunt's kitchen. Pastor Jackson and AC quickly followed behind, leaving the luggage in the car.

Micah stopped midstride when he saw Pamela and Jessica helping his aunt set the table.

"Micah!" Matthew screamed and ran to him. "Sorry about your mother," he said, "but I'm glad you're back." Matthew hugged him around the waist.

"Thank you, Matthew." Micah squatted and returned his hug, but his eyes were on Pamela. She was beautiful in the lime-green square-neck dress he'd bought her for her birthday. Her curls loose, resting on her shoulders. He wondered what she was doing there.

"Hello, baby." His aunt thought she would break the ice since she was the one who orchestrated this "chance" meeting between Pamela and Micah after Pamela called her, crying for help yesterday.

"Hello, Auntie." Micah returned her hug.

"How are you holding up, baby?"

"It's hard, but I'll be fine." Micah's eyes were back on Pamela. His answer had a dual meaning. He guessed she caught it when she looked away.

"I know you will, baby. Now go wash your hands so you can eat."

"Yes, ma'am." Before leaving the kitchen, Micah greeted Jessica, but didn't address Pamela. Matthew happily followed Micah.

"I don't think this was a good idea," Pamela said. "Micah won't even speak to me."

"In all fairness, he is grieving over his mother," Pastor Jackson said.

"And he's tired from his flight," Jessica added.

"He wanted to go straight home, but we talked him into

coming by. Of course, he didn't have a choice with Pastor in the car," AC explained.

"But did you see how he just stared at me?" Pamela hung her head and pouted.

"What I saw was a hurting man who loves you. He's hurting because he just lost his mother, but some of the hurt is from you rejecting him. But I'm not going to go there, because he is my nephew, and you know you were wrong." First Lady narrowed her eyes at Pamela. "Now get yourself together and handle your business!"

"Yes, ma'am," Pamela mumbled, then rolled her eyes at Jessica who was giggling behind Pastor Jackson.

Inside the bathroom, Micah listened to Matthew talk about the bike he wanted for his birthday, but his mind was on Pamela. He wasn't prepared to see her. He was still trying to figure out what she was doing there. And why did she have to look so beautiful? She looked as inviting as her voice sounded on his voice mail yesterday.

"Are you still going to teach me to ride?" Matthew asked while drying his hands.

"Yes, little buddy."

"When are you going to marry my mother?"

Micah stopped drying his hands and looked into Matthew's expectant eyes. He couldn't tell the boy he loved as a son that was not going to happen, at least not yet.

"We'll talk about that later, all right?"

"Okay. I can't wait for you to be my dad for real." Matthew leaned into him.

Micah swallowed the lump in his throat. He didn't know what to say, so he said nothing. He just took Matthew by the hand and led him back to the dining room.

Everyone was already seated, and, of course, Pamela sat between the last two empty seats. Micah looked around the table, but none of the culprits would make eye contact with him. He gave up and sat to the left of Pamela. The sooner he ate, the sooner AC could take him home.

During the meal, Micah and Pamela talked, but not to each other. Pamela tried to converse with him, but he would only give brief answers. When she asked him to pass her the salt, he did so without looking in her direction. When she asked him if he would like anything else, he responded by saying, "Not from you." She started to leave, but Pastor Jackson shook his head and she sat back down. Micah also noticed everyone seemed to be eating faster than normal. That made him happy. The faster everyone ate, the sooner he could leave.

"Baby, that was good." Pastor Jackson rubbed his stomach. "I think I'll go into the living room to watch TV." Pastor Jackson jumped up so fast that Pamela laughed. She hadn't seen him move that fast outside of catching the Spirit.

"I'll join you, baby," First Lady said.

"Me too, Pastor." AC pushed his chair back.

"Matthew, come on, let's go watch TV." Jessica grabbed the child's hand before he could protest. Matthew followed behind, still holding on to a half-eaten chicken leg.

"They could have shown a little discretion," Micah said once he and Pamela were alone.

Pamela gasped. "Do you think they're trying to get us to talk?" She failed at her attempt to make him laugh.

"Our relationship is over; therefore, we don't have anything to talk about," he replied harshly.

Pamela pushed back from the table and stood next to him. Without an intro or warning she began. "My life with Marlon Roberts was a living hell. When I met him, I was a naïve nineteen-year-old. Marlon was handsome and much more experienced. I was an easy target for his sweet talk and carefree lifestyle. Marlon was my first and only lover, but I wasn't his.

I should have known from the start he wouldn't be faithful to me. The night we met at Walgreens, he was purchasing condoms. I should have realized then, if he would ask for my phone number on his way to a rendezvous with someone else, he was nothing but a cheat. But like I said, I was naïve, and he was smooth and fine. While we were dating, I caught him with women, and he would swear that he wouldn't cheat again. I'd take him back and he'd be good, for a while." She looked down at Micah to see if he were listening. He was.

"One day, I went for my annual GYN checkup and discovered I had chlamydia. This time when he apologized, he asked me to marry him. Like a dummy, I said yes. I had the crazy idea that once we were married he wouldn't cheat anymore." Pamela chuckled at that thought. "I ran off to Las Vegas, against my parents' advice, to marry him. Standing in that strange chapel on The Strip was the loneliest and scariest time of my life. I had a gut feeling I was making the biggest mistake. Anyway, I ended up with gonorrhea three months after we were married.

"Marlon never had time or money for me. I had to borrow money from my parents nearly every month to keep us from getting evicted. When I became pregnant, I thought things would change, but they didn't. I thought being a father would slow him down and keep me from a monthly trip to the clinic." Pamela bit her lip and breathed deeply. "Marlon wasn't there for me during my pregnancy, and he wasn't there when Matthew was born. In fact, he had the nerve to deny his son. Matthew was four days old when Marlon decided to show up.

"That first year of Matthew's life, Marlon may have seen his son ten times, and he wouldn't even buy food or milk for his own child. By that time, he gave up on trying to hide his relationships from me. He openly talked on the phone with women. One woman came to our apartment to pick him up.

He suggested if I couldn't handle his lifestyle, he would leave. The ironic thing is, with all of his extracurricular activities, he claimed that he loved me. Then he was killed in a motorcycle accident on his way home from his girlfriend's house at four in the morning. Two women showed up at his funeral, claiming to be pregnant with his child. A third woman introduced a little girl to me. The woman said the girl was Marlon's three-year-old daughter."

"Matthew has a sister?" Pamela was so deep in recollection that Micah's voice nearly startled her.

"I don't know for sure, but the little girl did resemble Marlon. I haven't heard from any of Marlon's women since they found out Marlon didn't leave an insurance policy. In fact, he left me with nothing. Without my parents, I would have been homeless." Pamela watched Micah stand and walk to the opposite end of the table.

"Pamela, you really don't have to tell me all of this now."

She nodded. "Yes, I do. I have to be honest with you. I owe you that. You deserve the truth of why I couldn't accept you." She continued before she lost her courage. "I had help dealing with the heartache and broken promises. I smoked weed nearly every day. It didn't start off like that when Marlon introduced it to me, but every time Marlon pushed me away, I went to marijuana for comfort, to escape the pain. How Matthew came out healthy and normal is still a miracle to me. My son is truly special because God shielded him from my foolishness. Shortly after Marlon's death, I received salvation and haven't looked back." Pamela wiped tears from her cheeks.

"Micah, I'm so sorry, but when you told me about your past, I got mixed up. I didn't realize it then, but I hadn't forgiven Marlon for how he treated me, nor had I forgiven myself for allowing him to misuse me. I put you in the same category as

Marlon. You were always good to me, but so was Marlon in the beginning. I wasn't enough to satisfy him, and I was afraid I wouldn't be enough for you. It was one thing to compete with women, but I can't compete with a man. I know you said all that was in the past, but that's the same thing Marlon used to say in the beginning, after he got caught. I now know it wasn't my fault Marlon cheated. He cheated because that is what he chose to do."

Micah shrugged his shoulders. "So you rejected me because of what your dead husband did to you?"

Pamela nodded. "Yes, and because of the things I had heard about homosexuals not being able to be totally delivered. I've heard people say homosexuality is the 'big sin,' but now, I know it's not. It's no different from my drug use; we were both controlled by a spirit. The lust that controlled Marlon is the same lust that drew you into homosexuality. It just manifested itself in a different way.

"Micah, I know that lifestyle is part of your past and not your present or future. I'm your future. I also know that you're not Marlon Roberts. You love me. Marlon never really loved me."

Micah folded his arms across his chest and leaned back against the wall. "How is it that you're so sure of that now? Seven weeks ago, you were certain I was a pervert and a fagot. Just a few days ago, you thought I wanted Richard."

Pamela moved closer to him, but didn't dare touch him. "Micah, I know that because I know you. You are the greatest man I know outside of my father. Micah Stevenson, you are everything I prayed for. You're everything I need. The only time I feel complete is when I'm with you. You bring out things in me I never knew were inside, and you gave me what I didn't know I needed. You brought laughter back into my life, and you allow me to freely be myself."

Micah moved to turn away from her, but stopped.

She took a step forward. "You know me so well. You anticipate my needs, and you give me your all. And if all that weren't enough, you're a wonderful father to Matthew."

Pamela wiped her face again and moved so close to him she could feel his breath against her face. Micah turned his head, but she gently turned it back to her and looked him dead in his eyes. "Micah, you once told me you wanted a woman who wouldn't intentionally break your heart. I know I broke your heart, and for that I am so sorry. But it wasn't on purpose. Micah, I love you. I love you so much. I know you're the husband God sent for me, and I'm the wife He created for you. I don't want us to miss out on our destiny. I don't want to rob us of the greatest gift; love. I don't want to live the rest of my life incomplete and unfulfilled. I want to be with you. I want to love you and feel you love me back."

Micah breathed deeply and flexed his jaws.

Pamela unfolded his arms and exhaled when he didn't resist. She wrapped her arms around his waist and laid her head against his chest. "Micah, you're my present, and I'm not giving you back. I'm not letting you go. I know you don't really want to let me go. I know you still love me."

Micah's emotions raged like a violent storm within him. He felt it all: anger, relief, hurt, happiness, fear, and love. His body tensed and stiffened to her touch. His thoughts were divided. Could he trust her? Should he trust her? His heart was both willing and resistant to the thought of opening up to her yet once again. He wanted to trust the sincerity he saw in her eyes and heard in her voice, but he'd been down that road before and ended up broken.

With every labored breath he took, Pamela squeezed him

tighter. She squeezed him so tight her arms hurt, but she refused to let him go. This was her last chance. Then it happened. His strong arms enveloped her like a warm blanket, and his body relaxed. His wet chin leaned against her head. His tears met hers and flowed down her cheeks.

Listening to the beat of his heart, Pamela felt she was right where she belonged. They remained that way until Micah broke the embrace and lifted her chin, then gently kissed her on the lips.

He wiped her cheeks with his thumbs. "When do you want to get married?"

"When are you going to propose?" she smiled.

"What are you talking about?" he frowned. "I asked you a long time ago."

Pamela shook her head. "No, you didn't. What you said was that you want me to be your wife. Not will I be your wife."

Micah laughed. "So you want to be technical?"

"I'm worth it, aren't I?"

"You sure are." Right there in the dining room, Micah knelt on one knee and held her left hand in his. "Pamela Roberts, will you please be my wife?"

"Oh my Lord!" First Lady and Jessica nearly tripped over one another bustling into the dining room. Pastor Jackson and AC were on their heels, just smiling. None of them tried to conceal the fact that they'd been eavesdropping. Matthew heard the commotion and came running in from the porch.

Pamela and Micah shook their heads at their family and friends.

"Pastor, I guess you've forgotten about your sermon on how we should mind our own business?" Micah teased his uncle.

Pastor Jackson discarded the rebuke with the wave of his hand. "Boy, hush, and let the girl answer."

Everyone's eyes were glued on Pamela. Matthew didn't

know what the excitement was about, but knew it was something good because his mother was smiling.

"Yes, Micah, I will marry you," Pamela finally said.

Micah stood and lifted her off her feet and spun her around while she giggled uncontrollably. Then he did something he hadn't done before. While still holding her in the air, he kissed Pamela. At first she thought it was going to be his usual peck, but he parted her lips and invaded the inside of her mouth. Pamela wrapped her arms around his neck and yielded completely, even offered him a moan of satisfaction.

Pastor Jackson cleared his throat. "That's enough of that. There will be plenty of time for that later."

"Yes, sir," Micah said, then lowered Pamela to the floor, but not without one more quick peck.

As soon as they separated, Matthew ran to Micah and pulled on his arm. "Now, you can be my dad?"

Micah picked him up. "That's right. I'm going to be your real dad. I'm going to adopt you." That announcement didn't surprise Pamela or anyone else.

Matthew wasn't sure what that meant, but he knew having a dad was a good thing. "Okay," Matthew giggled.

"I have to call my parents," Pamela announced.

While she shared the good news with Henry and Dorothy, Micah talked with AC.

"Man, I told you God would work everything out," AC said, after the two shared an embrace.

"You were right, man, and He's going to work it out for you too."

"Man, what are you talking about?"

"Micah, my dad wants to talk to you," Pamela called out. Before accepting the phone from her, Micah kissed her cheek and said, "I love you."

Pamela was still blushing when Jessica walked over.

"Girl, I'm so happy for you." Jessica hugged her. "I knew you would come to your senses and beg that man for another chance. You beg quite nicely, I might add."

"Whatever. I hope you come to your senses soon," Pamela responded.

"What are you talking about?"

Micah joined them before Pamela could answer.

"It's been fun, but we have to go. We have some shopping to do," Micah said putting his arms round Pamela, his earlier fatigue completely gone. "Can you watch Matthew for a few hours?" he asked Jessica.

"Sure," Jessica answered. "But what are you shopping for?"

"My future wife needs a ring and a house."

"You're not going to buy a house today, are you?" his aunt asked.

"No, but we're going to start looking," Micah answered. "I don't anticipate a long engagement," he added after he lowered his head and kissed Pamela.

"Neither do I," Pamela agreed, stretching and kissing Micah again.

"Humph, the way y'all carrying on, y'all need to get a marriage license and get married tomorrow before y'all burn up," First Lady said, and then pulled them apart.

"Auntie, nothing's going to happen before time," Micah responded, then asked Pamela, "How much time do you need to plan our wedding?"

"Thirty days," she answered without hesitation.

"So soon?" Micah was surprised. "I was thinking you would need more time."

"Why wait when you know what you want?" she smiled. "I want you, I want us."

"Dad, can you get a house with a big yard, so we can play catch?" Matthew asking him that question was the only thing that prevented Micah from kissing Pamela again.

Hearing Matthew call him Dad always made Micah feel proud. "Yes, son, I can," Micah answered and rubbed Matthew's head. Matthew giggled, then skipped out of the room.

"Ready, sweetheart?" Pamela took his hand and happily followed her man. Then, as if suddenly remembering something, she stopped and turned around just before reaching the door. "Jess, you should tell Anthony that you're the one who's been sending him those cakes, pies, and banana puddings through First Lady. Life is too short not to enjoy the love of a good man," Pamela said, smiling back at Micah.

Micah added his two cents. "And AC, you should tell Jessica she's the reason you've stopped wearing those bright, shiny suits and started going to the gym."

AC and Jessica were speechless.

Pamela sat on her couch with her eyes glued to her left hand. The ring Micah purchased for her was gorgeous. She would have settled for a plain band, but Micah insisted she get something she really liked. She really loved the one-carat solitaire, especially since she wouldn't have to worry about Micah making payments for five years. He paid cash for it. Neither wanted to postpone their wedding date, so they agreed Micah would move into the town house once they were married until they found a house to their liking.

All day, she constantly thanked God for allowing Micah to open his heart to her once again. This time she was not going to blow it. She was healed. The test came when Micah voluntarily shared the details of David and his meeting with Richard. Pamela didn't second-guess his motives, and she didn't pull away from him. Listening to him share those painful details made her draw closer to him both emotionally and physically. She found herself touching Micah more today than she ever had. She could tell he liked it by the kisses he kept planting on her cheeks and hand. "Thirty days, just thirty days," she mumbled as Micah started down the stairs after reading Matthew a bedtime story.

"What are you thinking about?" He joined her on the couch and pulled her to him so that her head rested against his chest.

"You know you're the only thing on my mind." She snuggled closer to him. This was her favorite position, in the warmth of his arms listening to his heartbeat.

Micah hand-brushed her hair. "It has been some day. When I left Chicago this morning, I had no idea my day would end like this." He sighed. A few minutes passed without Micah saying anything.

"Are you thinking about your mother?"

"Yeah," he exhaled. "I miss her already."

"Do you want to talk about her?"

"Maybe later. Right now I want to enjoy this moment." He kissed her forehead.

"Thank you." She lifted her head so that she could see his face.

"What did I do?"

"You gave me another chance." She attempted to lay her head back down, but he held her chin so he could maintain eye contact.

"I love you. I'll always love you even when you hurt me. But from here on out, I need you to be open and honest with me about everything. Some of the drama could have been avoided if you had been truthful with me about what was going on inside of you."

"Micah, I was not honest with myself. I could not be honest with you."

"I understand, but as of right now, it's just me and you. No Richard and no Marlon. Not my past and not your past. I love you for the woman you are now, and I'll give you all of me except that part reserved for God alone. I will do everything possible to make sure you and Matthew are taken care of both emotionally and financially. All I ask is that you do two things."

"What's that?" she asked barely audible.

"Trust me with your heart like I trust you with mine and love me freely and uninhibited."

"I do," she whispered.

The kiss that followed was not sweet. It was passionate, too passionate. Seconds before all four hands started to roam, both of them quickly separated.

"I cannot wait for AC to pick me up," Micah said, trying to catch his breath.

"I'll call him," Pamela offered and jumped to her feet.

"Twenty-nine days and thirteen hours," Micah mumbled after looking at his watch.

Chapter 29

Sunday morning when Richard pulled into his reserved parking stall, Deacon Upshaw, the president of the board, was waiting for him.

"Good morning, Deacon Upshaw. How are you doing this fine Sunday?" Richard was so programmed to giving responses that he didn't notice the hardness in the deacon's eyes.

"Richard, the board is waiting for you in the conference room."

Richard momentarily paused. The deacon's choice to call him by his first name instead of the usual pastor caught him off guard. And why was the board assembled on a Sunday morning? "Let me get my briefcase—"

"You won't be needing it this morning." Deacon Upshaw cut him off before Richard could get the sentence out.

Richard anxiously followed the deacon inside the church and into the conference room. He started to give his rehearsed Sunday morning greeting of "Hallelujah, bless the Lord," but the cold reception made him think twice. No one showed their natural teeth or the ones they had glued in. Looking around the table at the twelve stern faces, Richard suddenly became nervous.

"Sit down, Richard," Deacon Upshaw ordered. Richard quietly obeyed. "We called this special session in response to the tape each of us received yesterday morning," Deacon Upshaw began. "Based on this tape, we are removing you from your position as pastor of Life Changing Ministries, effective today."

"What?" Richard jumped up and pounded the desk. "You can't do that! I've been pastor here for over fifteen years! You can't fire me without cause!"

"That is what makes this even more troubling. We've trusted you for fifteen years as our spiritual leader. But now we have to fire you, and we have a very good reason to end all ties with you," Deacon Upshaw said and instructed one of the members to press the play button on the VCR/DVD combo.

Richard sank into the chair as he heard with his own ears and saw with his own eyes a complete replay of his last conversation with Micah. He watched himself practically beg a man to have sex with him, then get angry when he refused. His stomach turned while listening to his voice describe what he was going to do to David. At the conclusion of the tape, Richard didn't say anything. He couldn't. Everything was right there, stamped with the date and time.

After everything I've done for him, how could he do this to me? Richard wondered without taking responsibility for his actions.

"Richard, we cannot and will not tolerate that kind of behavior from the pastor of our church. If you want to live a homosexual lifestyle, that's your choice, but you won't do it from this pulpit. We only pray that the church is not bombarded with lawsuits from individuals you have taken advantage of over the years. We also pray that you would allow God to deliver you.

"You'll be compensated for the remainder of this year. You have twenty minutes to clear out your office. When you're done, hand your set of keys over to security, and they will escort you off the premises." At the conclusion of the head deacon's words, the board members stood and prepared to leave. "May God have mercy on your soul," Deacon Upshaw said before closing the door behind him.

Richard sat dumbfounded. He couldn't believe his empire was crashing down around him, and at the moment, there wasn't anything he could do to stop it. In time, he would figure out how to get his job back and repay Micah for his betrayal.

"I can't believe I underestimated him," Richard mumbled while shaking his head. "I didn't know Micah had it in him." Richard started toward his office. The power he usually felt upon entering his shrine was gone now that the forbidden things he'd done behind closed doors were out in the open. Richard felt several emotions: anger, rage, and wrath. He even spat a few profanities as he packed. The one emotion he didn't feel was remorse.

Chapter 30

One year later . . .

"Good night, Mommy, and give Daddy a hug for me."

"I will." Pamela kissed her son good night, then turned off his light and closed his bedroom door. She then hurried down the hall to her bedroom.

The spacious bedroom was her favorite room in her newly built-from-the-ground-up, four-bedroom home. Of all the houses she and Micah looked at, this house won her over. The sunken bathtub with adjoining sauna in the master suite was all it took for her to sell her town house and follow her new husband to El Sobrante. The big backyard and large eat-in kitchen also helped, but she loved having her private getaway.

Pamela quickly lit the candles around the bedroom and turned on the music. She then sprinkled rose petals over the king-sized bed. She smiled at the wedding picture she kept on her dresser.

"I can't believe it's almost been a year since our wedding," she whispered en route to the bathroom.

What a wonderful wedding it was. The warm September weather was perfect for their simple wedding on Crown Beach in Alameda with the great Pacific Ocean as a backdrop. Pamela always dreamed of pledging her undying love to her soul mate on the beach with the sand flowing between her toes. That's exactly what they did. In place of traditional attire, Pamela wore a long flowing off-the-shoulder white linen dress, and instead of a veil, her head was adorned with a wreath made of roses. Micah was dressed in white linen pants and a button down shirt. Like his bride, he stood at the makeshift altar barefoot.

The small crowd of less than a hundred people consisted of her parents, a few of Micah's relatives and coworkers, along with well wishers from Praise Temple. AC and Jessica served as best man and maid of honor. Micah and Pamela would return the favor in their wedding next month.

Pamela would never forget the love she saw in Micah's eyes as she walked down the sandy aisle with both her father and Matthew on each side of her. The entire time Pastor Jackson performed the ceremony, Pamela felt at peace, like she was fulfilling her destiny. She knew in her heart she was marrying her soul mate. The moment Pastor Jackson pronounced them husband and wife, she shed tears of joy and almost did a victory dance.

The first night in the Bahamas on beautiful Paradise Island would be forever etched in her memory. She was nervous because it had been almost six years since she'd been intimate with a man, and she wasn't sure if she had done it right then. With Marlon, she mainly laid there, letting him have his way, but with Micah she wanted to participate. She wanted to give him as much pleasure as she would receive.

Micah was nervous too, but for a different reason. As far as he was concerned, this was his first time being intimate. He was so concerned about pleasing Pamela that he laughed, but listened attentively to the pointers tossed around at the bachelor party AC had thrown for him.

The knowledge he gained was lost when Pamela finally came out of hibernation wearing very little white satin and lace. Micah couldn't think; he could barely breathe. After slowly undressing one another, the anxiety left, and instinctively they went after each other like they'd always been together, exploring and cherishing one another like new Christmas presents. Micah was so considerate of her feelings that he made sure at every segment she experienced pleasure.

In the end, the beauty of their lovemaking left them both raw with emotions.

So far, their life together had been wonderful. Pamela transferred from the title company to one closer to her new home. Micah was the best husband and father. He still worked at the cable company, but now he was in management. He didn't have to climb telephone poles anymore, and the salary was higher, but he did have to put in long hours, which he did without complaining. Micah didn't mind as long as he had his Pooh (his nickname for Pamela) and Matthew to come home to. They were his world, his reason for being. His adoption of Matthew was completed two months ago. Matthew was officially Matthew Stevenson, his son.

Every morning before Micah left for work, after he prayed, Micah kissed his wife and son and told them how much he loved them. Just in case anything happened to him, Micah wanted his family to always know they were loved. He never went to bed with any disagreements dangling between him and Pamela either.

Tonight, Pamela was going to show Micah just how much he was loved, but in a different way. Micah had given her everything she wanted and needed, and now she wanted to give him the best gift she could give him; a baby. Micah never pushed her to have another child, but she knew he would love to have a biological child and would love their child as much as he loved Matthew. That's why she stopped taking her birth control pills three months ago, without telling him. Tonight, after a hot bubble bath and their playtime, she was going to tell him the good news of her pregnancy.

She returned from undressing in the bathroom to find Micah standing in their bedroom removing his watch.

"I like this kind of greeting." His grin expressed his appreciation of his wife's nude body. "I should work late more often." He kissed her passionately and roamed her body with his big hands, and as usual, Pamela's knees grew weak.

"How was your day?"

"Dull compared to how my night's going to end." Micah nibbled on her ear and Pamela almost forgot she'd left the hot water running in the bathtub.

"Come on." Pamela took him by the hand and led him to the bathroom where she helped him undress, and then joined him in the oversized bathtub.

"This is the best part of my day, coming home to you." Micah positioned himself so that his head leaned back against her bosom.

"Aren't you forgetting somebody?" Pamela squeezed the sponge over his chest.

"I love Matthew, but he can't do for me what you do." She giggled as his fingers traveled under water and found one of her sensitive spots. "I like playing with you, Mrs. Stevenson."

"I like playing with you too, Mr. Stevenson." The upside-down kiss she planted on his lips nearly made him jump from the tub. "And in a few minutes, I'm going to show you just how much, but first, how about a little contest?"

"What's the prize?" He sat up and turned around to face her.

"Me." She kissed him again, this time more deeply.

"Let's do it." His voice was husky and filled with desire.

They kissed once more before Pamela leaned over the side of the tub for the tray containing the chocolate crème-filled cookies and milk. After handing him a cookie, she slowly licked her lips to break his concentration, then called out, "On your mark . . . get set . . . go!"

"Wow! That was some consolation prize." Micah leaned on his elbow and ran a rose petal along Pamela's cheek.

"Just think what you would have gotten if you'd won," Pamela teased.

"What about a rematch?" The desire in his eyes told her it was going to be a very long night. *Thank God it's Friday,* she thought.

"Sure, and this time, I'll let you win." Pamela winked, then had to squirm away from him before he devoured her again. "Baby, hold on. You have some mail."

Micah pouted and watched Pamela sit up and reach into her nightstand drawer for the envelopes. She handed him the letter-sized one first.

"I wonder who this is from," Micah stated after reading the return Chicago address without a name. He knew it wasn't from Ms. Lula because he knew her address. It couldn't have been from Richard since he didn't know Micah's address or cell number anymore. He changed his number after Richard called harassing him after the firing. Micah quickly ripped open the envelope and was surprised to find the letter was from David. Pamela listened attentively as Micah read out loud.

Hello, Micah,

I would have written sooner, but I'm been very busy with school and work. I hope you don't mind Ms. Lula giving me your address. Don't worry; I won't pass it on to Richard. I don't associate with him anymore. After he lost his second lawsuit against the church, Richard left Chicago. Rumor has it, he's starting a church of his own in Indiana. Anyway, my foster parents are allowing me to stay with them rent free until I finish college.

The purpose for this letter is to thank you. When Richard was fired and barred from any contact with the mentoring program, I was angry at you and the church. Richard told me he was fired over lies you told the board about him misappropriating funds. He was still coming by to see me at my foster parents' house and taking me places.

Then one day, Ms. Lula invited me over to her house and showed me the tape you made the night before you left. I literally got sick listening to the plans Richard had for me and how he wanted to have sex with you.

I was completely stunned. I honestly didn't know Pastor Richard Lewis was trying to get at me like that. I thought he was just being a good Christian and mentor. I trusted him way too much. I was even considering calling him Dad. He offered, and I accepted his offer to move in with him after I turned eighteen and graduated from high school. I would have done just that if Ms. Lula hadn't shown me that tape.

Micah, I just wanted to say thank you, and I appreciate you for putting yourself out there like that. That helped me to see that God really does exist and that there are some really good people in the world. You barely knew me, and yet, you cared enough to put your business out in the open to help save me.

I spend a lot of my free time with Ms. Lula. She tells me you're married now with a son. I'm glad you were able to get your life back on the right track.

I have to go. I'm in the middle of finals. If you want, you can write me back or give me a call.

Thanks again,
David.

P.S. Keep an eye out for Beyoncé and Ciara. Make sure you give them my number. Tell them to call me anytime.

Micah chuckled at David's closing comment, then placed the letter back into the envelope.

"That was nice," Pamela said, and Micah nodded in agreement.

"I'm happy he's on the right track," Micah said. "I'll give him a call in a few days, but now I'm ready for a rematch."

Once again, behind those curly eyelashes she loved so much, his eyes told her she wouldn't get much sleep tonight. In no time his lips were on hers and his arms around her.

"Hold on, there's one more." She pulled away before he could consume her mind along with her body.

Micah pouted like a two-year-old and tore open what appeared to be an invitation. He opened the card decorated with balloons and confetti and read out loud again, but this time in a whiny voice.

To: Micah Stevenson
You are cordially invited to attend the birth of your child
When: Approximately nine months from now
Where: Summit Medical Center
Time: TBA

Micah stared motionless at the invitation in his hand and Pamela knew he was reading it over and over again in his head. When he finally did look up, he wasn't pouting anymore, and instead of his eyes only showing his desire for her, they revealed his appreciation as well. "You're having my baby?" He timidly touched her abdomen with his fingertips.

"I'm having our baby." She placed her hand on top of his. Pamela read her husband's confusion. "I stopped taking my pills three months ago. I love you so much that I want to give you a child." Pamela didn't realize she was crying until he kissed the tear that had slid down her cheek. He didn't stop there. He kissed every inch of her face, then proceeded to make the sweetest and most passionate love to her.

Epilogue

"Pamela, push!" Dorothy ordered.

"No! I'm not having this baby until Micah gets here," Pamela yelled between pants.

"You can't stop the baby from coming."

"Your mother is right." Jessica tried to talk some sense into her friend. "You might have to have the baby without him."

The sweat dripping down her face and the horrendous pains that shot across her back would not change Pamela's resolve. "Micah wants to see the birth of his child, and I'm not having this baby until HE GETS HERE!" She screamed the last part as she rode the peak of a new contraction.

Dorothy and Jessica looked at each other, then up toward heaven. There was no getting through to Pamela. They'd been in this same position nearly eight years ago at the birth of Matthew. Just like before, it wouldn't be long before Pamela would scream, "GET IT OUT!"

Pamela rested her head back against the pillow with her eyes closed, crying softly. This was not the way it was supposed to be. She wasn't supposed to go into labor three weeks early. Micah wasn't supposed to be away at a management training session in Sacramento. He was supposed to be here with her, coaching her with her breathing while holding her hand and stroking her back. "I want my husband," she cried.

"I know you do, baby." Dorothy rubbed Pamela's back trying to relieve some of her discomfort. Jessica tried calling

Micah on his cell phone to see how close he was, but didn't
get an answer.

"Oh God!" Pamela screamed. Her contractions were getting stronger and more frequent. She didn't want to admit
it, but if Micah didn't get here soon, he'd have to catch the
birth of his first biological child on video. That's not what
Pamela wanted. She wanted to see her husband's face when
their baby entered the world. Outside of their wedding day
and the day Matthew's adoption was final, this would be the
happiest day of his life, and she wanted him to enjoy every second, even if she couldn't. "Micah, please hurry," she pleaded
as if he could hear her.

"I'm here, Pooh." Micah rushed into the room, not really
knowing what to do beside kiss her and take his wife into his
arms. Pamela hugged him back, and for a moment allowed
herself to relax. Micah was here and the world was all right
again. "Baby, I'm sorry I wasn't here for you," he whispered in
her ear and stroked her hair.

"All that matters is that you're here now," Pamela responded, then braced herself for another contraction. Micah was
stunned when his sweet, loving, beautiful wife gripped his
shoulders and with her face contorted screamed, "GET IT
OUT!"

Dorothy and Jessica looked at each other and laughed. "I
knew it," Jessica said, pushing the nurse call button.

Twenty-five minutes later, Micah was overwhelmed with
emotions from cutting his daughter's umbilical cord. While
the medical team cleaned and assessed their baby, Micah sat
on Pamela's bed squeezing her hand and breathing heav-
ily. Pamela read his need and motioned for her mother and
Jessica to leave the room. Then she pulled her husband to her
and allowed him to release his deep emotions on her shoulder.

"Thank you," he managed to say between sniffles. "I love you, Pooh." He brushed her hair from her face and kissed her.

"I love you too."

"Would you like to hold your baby?" the nurse asked Micah, breaking the tender moment.

Micah quickly received his bundle of joy. Holding his daughter, he thought his heart would burst from the instant love he felt for her. Little Micala was just a few minutes old and already she had her father wrapped around her finger. A million thoughts of the things he wanted to do and say to his daughter ran together in his mind. The little curly haired bundle with his long eyelashes was really part of him, his own flesh and blood. Pamela watched proudly as her husband constantly kissed and smiled at their baby.

There was a knock on the door and Dorothy entered with Matthew, then left. Both Pamela and Micah felt it was important for Matthew to be present after the delivery so he wouldn't feel left out. They wanted him to have his time with the baby before everyone else showered her with attention.

"Wow!" Matthew said, looking at the package in his father's arm. "Mommy, how did you get that big baby out?" Little Micala weighed over eight pounds.

"With a lot of hard work," Pamela answered after kissing her son.

Matthew smiled watching his father place the baby in Pamela's arms. "Can I hold her?" he asked.

"Sure."

Matthew sat on the bed against his mother and held his little sister. Then he did what he'd seen his father do moments earlier, he kissed her on the forehead.

"Am I going to get a little brother too?" Matthew asked, looking at his mother's stomach.

"We'll talk about that later," Micah answered before Pamela could roll her eyes and snap her neck. "It's Thanksgiving time." That's what Micah called their family prayer time. With the baby back in her arms, Pamela bowed her head and Matthew followed as Micah led his family in prayer.

"Heavenly Father, we thank you for blessing our family today. I thank you for giving my wife a safe delivery. I thank you for giving my wife and me a healthy daughter and my son a sister. We thank you for the love we have today and ask that you continue to bless our family with your love and kindness. We ask that you continue to show this family how to love one another and grow in you. We pray that our family will forever be a living example of your love and grace. In your son Jesus' name we pray. Amen."

"Amen," mother and son echoed in agreement.

Group Discussion Questions

1. Did you agree with Micah's decision to share his complete history with Pamela? Why or why not?
2. Pamela is a devoted Christian who attends church regularly, yet she is also very judgmental. Are her actions and behavior typical of today's Christians?
3. Was Pamela's response to Micah's disclosure an overreaction or was it justified?
4. Jessica believed the sin of homosexuality wasn't any worse than promiscuity and physical abuse. Do you agree with her assessment?
5. Pamela stated on more than one occasion that God told her Micah was her ordained mate. However, after he revealed his past, Pamela discarded those words. Are there times in our life when we should discard God's plan for our life just because it doesn't appear ideal?
6. Did Micah make the right decision by not sharing the details of his relationship with Richard with his mother once he learned she was attending Richard's church?
7. Micah felt he would always be judged by his past, especially in the "church." Do you agree with his belief that the "church" is willing and ready to forgive every sin except homosexuality? Does the "church" have the power and right to hold anyone's past, regardless of what it is, against them? Why or why not?
8. Have you ever prejudged or condemned a brother or sister because their past was "worse" than yours?

9. Micah couldn't, in good conscience, allow Richard to take advantage of David, even if that meant placing himself on display. Are you willing to go the extra mile to help someone if it means displaying your frailties? How far are you willing to go in order to prevent someone from making the same mistakes you have?

10. Why do you think Richard had no remorse?

About the Author

A romantic at heart, Wanda uses relationships to demonstrate how the power of forgiveness and reconciliation can restore us back to God and one another. Wanda is a graduate of Western Career College. In addition to building a career in health care, she is also a licensed real estate agent and is currently pursuing her bachelor's degree in biblical studies. She currently resides in the San Francisco Bay Area with her husband of twenty years and two sons.

Right Package, Wrong Baggage is her third Christian fiction novel. Visit the author's Web site at www.wandabcampbell. net or contact her at wbcampbell@prodigy.net.

Urban Christian His Glory Book Club!

Established in January 2007, **UC His Glory Book Club** is another way to introduce **Urban Christian** and its authors. We are an online book club supporting Urban Christian authors by purchasing, reading, and providing written reviews of the authors' books. *UC His Glory Book Club* welcomes both men and women of the literary world who have a passion for reading Christian-based fiction.

UC His Glory Book Club is the brainchild of Joylynn Jossel, author and executive editor of Urban Christian and Kendra Norman-Bellamy, author and copy editor for Urban Christian. The book club will provide support, positive feedback, encouragement, and a forum whereby members can openly discuss and review the literary works of Urban Christian authors. In the future, we anticipate broadening our spectrum of services to include online author chats, author spotlights, interviews with your favorite Urban Christian author(s), special online groups for *UC His Glory Book Club* members, ability to post reviews on the Web site and amazon.com, membership ID cards, *UC His Glory* Yahoo! Group and much more.

Even though there will be no membership fees attached to becoming a member of *UC His Glory Book Club*, we do expect our members to be active, committed, and to follow the guidelines of the book club.

Urban Christian His Glory Book Club

UC His Glory Book Club members pledge to:
- Follow the guidelines of *UC His Glory Book Club*.
- Provide input, opinions, and reviews that build up, rather than tear down.
- Commit to purchasing, reading, and discussing featured book(s) of the month.
- Respect the Christian beliefs of *UC His Glory Book Club*.
- Believe that Jesus is the Christ, Son of the Living God.

We look forward to the online fellowship.

Many Blessings to You!

Shelia E. Lipsey
President
UC His Glory Book Club

**Visit the official Urban Christian His Glory Book Club
Web site at www.uchisglorybookclub.net

ORDER FORM
URBAN BOOKS, LLC
78 E. Industry Ct
Deer Park, NY 11729

Name:(please print):_____

Address:　　　　_____

City/State:　　　_____

Zip:　　　　　　_____

QTY	TITLES	PRICE
	A Man's Worth	$14.95
	Abundant Rain	$14.95
	Battle Of Jericho	$14.95
	By The Grace Of God	$14.95
	Dance Into Destiny	$14.95
	Divorcing The Devil	$14.95
	Forsaken	$14.95
	Grace And Mercy	$14.95
	Guilty & Not Guilty Of Love	$14.95
	His Woman, His Wife His Widow	$14.95
	Illusions	$14.95
	The LoveChild	$14.95

Shipping and handling - add $3.50 for 1st book, then $1.75 for each additional book.
Please send a check payable to:
Urban Books, LLC
Please allow 4 - 6 weeks for delivery

ORDER FORM
URBAN BOOKS, LLC
78 E. Industry Ct
Deer Park, NY 11729

Name:(please print):_____

Address: _____

City/State: _____

Zip: _____

QTY	TITLES	PRICE
	16 ½ On The Block	$14.95
	16 On The Block	$14.95
	Betrayal	$14.95
	Both Sides Of The Fence	$14.95
	Cheesecake And Teardrops	$14.95
	Denim Diaries	$14.95
	Happily Ever Now	$14.95
	Hell Has No Fury	$14.95
	If It Isn't love	$14.95
	Last Breath	$14.95
	Loving Dasia	$14.95
	Say It Ain't So	$14.95

Shipping and handling - add $3.50 for 1st book, then $1.75 for each additional book.

Please send a check payable to:
Urban Books, LLC
Please allow 4 - 6 weeks for delivery

ORDER FORM
URBAN BOOKS, LLC
78 E. Industry Ct
Deer Park, NY 11729

Name:(please print):_____

Address: _____

City/State: _____

Zip: _____

QTY	TITLES	PRICE
	The Cartel	$14.95
	The Cartel#2	$14.95
	The Dopeman's Wife	$14.95
	The Prada Plan	$14.95
	Gunz And Roses	$14.95
	Snow White	$14.95
	A Pimp's Life	$14.95
	Hush	$14.95
	Little Black Girl Lost 1	$14.95
	Little Black Girl Lost 2	$14.95
	Little Black Girl Lost 3	$14.95
	Little Black Girl Lost 4	$14.95

Shipping and handling - add $3.50 for 1st book, then $1.75 for each additional book.

Please send a check payable to:
   Urban Books, LLC
Please allow 4 - 6 weeks for delivery

ORDER FORM
URBAN BOOKS, LLC
78 E. Industry Ct
Deer Park, NY 11729

Name:(please print):_____

Address: _____

City/State: _____

Zip: _____

QTY	TITLES	PRICE

Shipping and handling - add \$3.50 for 1st book, then \$1.75 for each additional book.

Please send a check payable to:
Urban Books, LLC
Please allow 4 - 6 weeks for delivery

Notes

Notes